A Beginner's Guide To Salad

JENNIFER JOYCE

For Chris, Rianne and Isobel.

ABOUT THE AUTHOR

Jennifer Joyce is a writer of romantic comedies. She's been scribbling down bits of stories for as long as she can remember, graduating from a pen to a typewriter and then an electronic typewriter. And she felt like the bee's knees typing on THAT. She now writes her books on a laptop (which has a proper delete button and everything).

Jennifer lives in Oldham, Greater Manchester with her husband Chris and their two daughters, Rianne and Isobel, plus their Jack Russell Luna.

Find out more about Jennifer and her books or subscribe to her newsletter at jenniferjoycewrites.co.uk. You can also find her on social media:

Twitter/Instagram: @writer_jenn

Facebook: facebook.com/jenniferjoycewrites

ALSO BY JENNIFER JOYCE

The 12 Christmases of You & Me
The Accidental Life Swap
The Single Mums' Picnic Club
The Wedding That Changed Everything
A Beginner's Guide To Saying I Do
The Little Bed & Breakfast by the Sea
The Little Teashop of Broken Hearts
The Wedding Date
The Mince Pie Mix-Up
Everything Changes But You
A Beginner's Guide To Christmas
(short story)

PROLOGUE

Ruth's hand shook as she applied a coat of the lipstick she'd swiped from her mother's dressing table. She should have asked to borrow it, really but she never wore make-up and didn't want anyone to know why she needed to tonight. Vera would have been thrilled her eighteen-year-old daughter was finally going on a date – and that was the problem. It was Ruth's first date and she wasn't entirely sure he would show up.

Imagine the humiliation of being stood up and everybody knowing about it!

How did the date go, love? It didn't. I sat in the restaurant with your too-bright pink lipstick zigzagged across my gob and waited on my own until closing time. Thanks for asking, Mum. Goodnight.

Ruth paused, lipstick hovering in front of her face while she gave her reflection a good talking to. Zack would show up. They had a connection, a real connection, and it didn't matter that he'd been cruel towards her throughout their school lives. It wasn't Zack's fault – everyone had been cruel to her. It was what happened when you were the fat kid. People teased you, they called you names – and inventive ones like Fat Twat (rhyming), The Jelly Green Giant (word play) and Mrs Blobby (Noel Edmonds had a lot to answer for) – and they excluded you from absolutely everything. School had been hell for Ruth. She'd never been physically bullied, but the name-calling had been relentless. She didn't have any friends, unless you counted her older brother, Stephen and his best friend. Stephen and Billy had always stuck up for Ruth as best as they could, but they were older than Ruth and had moved away to the other side of Manchester for university, so she didn't see them very often anymore.

And they didn't really count as friends. Ruth knew that deep down.

She wished she had a friend more than anything, even more than she wanted a boyfriend. A real friend to share secrets with, to joke with and to swap make-up tips with. She could use a friend right now, judging by the mess she'd made of her lips. Lipstick was smeared beyond her lip line and was it... yes, it was on her teeth. Panic bubbled from her gut and spread throughout her body. She lifted her wrist to check the time. Relax, relax, *relax*. Deep breaths. She wasn't due to meet Zack at the restaurant for another twenty minutes and, as she was already camped out in the restaurant's loo, she had plenty of time to sort her face out.

After removing the lipstick with a damp tissue, Ruth took a chest-achingly deep breath and tried again, this time smoothing the lipstick over her puckered lips almost perfectly. It needed a touch up here and there, but all in all it was a vast improvement. Shame about the colour, but beggars couldn't be choosers and all that.

Ruth blew her reflection a kiss before she headed back into the restaurant and to the table the waitress had already seated her at. The restaurant was quiet, with only three other tables occupied but that could have been down to a number of factors: the restaurant being way out of town, the questionable décor and mismatched furniture, or the unidentifiable whiff about the place, which was somewhere between cat piss and BO. But to Ruth it was perfect. This was the setting of her first date and with Zack O'Connell too. Zack had been the most popular boy in her year and she'd always had an (obviously unrequited) crush on him. Zack had mostly ignored her during their fourteen-year acquaintance and when he had spoken to her, it was only to throw jibes her way. It had been only a few weeks ago that he'd snarled 'fuck off, fatso' when she'd asked him to sign her shirt on their last day of school, but here she was, waiting for him to wine and dine her.

Wasn't it funny how life worked out? How a simple walk through the park with your elderly neighbour's dog could change your life. Ruth hadn't expected to run into Zack and his friends in the park and when she had, she'd turned and stumbled away in the opposite direction. But Zack had caught up with her and asked if they could talk.

Talk? Zack wanted to talk to *her*?

Of course she'd been suspicious. She wasn't stupid. But it turned out Zack had been dumped by his beautiful and equally popular girlfriend and he couldn't talk to his friends about it. They were all idiots. They didn't have *feelings*, not mature ones that didn't involve their dicks anyway.

'Sasha dumped you? But why?' Sasha Bloom had been the most popular girl at school and she and Zack made an obscenely gorgeous couple. Ruth had always known she was a superficial bitch, but she'd never suspected Sasha could be so dumb. Why on earth would any girl dump Zack?

'She's going away to uni and doesn't want to be tied down to a boyfriend.' Zack's head was hung low and Ruth wanted to reach out to touch him, to offer him some sort of comfort. But she didn't dare. 'Can we meet up and talk properly? Tomorrow?'

She'd said yes. She wasn't a fool. They'd met and talked – not only about Sasha but about everything. It had been amazing, like having a real friend, and the afternoon flew by too quickly. Suddenly meeting up with Zack seemed cruel. It had given her a taste of what friendship was like but was now being snatched away.

But then he'd asked her out. On a date. In a restaurant and everything.

Ruth prayed he'd turn up.

Not normally a fiddler, Ruth found herself toying with the condiments on the table, reading the sticky, faded label on the bottle of vinegar and spinning the pepper pot on its rounded top. It seemed her stomach was having a bit of a party, twisting and jiving as she waited on her wobbly chair. She doubted she'd be able to eat a thing when Zack did arrive – both minor miracles as far as Ruth was concerned.

The door opened and Ruth turned in her seat, her sickly-pink mouth gaping as she saw Zack striding towards her. He was wearing the leather jacket she'd always thought he looked hot in and she gave her thigh a good pinch to make sure she wasn't dreaming.

'Zack, hi!' What did she do now? Did she stand up to greet him? Before she could make a decision, Zack had thrown himself into the seat opposite.

4

'Hey. You look nice.'

Ruth's cheeks turned as pink as her lipstick at the compliment. She was beginning to believe he really did like her. That was the second compliment he'd given her since they'd struck up their friendship, having already told her she'd be beautiful if she lost the weight. Nobody had ever told her she was beautiful, unless you counted her parents, which Ruth did not.

'Thanks. So do you. I like your jacket.' Ruth wanted to reach out and stroke the leather, to throw her face into its collar and smell it. She sat on her hands to take away the temptation.

'Shall we order then?'

Ruth nodded, though her appetite had deserted her. She couldn't imagine ever feeling hunger again. Although, when her pizza arrived, oozing with extra cheese, it did smell divine. Zack had no qualms about eating and immediately set about shovelling his food into his mouth. Ruth watched him for a moment, wondering whether he would pause long enough to chat. Or even chew.

'How do you think you've done in your exams?' It was an inane question, but Ruth couldn't think of anything else to say and their date was turning out to be more like feeding time at the zoo. They'd recently sat their A Level exams and would be picking up their results in less than a week.

'Dunno.' Ruth looked away as Zack flashed his food as he spoke.

'I think I've done alright. No As or anything, but I think I've done enough to get on my course.'

'Yeah?'

'I hope so.' Nervous laughter seeped from her lips. It was true that she was in no way experienced when it came to dates but she had imagined it would be different to this. More romantic. And with more conversation. 'Zack, are you really over Sasha?' The question was out of Ruth's mouth seemingly before she'd even thought it and she took a huge bite of pizza to keep her from saying anything else moronic.

'Yeah, course I am. Why?'

Ruth chewed and chewed at the pizza, wishing she hadn't shoved quite so much into her mouth. Unlike Zack, she couldn't bring herself to talk with her mouth full.

'It's just that I like you. I have for ages.' Ruth suspected she was in love with Zack O'Connell but then most girls in her year had been and so she kept it to herself.

'I like you too.'

Ruth's mouth spread into a wide smile until half of her face was made up of Barbie-pink lipstick. 'Really?'

'Really.' Still chewing, Zack dropped his cutlery with a clang. 'Come here and I'll prove it.'

Ruth leant across the table, eyes squeezed shut and lips puckered. Her first kiss was heavenly, and she only wished she had a friend she could gush over the details with later. She wasn't quite sure about Zack's tongue swirling round and round her mouth like a washing machine on a fast spin, but she was sure she'd get used to it with a bit of practice.

Ruth was so busy savouring the sensation of Zack's warm lips on hers that she wasn't aware of the commotion as half a dozen teenagers clattered into the restaurant, pointing and jeering.

'Oh my God, I can't believe you actually did it!'

'You're a sick bastard.'

'That's fucking gross, man.'

Zack's lips wrenched away from hers and as his body slumped back into his seat, Ruth took in the scene around her. Zack's friends were heading towards them, led by Sasha Bloom.

'Oi, fat bitch. Who said you could touch my boyfriend?' She cackled as Brad, Zack's best friend, stepped closer and slapped Zack on the back.

'What was it like?'

Zack swiped at his mouth with the sleeve of his lovely leather jacket. 'Like sucking a marshmallow.'

'I bet you enjoyed it really,' Ryan, another friend, jeered from within the crowd. 'You looked well into it.'

'Was I fuck.' Zack jumped out of his seat, grabbed a fistful of chips and turned to face his mates. 'You all owe me fifty quid. Each.'

And then they were gone, Zack and Sasha arm in arm, everybody laughing and ribbing Zack. Ruth watched them leave, refusing to move from her seat even as she realised Zack had left her with the bill. It had all been a joke. Nothing but a prank and the opportunity for Zack to make a bit of cash. He didn't like Ruth. She was nothing but a freak show.

Ruth took a bite of her pizza, but it lodged in her throat, a great big clump that refused to go down. Ruth's lips became a thin pink line and she squeezed her eyes shut, but it was too late and a tidal wave of tears poured down her cheeks and plopped onto her stuffed crust.

ONE

Ruth

Is there anything more joyous than glancing at the clock and realising you have a mere five minutes until you can go home? My mood shifted up a gear as I clicked print and swivelled in my chair to scoop up the document. There wasn't much point in starting anything new this late in the day, so I stapled the document, slipped it into its file and shut down my computer. Freedom was just four minutes away.

I was preparing for the journey home, touching up my lipstick, running a brush through my hair (you never know who you're going to run into on the bus), when the phone shrilled beside me, the sudden noise almost causing a catastrophic smear of fuchsia up to my ear. Snapping the lid back onto my lipstick, I snatched up the receiver, knowing exactly who was phoning me at three minutes to five. Gideon. Cancelling our date tonight. At the last minute, yet again.

'Good afternoon, Kelvin Shuttleworth's office, how may I help you?'

Of course I'd wanted to snap at my useless, unreliable boyfriend but I had to be professional. At least until I knew for certain that it *was* Gideon. I'd fallen into that trap once too often. The last time it had happened, I'd roared 'what the bum fluff do you want this time?' into the receiver after he'd phoned me seven times in six minutes. Seriously, if you have a memory like a goldfish, make a list of the topics you want to cover and *then* phone me. Did he think I sat at my desk doing nothing all day (I did mostly, but that's not the point here), waiting for his scintillating calls? By this, the eighth call, I was pretty narked.

'It had better be urgent or I swear I'm going to twist your bollocks until they ping off.'

Luckily it had only been Glenn from Accounts on the other end and not somebody *really* important otherwise I wouldn't be sitting at my desk right now. I'd be in the dole queue. So I answered politely now, just in case.

'You can help me by getting your arse in my office. Pronto.'

The phone call ended abruptly, and I checked the time. Three minutes to go and Kelvin was calling me into his office? Why was I even surprised? I'd worked for Kelvin Shuttleworth, General Manager, General Lazy Bastard and General Sleaze of H. Wood Vehicles for long enough to know he didn't give a toss about my free time. I'm sure he was under the impression I continually camped out under my desk awaiting new and exciting tasks.

'Yes, Kelvin?' I stood on the brink of the threshold, still on my side of the door, still ready to flee home.

'I want four copies of this.' He stabbed a thick wad of paper on his desk with a finger, not even bothering to pass it to me, lest he wear out his fat sausage fingers in the process. 'And I'll have a coffee.'

I flicked my eyes up to the clock on the opposite wall. Yes, it displayed the same time as the clock in my own office next door and it was in full view of Kelvin. 'But it's three minutes to five.' Not even that. More like two minutes and twenty-nine seconds. 'May I remind you that I finish at five?'

'May I remind you that you don't clock in and out?' I'd have to remind him of that fact when I rocked up at half past nine the following morning. 'May I also remind you that I have not forgotten your mishap with the photocopier?'

No, I didn't photocopy my arse. It would have been beyond repair if I'd somehow managed to perch my fat derrière on top of the photocopier and, as it turned out, it only took the repair man a couple of hours to fix it after I booted the hell out of it. You'd have done the same, I'm sure. It had been taking the piss all morning and then decided to chew up the pages in the middle of a 100-page document I was photocopying for an important meeting that afternoon. Not only did the pages refuse to come loose from the mechanism inside, I broke two nails while trying to free them. *That* had been the final straw.

'Do I need to show you the repair bill?' Kelvin made to reach into his desk drawer, even though I knew it wasn't kept in there. I did his filing for him, after all. The only things Kelvin kept in his desk drawer were a bottle of whiskey, an emergency Mars bar and an envelope containing several saucy photos of a woman half his age, who definitely wasn't his wife.

'That won't be necessary.' I grabbed the wad of papers, which must have been at least fifty pages. The photocopier had better be on its best behaviour otherwise it'd be me cancelling my date with Gideon for a change.

'Don't forget the coffee.'

Of course not, sir. We wouldn't want you dying of thirst. Or getting off your arse and making it yourself.

Dumping the document on my desk, I headed over to the staff kitchen. I say 'kitchen' but it was little more than a walk-in cupboard with a kettle, tiny sink and a fridge squeezed inside. I made Kelvin's usual coffee with full-fat milk, three sugars and four chocolate digestives on the side.

'There you are. Ooh, biccies.' Erin reached her slender fingers towards the saucer and grabbed one of the biscuits. 'Are you ready to go?'

I shook my head as I replaced the biscuit and explained the situation. I'd known Erin for three years, since I started working at H. Woods, a bus and coach manufacturers. We'd hit it off immediately, even though we couldn't have been more different, with Erin being slim and gorgeous with a dark and sleek Cleopatra sweep of hair while I was house-sized, okay-looking if you squinted enough and with short blonde curls. Erin was also a bit of a goer while I was chaste (not by choice, I should add. It's quite a challenge to be a slut when you're house-sized).

'You should have told him to piss off. It's after five.' Erin swiped another biscuit and I swallowed the urge to stab her with a teaspoon.

'I can't. He brought up the photocopier.'

'That was weeks ago. Is he going to hold you to ransom forever?'

'Probably.' I batted Erin's hand away as she lunged for another biscuit. How the hell did she stay rake-thin?

'Do you want me to stay behind with you?'

'Nah.' There was no point in us both losing part of our evening.

'Good, because I've got a date with Christian.' I gave Erin a blank look. I honestly couldn't keep up with all the men she dated. 'The gorgeous bloke from my salsa class.' Of which there were many, according to Erin, and therefore failed to narrow it down. 'He brings his girlfriend every week? The red-head bitch who kicked my ankle a few weeks ago?' Ah, yes. Salsa was an extreme sport where Erin was concerned, what with her flirting with every man under the age of sixty. 'Well, he turned up alone last week. His girlfriend broke her ankle – how's that for irony? – and I talked him into taking me out.'

'You've no shame.'

'Nope.' Erin grinned and swiped another biscuit before sauntering towards the staircase, waving a hand as she went.

Not bothering to replace yet another biscuit (it was nearly tea time and, well, I just couldn't be bothered), I carried the coffee through to an ungracious Kelvin before making a start on the photocopying. Luckily for both the photocopier and me, all went smoothly until I handed Kelvin the four documents. He didn't take them, simply nodded at his in-tray.

'Stick them in there. It's getting late. I'll deal with them tomorrow.'

I can't tell you how much I wanted to stick the documents in a far more unpleasant orifice than Kelvin's in-tray, but I restrained myself. Violence towards the photocopier was one thing, violence towards the general manager was another, however justified.

'Couldn't I have photocopied them in the morning?' I really couldn't help myself. My gob had a mind of its own at times.

'I suppose you could have, yes.' Kelvin glanced up from his computer screen. I could tell he'd been playing solitaire by the frantic clicking of his mouse. 'But I didn't realise how long it would take you to complete a simple task.'

I clasped my hands behind my back and clamped my lips together, determined to neither throttle my employer nor say something I wouldn't regret but would certainly lose my job over.

'I'll see you in the morning then.'

'Hmm.' Click, click, click. He was back to losing at solitaire.

The bus was late as usual, packed and sweaty with disgruntled commuters (of which I was most definitely one), meaning I had to stand for the entire journey in heels. I always wore heels, whatever the occasion. I'd already been cursed with being fat – I didn't want to be fat *and* stumpy, resembling a Weeble, and so my feet had to make the ultimate sacrifice. Still, my shoes were pretty fab that day – grey leopard-print lace-up ankle boots with a *massive* heel. They went perfectly with my knee-length charcoal dress overlaid with paler grey lace. To brighten the look (I did like to be bright, to show off my curves, rather than hide them away), I wore a pair of canary yellow cable and rib tights and chunky yellow beads around my throat and wrists.

The bus ride seemed to take forever, pausing at every stop to pile yet more disgruntled commuters on board, upping the sweaty, stuffy atmosphere. The others were already settled at home by the time I arrived. The 'others' being my housemates, Billy and Theo, and by 'settled', I mean they were camped out in the sitting room, eyes glued to the television screen while they hammered at the Playstation pads in their hands.

'Theo?' I remained in the doorway, afraid to enter. 'Why are you nearly naked?'

Theo, wearing just a pair of boxers and holey socks, didn't tear his eyes away from the TV. 'I've got no clean clothes.'

'What about the clothes you wore to work?' Please let him have worn clothes to work.

'They're in the washing basket. I spilled a pint over them at lunchtime.'

Ah. 'Spilled' in the case of Theo translated as 'propositioned a lady and was impolitely turned down'.

'Do you mind sticking the washing on for me?'

I told Theo where he could stick his washing. I'd had enough of being a skivvy for one day.

'There's some post for you. I've left it in the hall,' Billy called after me as I stalked away, muttering to myself about lazy bastard men.

By some miracle, Gideon didn't cancel our date and so I met him at Cosmo's, a restaurant around the corner from my house. I'd been seeing Gideon for about eight months and, while he was a bit of a slob and a bit of a moron, he'd do. At least he wanted me and what was the alternative? Sitting on my own night after night?

'Ruthie! Ciao *dolcezza*.' It wasn't Gideon who greeted me so enthusiastically, kissing me on each cheek, but Cosmo, the owner of the restaurant. Don't worry. He wasn't some sort of sleaze who pounced on all his female clientele. I'd known Cosmo for about ten years, even living with him for the briefest time (though not in any sort of sexual context).

'Is he here?' I asked as I removed my jacket.

Cosmo tried not to pull a face, but it was difficult and he was forced to turn his grimace into a smile, purely for my benefit. 'He's at the bar.'

'Pissed, I presume.'

'Getting there. Shall I show you to your table?'

We picked Gideon up en route, sitting at a table in a cosy corner of the restaurant. I ordered quickly, eager to tell Gideon my news. I'd taken my post upstairs with me so I could read it while I was getting ready and discovered an invitation to the Ultimate Highmoor Reunion. Highmoor was my old school, a great big building of misery for me but soon it would be no more. Highmoor was being bulldozed to make way for a shiny new academy and so a reunion was being held during the summer for all pupils who had attended during its sixty-year lifespan.

I was horrified to begin with and felt a bit queasy at the thought of having to face all the people who had made my life so depressing, all the people who had jibed and poked fun at me and were truly horrible and nasty, dismissing me purely because I was fat. The worst part would be facing Zack, my first love. I hadn't seen Zack in ten years, since he'd pretended to like me for a practical joke and shattered my delicate, teenage heart into a million pieces.

My first instinct was to tear up the invitation but something stopped me. I could go to the reunion with my head held high, my boyfriend on my arm, and show them all that I wasn't the same loser I once was. I wasn't alone anymore. I had a boyfriend – even if it was Gideon. I phoned the number on the invitation before I could change my mind and purchased two tickets. Now all I had to do was tell Gideon about the reunion and somehow talk him into wearing a suit, or a clean shirt at the very least.

'It's not working out, is it?' Gideon asked before our starter had arrived and before I had the chance to bring up the reunion.

'What isn't?'

'You and me. Us.'

Oh, God. I was being dumped. By *Gideon*.

What about the reunion?

TWO

Billy

Billy and Theo had barely moved from their positions on the sofa since Ruth arrived home from work, the only difference being the pink T-shirt Theo had found drying on the bathroom radiator when he'd been forced to leave the room to pee. It belonged to Ruth so it buried his smaller frame, but at least it stopped his nips from freezing off his chest.

'Shit! Quick!'

'Balls!'

'Fucking hell, Bill.'

'Sor -'

'Over there! Kill it this fucking time.'

Billy and Theo's conversation was far from intellectual as their characters trundled along the screen, hiding behind barrels and abandoned buildings, waiting to pounce and shoot the hell out of the enemy.

'Nice one, mate. Shit, move it. *Move it.*'

'I am. Give me chance to –'

'Fuck!'

'Don't worry. I've got it.'

Billy didn't have it. Taking his eyes off the screen to check the time as he heard the front door opening and then slamming shut, his character was done for.

'Ruth's back early,' he noted as Theo ranted about Billy's untimely death. It had been less than an hour since Ruth left the house with a cheery 'see you later, losers' to meet Gideon, who didn't even have the courtesy to pick her up. Not that he ever picked Ruth up for their dates. Or showed her any scrap of respect.

The sitting room door was flung open and Ruth stomped inside, kicking off her shoes and shrinking five inches.

'Why aren't you on your date with Giddy-up?' Theo had started the game again but he could talk and hammer the buttons on the Playstation at the same time. And people say men can't multitask. 'Did he stand you up? Or has his flea-infested beard taken over his entire face and he can't be seen in public anymore?' Or had Ruth finally seen sense and dumped the wanker?

'Leave it,' Billy muttered. There was clearly something going on, something that was upsetting Ruth so much she couldn't even bring herself to yell at Theo for wearing her T-shirt. 'Why don't you go and sort your washing out?'

Theo was about to protest. His washing could wait – his game couldn't. But then he noticed Ruth's eyes pool with tears and her lip started to wobble so he moved from the sitting room sharpish.

'Is it the reunion?' Billy and Ruth were alone now, Ruth perched on the edge of the sofa, her jacket still on. Billy wasn't sure if she'd opened the letter. He'd told her about it, but she'd taken the envelope upstairs and only emerged when it was time to leave for her date. Billy couldn't wait to catch up with everyone from school – Dom, Smithy, Tuck. Maybe Stephen would even fly over from New York. He wouldn't normally as it was too expensive to travel over for just a party, but he might this time, it being their last chance to see their old school before it was flattened.

But Billy knew it was different for Ruth. Her school days had been horrific and he couldn't blame her for being upset at the prospect of seeing the bastards from her year again.

'I'm not going.' Ruth lifted her chin, decisive and determined, despite feeling like jelly inside. 'I can't go. Not without a boyfriend.'

'But Gideon...'

'... is not my boyfriend any more.'

Oh. That explained the moodiness. Billy would be pretty miffed if he'd been binned by someone as repellent as Gideon too.

'What happened?'

Ruth pulled off her jacket and slung it on the back of the sofa before making herself more comfortable. 'I don't want to talk about it.'

Billy was relieved. He didn't particularly want to talk about Gideon either. That he was no longer a part of Ruth's life was enough for him.

'Do you want to watch *A Beginner's Guide*?'

'But we've already seen it.' *A Beginner's Guide To You* was their favourite sitcom and they never missed an episode, watching it together every Thursday evening with some variety of giant confectionery.

'When has that ever stopped us?' Now on its third season, Billy and Ruth knew the first two seasons word for word. 'And there's a massive fruit and nut in the fridge.'

'I'm not really in the mood. I'm having an early night.'

As Ruth heaved herself off the sofa, Billy realised how bad she must be feeling. Ruth never turned down an opportunity to watch *A Beginner's Guide* and she never *ever* rejected chocolate.

Billy had known Ruth from as far back as his memory could take him. They'd grown up on the same street and Billy was best friends with her older brother, Stephen. The Lynch's household became his second home and he spent the majority of his teenage years there, either holed up in Stephen's bedroom or sitting at the table eating Mrs Lynch's home-cooked food, which was far superior to the ready meals his father provided him with.

After completing their A Levels, Billy and Stephen enrolled in the same university and moved into a house share in Woodgate, a ten-minute train ride away. 184 Oak Road was already occupied by Cosmo, a trainee chef with aspirations of opening his own restaurant one day. The three hit it off immediately and the house was constantly filled with fun, laughter, good food and beautiful women. The beautiful women flocked to the house because of Cosmo but Billy and Stephen got to eat amazing food night after night so they couldn't grumble.

When Ruth turned up on the doorstep, her face pink and scrunched up with tears because she'd been dumped by some boy (Ruth had always been vague on the details), Billy and Stephen had offered to beat the boy in question up and the idea was so ludicrous – Zack being sporty and well-built and Billy and Stephen being your typical computer geeks – it cheered Ruth up enough to smile and dry her eyes with her sleeve. She'd been crashing on the sofa for a few days when Ruth learned Cosmo was moving out in a week to live with his latest girlfriend. She begged, literally begged, Billy and Stephen to let her move into the third bedroom and because they couldn't be bothered advertising for a new housemate, they agreed. Ruth applied for college in Woodgate and Cosmo helped her get a waitressing job at Café Katerina, the restaurant he was learning his trade in. The three lived together for a while until Stephen was offered a work experience position in New York and had shown such promise while over there that they offered him a twelve-month contract. Six years and several housemates later, Stephen was still in New York with his American wife and their three children.

Numerous occupants had taken Stephen's bedroom over the years, the first being Sindi, who lasted two months, as it transpired 184 Oak Road wasn't nearly glamorous enough for her. Ray lasted three years until he got married, moved to Wrexham and now just exchanged Christmas cards with Ruth and Billy. Leah lived with them for a year, but she never really gelled with her housemates and as soon as she was promoted at work she moved into her own flat. Christmas cards were never exchanged. Polly was next, living with them for eighteen months until she went on holiday to Cyprus and was never seen again. Jess was the shortest occupant, lasting a mere three weeks before she caught Billy 'fondling' her underwear, an accusation Billy hotly denies to this day. Louise was a classic tale: moved in, got together with Billy, broke up, moved out.

Billy and Theo worked together, and while they were

complete opposites in both looks and personalities, if you put them in front of a computer, they were as nerdy as each other, so when Louise moved out and Theo was looking for a new place it was the obvious solution for Theo to take the third bedroom. Theo had been living with Ruth and Billy for almost two years now, mainly because they had no idea how to get rid of him.

```
To: s.lynch
From: billy.worth
Subject: Reunion baby!

Hi mate,

How's everything in NY? Have you heard
about the reunion? Highmoor is getting
ripped down so they're having a
massive reunion in August. Will you be
able to make it? I'm looking forward
to it, but obviously Ruth isn't so
much.

Speaking of Ruth - great news. She
isn't with the prick Gideon any more.
She's upset about it (not good) but
she's better off without him. He's a
tosser and Ruth deserves better.

Let me know about the reunion, yeah?

To: billy.worth
From: s.lynch
Subject: Re: Reunion baby!

Yep, heard about the reunion. Someone
from the committee emailed me
```

yesterday. Think I'm going to be able to make it. We were planning a trip during the summer anyway so works out well.

Give Ruth a big hug from me. I only met Gideon once, when I was home last Christmas. You're right — he is a tosser. Spoke to Ruth like shit and was so rude to Mum. Was going to say something, but Mum said not to, that I'd only make matters worse.

Look after Ruth for me, will you?

To: s.lynch
From: billy.worth
Subject: Re: Re: Reunion baby!

You know I'll look after her. She's like a little sister to me.

THREE

Ruth

The bus driver shrank back in his seat as I thundered onto the bus, thrusting my monthly bus ticket towards his petrified face. He didn't even flick his eyes towards the expiry date in his eagerness to wave me past his little window. Nobody dared meet my eye as I stamped along the length of the bus, parking myself on the back seat where it was warmest. It was March and spring was supposed to be in the air but it seemed spring had abandoned me as well as Gideon and I was freezing in my floral tea dress. The fabric was thin and the sleeves short, and, although I was wearing a jacket, I may as well have been perched on an iceberg than the grubby back seat of the bus.

I shoved my earphones in, pretending my roughness hadn't hurt my delicate lobes, and turned the volume up on my iPod. Steps' *Greatest Hits* blasted my brain, the beat and bells of the intro to 'Tragedy' cheering me like magic. Faye started to sing and I found myself smiling as she neared the chorus. I wouldn't do the actions, I promise. Not in public.

My lifted mood drooped as soon as I stepped off the bus and the ugly business park loomed ahead. H. Wood Vehicles was the largest building in the gloomy park, lined with smaller manufacturing units and a purpose-built gym at the entrance. I tugged at my earphones, wound them around the iPod and trudged towards H. Woods' reception, dreading the next eight hours.

'Morning!' The receptionist smiled in greeting, but her grin depleted as she took in my down-turned mouth, narrowed eyes and lack of gait to my step. 'Oh. Is something wrong?'

I liked Quinn. She'd been the first contact I'd had when I arrived for my interview and had somehow put me at ease and there was nothing better than sneaking downstairs to have a bit of a skive and a gossip with her, so I did my best to soften my glare.

'I just got out of bed on the wrong side, I think.' I leant against the high reception desk, propping one foot against my calf and allowing the blood to return to one set of toes. 'I'll be alright once I've had a cup of coffee.'

'And how about...' Quinn rummaged in her drawer and pulled out a bag of Maltesers, selflessly handing them over to me. It was only a fun-size bag but it's the thought that counts and I managed a smile. 'I've got some magazines I've finished with as well if you want them.'

'Is Kelvin in yet?' Quinn shook her head. 'Then I'll take them. Thanks, doll.'

'No problem. Fancy a skive at ten?'

'I'll bring coffee.' I grabbed the stack of cellulite-ridden-celebrity type of magazines that Quinn favoured and carried them up to my first-floor office. I opened the blinds to reveal the March gloom before unlocking Kelvin's door and opening his blinds and switching on his computer, lest he break the old digits doing so himself. The magazines were deposited in my desk drawer bar the top one, which sat open on my desk while I munched my way through the tiny bag of Maltesers. I had to have a chuckle at the celebs the magazine had deemed fat. Fat! If having a miniscule pouch while wearing the tiniest bikini known to man was fat, I dread to think what the magazine world thought of me. *I* was fat. That poor size 10 girl was not.

I flicked the page. A celebrity was pregnant, which was fab news now and the magazine was piling on the praise. But wait a few months and the same celebrity would be ridiculed for having a single stretchmark and an ounce of fat while she wore her bikini. Alternatively, she would lose the baby weight before the umbilical cord was cut and the magazine would shake its head while it told everybody the new mum was 'too thin' and 'obsessed' with diet and exercise. She couldn't win.

The phone rang as I was reading an article rating women in order of 'hotness'. I picked it up and answered in my usual, automatic manner while still flicking through the magazine but was on high alert when Quinn informed me Kelvin was on his way up.

'Thanks, doll.' I dropped the phone in its cradle, shoved the magazine in the drawer and was busy tapping away at my keyboard by the time Kelvin puffed his way into the office. I had yet to switch my computer on but Kelvin wasn't to know that.

'Good morning, Kelvin.' I plastered an over-the-top smile on my face as Kelvin passed my desk. It wasn't returned.

'Coffee. And arrange a meeting with Sally and Hugh for lunchtime. Order food but none of that poncy pasta they brought last time.'

I saluted behind Kelvin's back. 'Yes, sir. Certainly, sir.' If Kelvin heard my response, he didn't show it as he strode through to his office and nudged the door shut with his foot. I was about to go off to make the coffee when the phone rang again.

'Good morning, Kelvin –'

'Is he in?'

'Can I ask who's speaking, please?' I already knew who was on the other end, rudely interrupting me. Only one person possessed such a shrill voice but I knew it pissed her off when I asked. How *dare* I make her address herself?

'It's Susan and I wish to speak to my husband, so stop wasting time and put me through.'

'Of course. You stupid old hag.' The last bit was obviously said while the phone was on mute as I transferred the call to Kelvin's office. Annoyed at being disturbed, Kelvin was further irritated when I told him, quite gleefully, who was on the line.

As soon as I put the phone down it rang again. Couldn't I get *any* work done today?

'Quinn says you look like a miserable cow this morning.' Erin was straight to the point, not wasting her breath on pleasantries.

'Paraphrasing?'

'Maybe.' I knew Quinn would never be so mean but Erin had no such qualms. 'So what's going on?'

Where did I start? I opted for chronological order, telling her first about the reunion and then Gideon dumping me in Cosmo's. He'd still wanted to eat but once Cosmo found out what had happened, he'd chucked Gideon out, napkin still tucked into his grimy T-shirt, knife and fork in hand.

'So now I can't go to the reunion *or* get my money back for the tickets. I phoned this morning but they said they're unable to issue refunds.' I adopted the snooty tone I'd been treated to earlier.

'Why can't you go to the reunion?' I couldn't blame Erin for not understanding. She'd never been fat or unpopular.

'I can't turn up without a boyfriend. Everyone thought I was a loser at school and they'll think I'm still a loser if I go alone. I can't turn up still fat and single.' Unless... My mind went into overdrive as I imagined gliding into the school hall in a slinky, sexy dress. I'd be thin and stunning, like the ugly duckling returning as a swan, and it wouldn't matter that I was single. Everyone would ask who I was, and their jaws would drop when they realised it was Ruth Lynch, former Mrs Blobby, now gorgeous and radiant. Zack's jaw would drop most of all and he would rue the day he ruined his chances with me.

'I've got it! I'll lose weight.' It sounded so simple. Why hadn't I thought of it before? 'I've got almost six months to get slim. It'll be perfect.'

'You know you don't *have* to go to the reunion, don't you?'

I bloody well did. 'The tickets cost me a hundred quid. *Each.*'

'What? Robbing bastards.'

'I know, but apparently there are thousands upon thousands of ex-pupils, so they're charging an extortionate fee to weed out those who aren't really into the whole reunion thing.'

'And are you?'

I wasn't sure. I'd never really considered the matter, but the thought of shocking everyone with my transformation had fired me up. 'I suppose I'm a bit curious to find out how everyone turned out.' Zack, I meant how Zack had turned out and Erin knew it too.

'Can't you just look him up on Facebook?'

'I tried to this morning. He isn't on there.' Which meant he was either hideously fat or disfigured now. I couldn't wait to gloat!

'Didn't I ask for coffee?' Kelvin barked from the doorway. I put up my index finger, indicating that Kelvin should shut his gob while I finished my call.

'That's great, Sally. Yes, down in Meeting Room One. Fabulous. Bye now.' I hung up on Erin and turned to Kelvin. 'You did ask for coffee and I was just about to go and make it. I thought organising the meeting was more important.'

Kelvin grunted in response. I hoped both Sally and Meeting Room One were available at lunchtime otherwise I'd be busted.

I used the rest of my morning productively, researching diets on the internet. In the end I chose the Simply Salad Diet as I was a terrible cook and Simply Salad required no real cooking at all. For breakfast, I was permitted one slice of wholemeal toast and then I could eat as much tomato, cucumber, lettuce and red pepper for lunch and dinner as I wanted. Snacks, which I would definitely need to get me through the day, were carrot sticks and apples.

Slipping out of work dead on five before Kelvin could throw a last-minute task at me, I hopped off the bus early to pop to the supermarket to stock up on my salad components. I felt immense pride as I swerved past the crisps and chocolate aisle, my basket full of nutritious goodness. They called out to me, and pretty loudly too, but I said no. I may have been a duckling now, but I was determined to flourish into a swan.

'What's that?' Billy asked when he arrived home from work and found me chopping salad in the kitchen.

'It's a tomato, you knob.' I popped a slice into my mouth and while it wasn't a cheeseburger, it wasn't bad and I'd had worse things in my mouth. I shuddered as an image of Gideon trespassed into my mind. 'Theo not with you?'

'Out on the pull, apparently.'

'Mid-week?'

Billy pulled out a chair and flopped onto it, leaning his elbows on the table. 'He says he hasn't had sex since Saturday and his balls are about to explode.'

The tomato churned in my stomach. 'That was *way* too much information.'

'You asked.' And now I wished I hadn't. 'So how are you feeling today? About Gideon? And the reunion?'

'I'm feeling fantastic.' I pointed at the bowl of half prepared salad. 'I'm on a diet. I'm going to lose weight and show all those morons how wonderful my life is now.' I couldn't wait to show them how happy I was, despite their taunts. I could already feel the pounds slipping off as I resumed chopping the tomatoes.

FOUR

Billy

The Playstation just wasn't the same without Theo
there to bellow swear words and put-downs, so Billy
switched it off and dumped the control pad at the side
of the TV before trudging up the stairs and switching on
his computer instead. Working in IT, Billy spent most of
the working day attached to a computer, but it didn't
impede his enjoyment of using his home computer.
He'd been obsessed with technology since his first
Commodore 64, which he and Stephen would play on
relentlessly: before school, after school, the entire
summer holidays. When it came to choosing a career,
there'd been no other option for either of them.

He was halfway through composing an email to
Stephen when he heard a strange sound through the
wall. His fingers froze over the keyboard while he
strained to hear it again. There it was! A strange,
muffled mewling sound coming from Ruth's bedroom.

Billy's fingers slid away from the keyboard, resting by his side as he listened, and it slowly dawned on him what the noise was.

'Ruth, are you okay?' Billy had knocked gently on the bedroom door and while he'd received no answer, the mewling had ceased. 'Ruth? It's Billy.'

There was another sound now but it was laughter rather than tears. 'I know it's you, you daft sod. If it was Theo, he'd be telling me to shut up, not asking if I was okay. Come in. Don't worry, I'm decent.'

Billy eased Ruth's bedroom door open and peered inside. Ruth was curled up on the bed, her normally bright face dulled by red eyes and a grimace. His first instinct was to gather Ruth into his arms, wrapping her up against the hurt. His second instinct was to track Gideon down and thump him in the face, but who was he kidding? Billy was weedy both in frame and nature. He'd never had a fight with anyone other than with Stephen when they were twelve and they'd both ended up wailing like a couple of sissies.

'He's not worth it, Ruth.' Billy perched on the edge of her bed but he made no attempt to soothe Ruth physically. Now up close, he wasn't sure how Ruth would react to his spindly arms trying to reach out to her. 'He's an absolute arsehole. I've never said anything before because it didn't seem right, slagging off your boyfriend, but I can't stand him. He's lazy and disrespectful, arrogant and rude.' Gideon constantly farted and scratched himself, even in front of Ruth's mother, and he was loud and opinionated, even though his views were utter bollocks. 'Don't waste your time crying over Gideon.'

Laughter spluttered from Ruth's lips as she shook her head. 'I'm not crying over Gideon. I agree with everything you've just said. He is an arsehole. And he's selfish in bed.'

All the pent up anger Billy had repressed over the last eight months seeped from his body. He'd despised Gideon, actually hated the man, and now it transpired Ruth didn't even like him herself. 'So why were you with him?'

Ruth reached for a pack of tissues on her bedside table and dried her eyes thoroughly before answering. 'I guess he was better than nothing. I didn't want to be on my own.'

'You're not on your own.' Billy reached out to pat Ruth on the knee but changed his mind. 'You've got me and Theo.'

Ruth gave a hoot. 'And that's supposed to cheer me up?'

Well, why not? They weren't perfect – especially Theo – but they cared about Ruth in their own way. They had their spats over the washing up, but they were mates deep down.

'If you aren't crying about Gideon, what's the matter?'

Ruth dabbed at her eyes before they met Billy's. She leant towards him and took his hands in hers, almost crushing them with her intensity. 'I'm so fucking hungry, Billy.' As though on cue, Ruth's stomach gave a loud growl. 'It's this diet. It's not filled me up at all. And neither has this.' Her gaze immediately dropped from Billy's face, even before she turned to reach under her pillow, dragging out the empty wrapper of a family-sized bar of Galaxy Caramel.

All the sympathy drained from Billy as he took in the wrapper. 'I bought that for us to share while we watched *A Beginner's Guide* tonight. And you've eaten it all.'

'You sound like Baby Bear.' Ruth flashed Billy a grin. He did not return one. 'I'm sorry, but I was starving. I've only had a bit of salad for tea.' She was dreading the next day where she'd be eating one measly piece of toast and yet more salad. Her stomach groaned in protest.

'You're hungry because just salad isn't enough to sustain a person.'

'But I need to lose weight.'

'And you're going to do that by snaffling my chocolate?' His eyes dropped to the empty wrapper, which Ruth shoved back under her pillow.

'Fine. I'll stop the stupid Simply Salad Diet, but I need to find another one. A better one.'

Billy rose to his feet as Ruth grabbed her laptop from under the bed. 'I'll leave you to it but don't take too long. *A Beginner's Guide* is on in twenty minutes.'

Ruth was already up and dressed when Billy emerged from the bathroom, his thick brown curls stacked on top of his head at an odd angle, his body still encased in a tatty dressing gown. It was Sunday so he had enjoyed a lengthy lie in.

'We'll be off to the pub in a bit if you want to come with us.'

Ruth paused at the top of the stairs and gave Billy an indulgent smile. 'You know I love nothing better than watching Theo chat up barmaids, but I have plans. I'm going shopping with Erin.'

Billy took a step back at the mere mention of Erin's name. The woman was like a vulture, sensing her prey and homing in with a fierce determination. She had never attempted to seduce Billy but he lived in fear that one day she'd run out of victims and pick on him.

'See you later.' Ruth blew Billy a kiss before skipping down the stairs, her mood much better now she'd changed her diet.

Theo emerged from his bedroom a while later, his hangover manifesting itself through heavy, bloodshot eyes, grey skin and a stomach that was ready to empty itself without a moment's notice. Billy didn't know what sorcery occurred within the confines of their bathroom, but Theo went in looking like he was about to keel over but came out radiant and ready for action, his hair its usual perfect black gleam, his skin smooth and glowing but not in a girly way, his teeth sparkling. Billy sometimes wished he knew what his housemate's secret was but then, if he was being completely truthful, he couldn't be arsed with all that metrosexual grooming crap, so the magic would be wasted on him.

Their local pub was the perfect place to spend their Sunday afternoon. The other patrons were young, the bar staff were hot, and the pool table charged a meagre 20p a game. Theo went to the bar for the drinks and to charm his way one inch closer to the inside of the barmaid's knickers while Billy staked his claim on the pool table and racked up. Theo had been after Caitlin for weeks and while he could move on to a million other girls, he was unwavering in his task of bagging the only one who had turned him down. Billy had set up the pool table, had a brief conversation via text message with Ruth and had a quick go on the fruit machine before Theo arrived with their drinks.

'Any luck?'

'Not yet, mate, but I'm getting there.'

Billy didn't doubt it. 'Whose break?'

Billy and Theo won a game each and were in a nail-biting decider, both now on the black. Billy consigned himself to losing as the ball hovered over the bottom right pocket but didn't quite make the leap to Billy's victory. Theo patted Billy on the back before lining up the shot, shooting a wink towards the two women who had been spectating since the middle of the first game.

'I'll give you a chance, mate. I'll take the shot with my eyes closed.' Theo grinned at the giggling women, closed his eyes and took his shot. The white ball shot up the table, missing the black by a whisker before rebounding off the cushion. The women gasped. Theo swore. Billy tried not to gloat, even as he potted the black and claimed ultimate victory.

'Bad luck,' one of the women cooed, placing a hand on Theo's chest. Her eyes widened as she came into contact with his shirt, feeling the contours of Theo's sculpted chest beneath. 'Can I get you a drink as a consolation prize?'

Caitlin was forgotten for the afternoon as Theo chatted and flirted with Becki, leaving Billy to try to entertain her friend. Clare was much quieter than Becki, though just as pretty with a blonde, fringed bob and fern green eyes. She accepted Billy's offer of a drink, returning the offer once they'd finished. Billy found Clare to be a sweet girl but with a wicked sense of humour and he was beginning to relax and enjoy himself when Theo pulled on his jacket and leaned in towards Billy.

'We're getting off. Don't wait up.' He winked at Billy as he grasped Becki's hand and led her towards the pub's exit, making sure to wave at Caitlin on his way out. Billy looked down at his drink. It was almost empty, as was Clare's, which meant she would be leaving too. She picked up her drink, drained the last inch and turned to Billy.

'Shall we have another?'

Billy couldn't believe there was a beautiful woman sitting with him. *Voluntarily*. Clare could have gathered her jacket and handbag ages ago, staying for one more drink purely out of politeness, but she hadn't. Two hours had passed and she was still there, laughing at Billy's jokes and bolstering his confidence by the millisecond. Women didn't generally get his jokes – Ruth aside – and they rarely found them remotely amusing.

'Will you excuse me?'

Here it comes, Billy thought. She was off. Not that he could complain. He'd had a good innings with Clare and had enjoyed their afternoon together. It had been a pleasant surprise and he was grateful for what it was.

'I just need to pop to the ladies. I won't be a minute. I'll grab another round on the way back, yeah?'

Billy knew Clare wasn't just being polite, that she wasn't planning to do a runner behind his back as she'd left her jacket behind. It was a nice jacket too, a belted black leather one that Billy bet Clare would look sexy as hell wearing. Billy usually felt self-conscious as he sat in a pub alone, but not today. Today he felt invincible. There was a beautiful woman willing to spend her afternoon with him, without even a hint of coercion. Billy felt his confidence raise another notch, a sensation he'd had little experience of before.

'There he is. I told you he'd still be in here.'

Billy cringed into the pint he was draining. Oh God, no.

'Hey, Billy. Where's your loser mate?' Erin cackled as she sauntered towards him, arms laden with shopping bags. She dumped them on the bench next to Billy and plonked herself on a low stool. Billy waved to Ruth at the bar and shook his head when she asked if he wanted a drink.

'You're not on your own, are you?' Ruth asked. 'Where's Theo?'

Erin wrinkled her nose. 'He's pulled, hasn't he?' She took Billy's shrug of his shoulders as an affirmative and turned towards Ruth, calling out across the pub. 'Theo's pulled some slapper. Probably shagging as we speak.'

'Becki's not a slapper, actually.'

Billy groaned, squeezing his eyes shut. Childlike, he convinced himself that if he couldn't see Clare, she wasn't there. Could she have timed her re-entrance any shittier? He wondered whether Clare would snatch her lovely jacket from beside him or mark it as a loss before she stormed out of the pub.

Thank you, Erin. Thank you very much.

From: s.lynch
To: billy.worth
Subject: Tickets

Good news! Bought the tickets for the reunion and booked the flights this morning so I'll see you in August!

How's Ruth?

From: billy.worth
To: s.lynch
Subject: Re: Tickets

Cool! I have good news of my own. I have a date. An actual date! And I didn't even meet her on the internet.

Ruth's friend almost ruined my chances but she must like me as she gave me her number before she left the pub. Result!

Ruth's fine. Over Gideon (turns out she felt the same way we did about him). She's really looking forward to the reunion too!

FIVE

Ruth

'Look at you, all domesticated. You'll be having dinner parties next.' Erin and I were in the kitchen, Erin perched daintily on the counter while I grilled a couple of salmon fillets and chopped the salad. It was hardly cordon-bleu-style cooking, but since I struggled to heat microwave pizzas, it was quite an achievement. 'Who would you invite? Not me, obviously. I'm way too common for dinner parties.'

'Do you think I'd host a dinner party and not invite you? You'd be my star guest.'

'Really?' Erin sounded genuinely surprised, her eyebrows and tone rising with the question. 'Thanks, doll.'

'You're easily pleased.'

'Ha! If only.' Erin slipped off the worktop and headed for the fridge, sticking her head inside and emerging with two bottles of beer. 'Did I tell you about Christian?

The salsa guy?' She proffered one of the bottles but I shook my head.

'I don't think I can drink beer on this diet.'

'Not even one?'

I caved in and grabbed the bottle. One would do no harm. 'So what happened with Christian?'

'Not a lot.' Erin dragged out a chair and sat at the table, slumping against the surface. 'Oh, he was going like the clappers, having a jolly old time. *I* barely felt a thing. No wonder his girlfriend always has a face like a slapped arse. Frustration. Pure *frustration*. Poor cow.'

'So you won't be seeing him again?'

'No, I will not be seeing him again. Total waste of time.' Erin rummaged in the kitchen drawers for a bottle opener and opened both our bottles before slumping back at the table. 'So who would you invite to your dinner party then? Apart from your star guest?'

I gave the salmon a prod. How did you know they were cooked? 'I'd have to invite Billy.'

'*Billy*? But he's your housemate. And quite boring. Why would you invite him?'

'Billy's not boring and he's one of my best friends. Plus, he's a better cook than me. I'd have him prepare everything while I made the table look pretty.'

'Good plan.' Erin tipped her bottle at me in appreciation. 'You wouldn't invite Theo though, would you?'

I spluttered. 'Course not. What do you take me for?' I gave the salmon another prod. 'Do you think this is cooked?'

Erin joined me at the grill and the pair of us peered at the fish, neither having a clue. Erin was a worse cook than I was.

'Shall we give it a go?'

Erin took a contemplative swig. 'Yeah, why not? What's the worst that can happen?'

We could die.

I kept my gob shut and served the salmon onto two plates instead.

'What's she doing here and why is she drinking my beer?' Theo paused on the threshold of the kitchen, leaning against the doorframe as he eyed Erin with deep suspicion.

'Erin's my friend and therefore welcome in my home. But sorry about the beers. I'll replace them.'

Theo remained in the doorway, observing us through narrowed eyes. I hoped he wasn't going to ask to join us. My diet was quite restrictive and the portions pretty small, so I wasn't in the mood for sharing. He stepped fully into the room and I held my breath.

'Where's Billy?'

'He's out on a date.' I slowly placed the plates onto the table, hoping the careful movement wouldn't draw any attention to my food.

'A date? Billy? Are you sure?'

'Yes, I'm sure. He's with some girl he met at the pub.' I placed the bowl of salad in the middle of the table, not bothering to hide it. There was plenty of salad to go around so there was no need to be stingy.

'There's a first time for everything, I guess.' Theo sauntered towards the fridge and I was relieved when he pulled out a massive, greasy meat feast pizza that had been tempting me since the weekend big shop. Not only was he disposing of the temptation, he wouldn't want to share my salmon with that yummy tyre-sized pizza all to himself. Although, if he wanted to swap...

'Do you have to be so horrible? Billy is a nice young man with a lot to offer.'

I gaped as Erin jumped to Billy's defence – hadn't she labelled him boring only a few minutes ago?

Theo sniggered. 'Name one thing our Bill has to offer any woman.'

'Well...' Erin filled her plate with salad while trying to fill her brain with an answer. The room fell into an unbearable silence. Could she really think of nothing positive about Billy? When Erin's plate was piled high with salad and she still hadn't mustered one measly point, I felt I had to wade in on Billy's behalf.

'He's kind and caring and mature. He can look after himself *unlike some people*. He's funny and smart and he makes a gorgeous curry. You should try it, Erin, it's amazing.'

'Sounds like someone wants to shag our Bill. I'll be listening out for creaking bedsprings tonight.' Theo winked at me while I glared back.

'Grow up. Billy and I are friends. A girl can appreciate a man's good points without wanting to jump into bed with him.'

'Hmm, yeah right. Erin, do you believe that?'

I turned to my friend who shot me an apologetic look before shaking her head. 'Utter bullshit.' Theo grinned in triumph, the smug bastard.

'She would say that. Erin jumps into bed with everyone. She'd probably even shag *you*.'

The kitchen erupted into gagging sounds and protests to the contrary while I sat back with glee and polished off my salmon. I wasn't entirely convinced it was cooked through, but I was hungry and had no alternative option.

I swallowed the last piece of chicken and fell back in my chair, rubbing my stomach. It was a shock to find that I was actually full. That day's grilled chicken and salad had turned out to be a huge success, unlike the previous day when the chicken had still been pink, practically *bleeding*, in the middle.

'That was lovely. Thank you.' Asking – or begging, if I'm being completely honest – Billy to cook the chicken for me had been a genius move.

'You're welcome. But you know this means you have to wash up, right?' I played along, giving a drawn out sigh as I gathered the plates but I'd happily wash the dishes if it meant someone else cooked my meals. At least washing dishes wouldn't poison me.

Billy made a cup of tea and sat at the table to chat to me while I cleared up but in the end he joined me at the sink to dry. He'd make someone a good husband one day.

'I'm just going to jump in the shower before *A Beginner's Guide*,' I told Billy as I dried my hands on his tea towel. Twenty minutes later I was nestled on the sofa in a pair of clean pyjamas, my wet hair still encased in a towel. The opening credits began and my mouth watered, anticipating a sugary treat I was no longer permitted. Damn this diet!

Billy jumped up from the sofa. 'Oh, I almost forgot…' The rest of his words were lost as he dashed off towards the kitchen. I heard the fridge open and close, followed by the rapid footsteps of Billy's return. I'd have to remind him that I couldn't eat chocolate on my diet. And then I'd let him talk me into eating a *tiny* piece.

'You know, I can't actually eat chocolate on my diet. Although I have been very good…' I paused as Billy stepped into the room. Something was wrong. Billy was carrying a large bowl, which wasn't unusual in itself as we sometimes shared a bowl of popcorn, but this didn't smell like popcorn. It didn't smell like sweet cocoa goodness either.

'It's okay. It's isn't chocolate.' This, I'd already established. 'How insensitive do you think I am?' So what was it then? A mountain of Haribo? Ooh, Jelly Babies! 'Ta-dah!' Billy presented the bowl with a flourish before flopping onto the sofa beside me. I looked inside the bowl. I looked at Billy. I looked back inside the bowl, my excitement well and truly slapped down.

'It's fruit.'

Billy beamed. I sat on my hands so I didn't swipe the grin off his chops. 'Not just fruit. *Fruit salad*. I made it myself.'

'You chopped up a load of fruit?' Big whoop. Give the guy a Michelin star.

'Yep.' He looked *pleased* with himself. 'I know it isn't technically allowed on your diet, but I figured fruit is healthy so it'd be okay as a treat.'

Who gave a toss about healthy? I wanted chocolate. Sweet, fattening chocolate. Screw the diet and screw the reunion. But no, let's not be hasty. Billy was right. Chocolate was bad for the next six months. I took a couple of deep, calming breaths, envisioning Zack's face when he saw me glide into the school hall looking svelte and glamorous.

Svelte and glamorous. *Svelte and glamorous.*

'Thank you, Billy. That was very considerate of you.' I plucked a slice of apple from the bowl and popped it into my mouth, choking back a sob at its lack of sugary creaminess.

SIX

Ruth

The bus ride into work was as hellish as ever, cramped and damp with the added bonus of vomit streaking down the back of the front seat and pooling on the floor, but the journey wasn't the reason for my drooping shoulders and downturned mouth as I shuffled into reception. It was a Monday morning, so of course I was feeling a little blue (it would be abnormal if I was happy to be at my place of employment first thing on a Monday) but again, that wasn't the reason for my slump. I had failed at another diet.

After the Simply Salad Diet hadn't worked out, I'd started a new diet, which was still heavily salad based (which worked out well as I still had a fridge full of the stuff) but had the luxury of adding a small portion of grilled chicken, salmon or tuna and I'd also taken it upon myself to add a second slice of wholemeal toast

for breakfast. The new diet was going well and I
managed to stick to it. Until Friday. And Saturday and
Sunday.

'Morning!' Quinn's bright features faded as she took
in my misery guts features. 'Don't tell me you're still
hung over after Friday.'

Friday, aka Diet Destroyer Day.

'No. I'm not hung over.' If only it were that simple.
I'd take a couple of paracetamol, buy a large strawberry
milkshake and a bacon butty and I'd be sorted.

'It was a great party though, wasn't it?'

I rested my elbows on the reception desk and
allowed myself to crash. 'Hmm, great party.'

Friday's party had been in honour of the purchasing
manager, who was leaving H. Woods and moving on to
somewhere far superior (or so I guessed. After working
at H. Woods, the only way was up, after all). The party
was in full swing and I was enjoying myself, drinking
vodka and diet coke and dancing away on the sticky
makeshift dance floor at The Bonnie Dundee. And then
the buffet was opened. Uh-oh. I tried, really I did, but
the lure of all those sausage rolls, greasy chicken legs,
crisps and cake was too much. I demolished the buffet,
not even giving the token bowl of salad a second glance.

I intended to resume the diet the following day, but
the weekend turned into a calorie disaster. I joined Billy
and Theo in a Saturday night takeaway curry, complete
with onion bhajis, popadoms and samosas on the side,
and I visited my mum and dad on Sunday where I ate a
huge roast followed by sticky toffee pudding.

'You should have seen me on Saturday. I thought I
was going to die. I couldn't get out of bed until three
o'clock.'

See, that's where I went wrong. I should have drunk

myself into oblivion like Quinn, rendering me comatose all weekend and thus unable to consume any calories. I made a mental note of the plan for next time.

Quinn looked over my shoulder, her eyes widening as she stood up straight. 'Kelvin's car just turned into the car park.'

With a yelp, I scurried through reception to the stairwell, racing up the first half of the stairs before I was reduce to a crawl. I still had plenty of time though as Kelvin was even fatter than me so he'd still be de-wedging himself from his car by now and he'd still be sweating on the first step by the time I reached the office. The blinds were open and both computers were switched on by the time Kelvin wheezed into my office. I was sitting at my desk, somehow controlling my breathing while composing an email. It was to Stephen and Billy, but Kelvin didn't have to know that.

'I've got a meeting scheduled with Angelina in ten minutes. Bring us coffee – and I spotted a packet of Jammy Dodgers in the kitchen yesterday.'

'Good morning to you too,' I muttered as Kelvin shut himself in his office. I raced to finish my email and sent it before heading off to the kitchen. I found the Jammy Dodgers, but they were labelled 'Lisa', so I shoved them to the very back of the cupboard, where Kelvin would be too lazy to look, and filled a plate with his usual chocolate digestives instead.

'Send Angelina straight through when she arrives,' Kelvin said by way of thanks as I placed the tray of coffee and biscuits on his desk. 'And we're not to be disturbed, under any circumstances. This is a very important meeting.'

'And quite urgent too, I should imagine.'

Kelvin narrowed his piggy eyes at me. 'And what do

you mean by that?'

'It's first thing on a Monday morning. You've barely had time to take your jacket off, so it must be urgent if you need to see Angelina right this second.'

'It is. Extremely urgent. We have important matters to discuss.'

And it had nothing to do with the bulge in his trousers, the randy, disgusting bastard.

'Knock, knock!' Angelina had arrived, singing out instead of actually knocking on the door like a normal person. 'Sorry I'm late. I was hoping to catch a glimpse of the new purchasing manager before I left the office, but Sammy's taken him on a tour of the building.'

'Never mind, you're here now.' Kelvin turned to me, his fingers itching to whip down his fly. 'Is that the phone ringing out there? Remember, we're not to be disturbed. Close the door.'

I did as I was told, shuddering as I imagined what was about to happen in there. Kelvin and Angelina had been having an affair for months. And by affair, I mean a series of quickies in his office.

I hurried away from the door, worried I may actually hear the affair in action, and answered the phone.

'Is Kelvin there?'

'Who may I ask is speaking?' I knew who it was, of course, but I had to do something fun to brighten my day.

'It's Susan. Put Kelvin on.'

I paused, relishing the thought of annoying the hell out of Kelvin's stroppy little wife. 'I'm afraid Mr Shuttleworth is in a meeting. Can I take a message?'

'No, you bloody can't take a message. What I have to say to my husband is none of your damn business. I want to be put through to him.'

'I'm afraid I've been asked not to disturb Mr Shuttleworth. I can ask him to call you back shortly.' Very shortly. Kelvin wouldn't last long enough to allow the coffees to grow cold.

'You'll put me through to him *now*.'

'I'm afraid I —'

'And I'm afraid you'll lose your pissing job if you don't put me through to my husband.' The more irate she became, the wider my smile stretched. 'So stop being an annoying bitch and let me speak to Kelvin.'

'Mr Shuttleworth is in an important meeting and was quite clear he is not to be disturbed.'

'But I'm his wife!'

'Still, I have to follow Mr Shuttleworth's instructions.'

'For fuck's sake.' A loud sigh hissed in my ear. 'Fine. Tell him to phone me back as soon as possible.'

The corners of my mouth itched as I fought to remain serious. 'Can I take your number?'

'He has my fucking number.' The phone was slammed down without so much as a goodbye. I was scrawling the message on a post-it when Erin wandered into the office, cups of coffee in hand.

'What so funny?' Erin asked as I tittered to myself.

'I've just been winding Susan up.' I took one of the cups from Erin and thanked her. 'What happened to you on Friday? The last time I saw you, you were doing your best to avoid the Ginger Bastard.' Richard Shuttleworth, aka the Ginger Bastard, was Erin's manager and he'd had a massive crush on her since she started at the company. He acted like a lost puppy, following her around, desperate to be petted.

'I avoided him completely by going home with Stuart from Accounts.'

'Again?' Erin had worked her way through the more good looking employees of H. Woods, but she rarely went back for seconds. She liked to explore new options and give other men a go. She was fair like that.

'Well, he is rather good.' Erin grinned and gave a contented sigh. 'Three times, Ruth. If it wasn't for my Get Out By Eight rule, it would have been four.'

With Gideon out of the picture, I couldn't imagine when I'd have sex again. And speaking of sex, Kelvin's door opened and he ushered Angelina out, pausing when he spotted Erin perched on my desk. Anyone else caught skiving would have been given a bollocking, but not Erin. Richard wouldn't allow his father to berate the lovely Erin.

'Did you get dressed in the dark this morning?' Erin asked Angelina, nodding at her skirt, which was tucked into her knickers at one side. 'Don't be embarrassed. It happens to all of us.' Angelina unhooked her skirt before scurrying out of the office, doing her best to keep her head held high.

'Susan called. She wants you to ring back as soon as possible.' I held out the post-it but Kelvin didn't deign to take it. Instead, he grunted and retreated into his office.

Erin hopped off my desk. 'She has no standards, that Angelina. Imagine having sex with *that*.' Shaking her head, Erin gave a wave and wandered back to her own office, leaving me to get on with some work. Opening Google, I began researching a new diet.

I settled on the Atkins Diet, assuming it would be a piece of piss. I could eat as much meat as I liked, for God's sake. I'd been dreaming of big fat steaks during my salad days and now not only could I eat them, my diet dictated that I must. I was glowing after three days of Atkins, full and 52olognese after my days of tomato misery.

'I'm going on my lunch break. Would you like anything from the kitchen?' See, my good mood was even allowing me to be helpful towards Kelvin.

'I've got my lunch here.' Kelvin prodded a plastic box on his desk without looking away from his computer screen. 'Shut the door on your way out.'

I skipped to the kitchen, actually looking forward to my lunch for a change, and was met by a delicious bottom as I stepped into the kitchen. An unidentified male was searching the only cupboard in the tiny kitchen. Had I been Erin, I'd have followed my desire to give it a good squeeze. But I wasn't Erin so I fought the urge and headed for the fridge to cool down instead.

'Oh, hello. I didn't hear you come in.' The unidentified male pulled his head out of the cupboard and rose to his feet, dusting off his trousers. I bit back a yelp as he looked up. Yikes, he was divine. Still unidentified, he was tall and lean with closely shaven blond hair and the beginnings of pale stubble. I imagined the roughness on my soft skin as he kissed me and felt my cheeks warming.

'I don't think we've met. I'm Jared Williams, the new purchasing manager.' He held out a hand and despite being warm, it sent a shiver along my arm as I took it.

'Ruth Lynch, Kelvin Shuttleworth's PA.' I stood gawping at him, wondering how it was possible for a man so amazingly gorgeous to be before me in H. Woods' grotty little kitchen, how he had found himself working at H. Woods at all. Surely there were better places for a man such as Jared Williams.

'Sorry, am I in your way?' Jared shuffled to the side as best as he could, pinning himself up against the wall while I shot towards the fridge, sinking my hot face into its glorious coolness. Had I really just stood staring at him, 53olognese53 by his beauty? I was pathetic beyond words.

'There isn't a ham salad in the fridge, is there? I've had a look but I couldn't find it. I thought maybe it had been moved to the cupboard, but it isn't in there either. My yogurt's gone too.'

Kelvin strikes again, I thought, recalling the plastic tub on his desk. As well as being a pervert and a grumpy sod, Kelvin Shuttleworth was a phantom lunch stealer.

I rose from the fridge and put a hand on Jared's arm to break the news. 'I don't think your lunch has made it, I'm afraid. It's a gamble storing your lunch in here. You've only got a fifty-fifty chance of it surviving. Did nobody warn you?' Jared shook his head, his brow furrowing ever so slightly. Lord, help me. He was even sexy while frowning. 'It's Kelvin. He's somehow under the impression that the kitchen is stocked for his personal use. Labelling food doesn't work either. He sees food and eats.' I'd given up trying to hammer the point home a long time ago. 'I'm sorry for your loss.'

To my relief, Jared didn't think I was a complete tit and he smiled at me. And what a sight that was! I'd forgotten I was clutching hold of my plastic tub until it almost slipped from my clammy hands.

'My chicken was lucky enough to have survived. There's plenty if you want to share.'

What was I doing? That was practically a lunch date. Why on earth would a man like Jared accept any kind of date with the likes of me?

'That's so kind of you. I'd love to share.'

Oh. Right then. 'It's just chicken. No salad or pasta or anything. You'd probably be better off going to the pub for one of their lunches.' Why was I talking him out of it? Shut up, Ruth. 'But they're a bit ghastly, to be honest. They only do two meals – rubbery spaghetti 54olognese or a sweaty ploughman's lunch.' Please, for the love of God, *shut up.*

'I'm not a fan of rubbery or sweaty food. I prefer chicken, even if there isn't any salad or pasta or anything. Do you mind sharing?'

I didn't and so we grabbed a couple of plates and divided the chicken between us. I expected Jared to wander off back to his office, putting as much distance between him and the crazy girl as he could but he didn't. We stayed put in the kitchen, despite the lack of seating, and ate our lunch while chatting. I couldn't get over it. Gorgeous Jared Williams, chatting to me. *Me*!

That night, I dreamt about Gorgeous Jared Williams but then he turned into a baked potato, dripping with butter. I didn't know it yet, but not only was I craving Gorgeous Jared Williams, I was also beginning to crave carbs. The cravings intensified over the next few days and I found my dreams muddled with potatoes, I hallucinated about eating stodgy pasta and the sight of bread brought me out in a cold sweat. I could feel the end of Atkins was nigh but the final straw came when I weighed myself. I'd lost a pound. *One sodding pound.* I needed to slim down to at least a size 14 to wow at the reunion so one pound wasn't going to cut it. I needed another diet and fast.

After scouring the internet, the answer became clear. Instead of depriving myself of food groups, I simply had to cut down on what I ate and follow a calorie controlled diet. I found a weekly food plan online that looked reasonable and even allowed the odd treat. Perfect. Except there was one massive downside to a calorie controlled diet. I had zero control.

SEVEN

Billy

The bathroom shelf was crammed with all sorts of crap, from 56olognese56r, self-tan, hair serum, face washes and scrubs to night cream. And worst of all, it all belonged to Theo. Billy's grooming consisted of shampoo, shower gel, deodorant and running a comb through his hair, but then he didn't have a tiny proportion of the luck Theo had with women so maybe over grooming was the way to go.

Billy peered at Theo's shelf, at the pots and bottles of magic. He was preparing for his second date with Clare, so he wanted to present himself to the best of his ability and if that meant rubbing a bit of poncy cream in his hair and face, then so be it.

Billy was surprised it had come to a second date at all as they hadn't got off to the best start. Billy had assumed his chances with Clare had been torn to shreds due to Erin's gigantic gob. Clare had obviously jumped to her best friend's defence after Erin unwittingly insulted Becki and Billy feared things were about to get ugly. Luckily for Billy, Ruth was on hand to calm the situation and the four of them had shared the briefest drink known to man before Clare made her excuses and left. Inexplicably, she'd left her number and they'd embarked on a disastrous first date a few days later.

It had started off alright with a trip to the cinema and, while the film was a bit naff, it wasn't anything too damning. They went for a drink afterwards and that's where the trouble began. Billy had been to the bar and when he returned he found there was a bloke – the preened kind who probably used everything on Theo's shelf and more – chatting Clare up. And what did Billy do? He stood back and let him. Well, what else could he do? The bloke was tall, broad and toned while Billy was a floppy haired, skinny geek. Clare shouldn't have been out with him at all. He was punching way above his weight and so he quietly slid Clare's drink onto the table and nursed his own a couple of seats away.

'What are you doing over there, Billy?' Clare had patted the bench she was sitting on, opposite the preened guy who was perched on a stool looking cool, slick and smug. 'Come and sit here. Callum was just keeping me company while you were at the bar but you're here now.' She turned to the preened guy with a sweet smile. 'Thank you ever so much.' Now bog off, her smile continued.

Clare had rolled her eyes as Callum swaggered back to his mates. 'What an idiot. His head is so far up his bum I'm surprised he can breathe.'

It turned out Clare wasn't into the hyper grooming thing and had agreed to see Billy again. So why was he studying Theo's shelf? Clare liked Billy as he was.

Shaking his head at his lack of confidence, Billy ignored the products on the shelf and left the bathroom. He was showered and shaved and that was good enough.

'Fancy a game?' Theo held up the Playstation pad and made room on the sofa. It wasn't yet seven pm, but the coffee table was already littered with beer bottles and takeaway cartons.

'I can't. I'm going out on a date.' Billy tried not to sound smug as the words left his mouth, but dates happened so infrequently for him that it was difficult not to.

Theo swivelled round to take a proper look at Billy, noting that he wasn't wearing his usual scruffy jeans and game-based T-shirt. 'With who?'

'Clare.' The name was met by a blank look. 'We met her in the pub a couple of weeks ago. You went home with her friend, Becki.'

'Becki... Becki... Ah, yes.' Theo nodded in approval. 'Dirty, *dirty* girl. Is Clare as mucky as her friend?'

'Like I'd tell you.' Like Billy would know. Clare wasn't like that and, to be honest, neither was Billy. He preferred to get to know a girl before they had sex. Theo wasn't even fussed if he knew the girl's name. 'Anyway, I'm off.'

'Have fun,' Theo called over his shoulder, having already turned back to his game.

Billy took the opportunity to calm his nerves during the walk to Clare's house, but it seemed his nerves were unwilling to be soothed and the nauseous feeling remained, doing laps in his stomach until the moment Clare opened the door. Looking casual but pretty in a pair of skinny jeans and a cream T-shirt with a peach, leafy floral print, Clare hooked on a jacket, hopped over the threshold and gave Billy a peck on the cheek before linking her arm through his and chatting away for the duration of the short walk to Cosmo's. With Clare obviously feeling so at ease with Billy, he found the feeling reciprocated and his jitters wafted away into the cool evening air.

Cosmo met them at the door with a pre-arranged glass of champagne. 'Mr Worth, Ms Rathbone, would you like to follow me? Your table is ready.' Billy and Clare were seated by the window where a bucket of ice held the remainder of the bottle of champagne. Cosmo gave the pair his undivided attention for the evening and by the time they left, tipsy on champagne and full of Cosmo's finest food, Clare felt thoroughly wined and dined.

'Does he treat all his customers like that?' Clare asked as she zipped up her jacket outside the restaurant. The sun had completely died out by now and the temperature had dropped severely.

'He's never treated me like that before so it must just be you.'

'And you had nothing to do with it?' Billy had let slip that Cosmo was an old friend of his but Clare thought it was sweet that he had gone to such efforts for her. Rising on her tiptoes, she kissed Billy lightly on the lips. With her back to the window, she didn't see Cosmo flashing Billy a wink from within the restaurant.

'It's still quite early. Do you want to come back to mine for a coffee?'

Clare slipped her hand in Billy's as they began to walk away from Cosmo's. 'That would be lovely.'

Billy clasped his hands together and thanked a higher power when they returned to an empty house. Theo must have grown bored of his own company and wandered down to the pub for another crack at Caitlin and Billy hadn't seen Ruth since breakfast.

'How do you take it?' Billy asked as he filled the kettle.

'White, no sugar please.' Billy bit his tongue, unwilling to utter 'sweet enough?' as that would be beyond cheesy, even for him. 'This is a lovely house. Do you share?'

'Yep, I have two housemates, Theo and Ruth. You met them, remember?'

Ah, yes. Theo. He'd promised to phone her friend but never did. Bastard. 'Ruth seems nice. Have you known her long?'

'I've known her forever. She's my best mate's little sister and we've lived together for about ten years.'

'And you two have never...' How did she phrase it? '... Hooked up?'

Billy spluttered and spilled the coffee granules he'd been scooping into mugs onto the counter. 'God, no. Stephen would kill me. And she's like a sister to me. We grew up together. When my mum died, I spent more time with her family than my own.'

'So there are no feelings there? For either of you?'

'Not in that way, no.' Billy finished making the coffees and they wandered into the sitting room where Clare slipped off her boots and curled up on the sofa. 'So who do you live with?'

Clare scrunched up her nose, which Billy thought looked adorable, like a little bunny. 'My parents. I know, I know, I'm too old to be living with Mum and Dad but it's only a recent thing. I split up with my ex six months ago and I tried to manage the mortgage on my own, but it wasn't happening so I had to go home to Mum and Dad. But it's only until I've scraped a deposit together to rent my own place.' She blew on her coffee but it was still far too hot. After standing to place it on the coffee table, she sat back down, much closer to Billy this time. 'I've had a fantastic time tonight. Thank you.' Reaching up, she pulled Billy towards her and kissed him but this time it wasn't a quick peck. He began to suspect she was as mucky as Becki when her soft, warm hands slipped under his shirt, tracing up towards his hair-free chest. Billy had experienced quite a lengthy dry spell since his ex-girlfriend, Louise moved out and his body sprang into action from the lightest touch, more than ready to rectify that fact. Clare murmured against his lips as Billy drew her closer to his body and a celebration began in his trousers. *Yes! Yes! She is as mucky as Becki. Finally, some action!*

But action wasn't to be. The door swung open and Ruth bounded into the room, her face flushed and grin wide.

'You'll never guess how much I lost at Weight Watchers. I was – oh, shit, sorry. You're busy.' Ruth backed away from the sofa, retreating into the hallway but Clare stopped her.

'No, no, it's fine. Really.' She removed herself from Billy's lap and smoothed her T-shirt. 'Hello again, Ruth. We met at the pub a couple of weeks ago.'

Ruth nodded and extended a hand. 'Hello. It's nice to see you again.' A moment before Clare took her hand, it dawned on Ruth that there was a good chance Clare's hand had just been acquainted with Billy's 'little friend', and, although the thought made her grimace it was too late and Clare's hand was wrapped around hers.

'Since when do you go to Weight Watchers?' Billy asked. 'I thought you were just cutting back.'

'I was.' Ruth tried to be subtle in wiping her hand down her T-shirt. 'But it didn't work. It turns out I'm a greedy pig without control. Funny that. So I decided to sign up for Weight Watchers. There's no motivation like the humiliation of standing on the scales in front of an audience. I was lucky and lost weight this week – *four pounds* by the way – but imagine if I'd put weight on. I'll picture the mortification next time I want a Mars bar.'

'Well done. Four pounds is fantastic.'

Ruth beamed at Clare. 'Thank you. It feels amazing to have lost it.' She was about to plonk herself in the armchair when she caught Billy's eye. His face was screaming *fuck off, Ruth* and she decided it was best to follow its instructions. 'Anyway, I'm exhausted after all that weight loss. I'm going to go up for an early night.'

'Goodnight, Ruth.' Billy, eager to be alone with Clare again and finish what they'd started, had to repel against the desire to elbow Ruth out of the room and shut the door.

'I should be getting home, actually.'

'But it's still pretty early.' Billy wasn't sure whether it was his mouth or his penis that cried out as Clare shoved her feet into her boots and grabbed her jacket.

'Dad will be waiting up. Sorry.' She gave Billy another chaste peck before heading for the door. 'It was nice to meet you properly, Ruth.'

'Yes, you too.' Ruth was already halfway up the stairs as Clare wandered into the hallway. Billy would be pretty pissed off by the time he'd closed the front door and she wanted a head start.

'Phone me tomorrow, yeah?' Clare pecked Billy on the cheek and then she was gone, leaving her coffee cold and Billy colder, his dry spell still reigning.

EIGHT

Ruth

Billy was pissed off with me. He tried to hide it but the slamming of doors and the inability to be in the same room as me were dead giveaways. Not that I could blame Billy for being annoyed after I ruined his chances of getting laid. I didn't think he'd had sex in a long, long time, possibly since he broke up with Louise. Wow. Nearly two years ago. I was surprised Billy wasn't hurling furniture at me.

Still, being in Billy's bad books wasn't enough to dampen my mood. I skipped out to work that morning, early Spice Girls blasting in my ears, and I didn't even grumble when I was forced to sit next to a BO-reeking teen with bad breath and fidgety fingers that drummed on the window for the duration of my journey.

'You're looking very pleased with yourself this morning.'

'Very observant, Quinn. I *am* very pleased with

myself.'

'Weight Watchers went well then?'

I strolled towards the reception desk, savouring the moment. 'It went extremely well. I lost four pounds.'

Quinn looked as thrilled as I felt as she clapped her hands like a performing sea lion. 'Well done. That's amazing. Let's have a look at you.' Ever obliging, I took a couple of steps away from the desk and gave a twirl. I knew you couldn't *see* the weight loss but sod it, I was relishing my little victory. 'I'm so pleased for you, Ruth.' Her smile slipped a little and she leant across the desk. 'But I should warn you. Kelvin's already upstairs.'

'What?' I checked my watch. It was only ten to nine.

'He's been here since half past eight.'

I wasn't late for work, yet I still raced up the stairs, puffing and panting my way to the top. Quinn was right – Kelvin was in his office and in the process of wrecking the joint by the looks of it.

'What are you doing?' Files were slumped over the carpet, bits of paper spilling out everywhere while Kelvin rustled through the cabinet, dumping yet more files by his feet. Had he misplaced a Snickers?

'I'm looking for the Westerly file. Where is it?'

Stepping between the files on the tiny patches of available carpet peeking through, I paused half way between the door and Kelvin. 'It's on your desk.'

'It isn't. I haven't touched it.' Kelvin swung around, almost taking out a pot plant with his girth. 'Oh. There it is. Very good. Would you mind sorting this lot out? I have a meeting with Glenn and I'm late. Can you also 64olognes coffee for four down in Meeting Room One?' Without waiting for a reply, Kelvin thumped out of the room, Westerly file tucked under his arm while I took in the mess surrounding me. But then I'd lost four pounds, so I didn't care and quickly dropped to my knees to pick up the files.

My good mood swept me through the rest of the morning and not even Susan Shuttleworth's shrill, whiny voice double checking the arrangements for Kelvin's birthday party could bring me down. I was four pounds lighter so I couldn't have cared less about anything else.

'It's lunchtime.' Kelvin strode towards me, having returned from his meeting, his office now clear of clutter and the files in correct order. 'Can you bring me something from the kitchen?'

'But it's only half past eleven.'

'So? I'm hungry now.'

'Did you actually bring any lunch with you?' I couldn't imagine him whipping up a sandwich that morning, wrapping it in tinfoil and popping it in the fridge with a yogurt and an apple.

'No, but there's always food in there.'

'That belongs to other people.' What did he think the poor sods ate after he'd snaffled their lunch? 'I can nip out to the shop if you'd like.'

'Don't bother.' Kelvin huffed into his office and slammed the door so I took the opportunity to go on a break, making a couple of coffees en route to the Sales and Marketing department. Erin gasped when she saw me.

'Who is this skinny bitch? You remind me of someone but I can't put my finger on who.'

I nudged her with my elbow as I placed one of the coffees on her desk. 'Get lost. I'm not skinny. *Yet.*' We grinned at each other and I pulled an empty chair over to her desk to settle myself in for five minutes. 'You'll never guess who I caught going at it with some girl on the sofa last night.'

Erin yawned and checked her manicured nails for imperfections. 'I'd take a wild guess at Theo. The man has no standards at all. Imagine shagging someone in a communal area.'

'It wasn't Theo.' I wanted to pause for effect but the gossip was too juicy and I ended up blurting it out. 'It was Billy. And they weren't actually having sex, but I bet they would have been if I hadn't interrupted them.'

Erin pulled a face. 'Billy? How?'

'Hey.' I didn't fancy him myself, being Billy and all, but he was no ogre. 'He's quite cute in a geeky way. It's quite cool now, isn't it, geek chic?'

'Geek chic, yes. Billy, no. Where did he find someone willing to shag him?'

'The pub.'

'Is she hideous?'

I was starting to feel a bit sorry for Billy. I knew he wasn't Erin's usual type, but there was nothing wrong with him. Perhaps he could have done with a decent haircut but nothing more drastic.

'We met her. It's the girl you nearly had a catfight with.'

'Oh *her*. She was very pretty, actually. Tiny and blonde, like a life-sized Tinkerbell. Did she have a concealed white stick?' Erin howled at her joke while I scowled, forgetting my weight-loss joy momentarily. Erin could take her cruelty too far sometimes. 'Uh-oh. Ginger Prick's on his way. Hide me.'

'Nope.' After her jibes at Billy, a very dear friend of mine, she was on her own. 'I have to get back to Kelvin before he ransacks his filing cabinet again.' Ignoring Erin's scowl, I made my way back to my office, stopping off at reception for a quick chat on the way. Kelvin shifted guiltily when I stepped into his office, swiping at his mouth with one hand while elbowing a tub into his open drawer, forgetting all about the fork still clutched in his other hand.

'I was going to ask if you were sure you didn't want me to nip out for some lunch, but you've obviously sorted yourself out.'

Kelvin avoided my accusing glare. 'No, I'm fine as far as lunch goes, but do bring me a coffee.'

'Anything else?' Perhaps I could steal someone's dessert for you to pig out on?

'Coffee will be fine. But don't forget my biscuits, will you?'

I wouldn't dare.

I was met by a familiar pert bottom sticking out of the cupboard when I arrived at the kitchen. I paused in the doorway, enjoying the sight for a moment until Jared straightened and turned around.

'What have you lost this time?' I moved swiftly into the kitchen and busied myself with the kettle.

'My pasta.'

I thought of the plastic tub falling into Kelvin's drawer. 'I did warn you, didn't I?'

Jared hung his head. 'You did.' When he raised his eyes to meet mine, they were bright with amusement. 'I don't suppose you have any chicken to share?'

'I'm afraid not.'

Jared clicked his fingers. 'Damn. I guess it's rubbery spaghetti bolognese for lunch then.'

'It'll be your punishment for not listening to my advice.'

'Wow, you're harsh. There wasn't even a hint of sympathy then, was there?'

*　*　*

I waltzed into my third Weight Watchers meeting with an air of confidence that hadn't been present the previous weeks. Then, I'd worn jeans and a plain T-shirt with a black cardigan over the top, trying my best to blend into the background. I was sure I'd be the biggest person in the room, but there were people even bigger than I was, can you believe? The following week, I was back to my usual bright self in a fifties-style black dress with a cherry print and netting under the skirt, teamed with a pair of red peep-toe wedges.

'You're back then,' a dull voice said as I entered the church hall. In my eagerness, I'd arrived early and there were only the two of us there. 'We see loads of people who come for their first proper weigh in and never return. Some don't make it past the initial meeting. I nearly didn't come back, you know.' I did know. She'd told me the previous week as we waited to weigh in. 'I didn't lose a pound at that proper weigh in. I went home and cried and said I wasn't coming back, but my mum dragged me here the next week and that was it, really. I kept coming and look at me now.' She smoothed her hands down across her hips and turned side on so I could see her size 12 frame. 'I used to be a size 20, you know.' I did know. She'd told me the previous week and it was fantastic that she'd lost so much weight, a real inspiration and all that, but did she have to look and sound so miserable while she told the story?

'You must have worked really hard.'

'Yeah.' Monotone. 'I did. It was worth it though.'

'I bet you can fit into fabulous clothes now.' It was the thing I was looking forward to most of all after wowing everyone at the reunion. I longed to wander into any shop on the high street and pick out gorgeous clothes, knowing they'd stock them in my size.

'I'm not really into shopping.'

I could have slapped her. Didn't she realise how lucky she was? To have so much choice and so freely available? I had to buy my clothes from specialised shops, paying over the odds to dress young instead of like a sack of potatoes.

'What *are* you into?'

She shrugged her slim shoulders. 'Don't know really. Oh look. Here's Lesley and Brenda. Hello girls.' Her features didn't even brighten when she greeted her friends. I made a vow, there and then, that when I lost the weight, I'd be bloody happy about it. I'd shout it from the sodding rooftops to let everyone know how ecstatic I was, and I'd bankrupt myself stuffing my wardrobe with beautiful garments.

I had a good weigh in, losing a further two pounds. Added to the four from last week, I'd lost almost half a stone in a couple of weeks. If I carried on at this rate, I was going to look stunning at the reunion *and* I'd need an extra wardrobe.

The sight of Susan Shuttleworth standing in my office was enough to have me hurtling towards the window and throwing myself, elbow first, through the pane of glass in a bid to escape. As tall as she was wide, giving her the appearance of an egg on legs, and with a protruding arse that put mine to shame, Susan was somehow under the delusion that she was something of a glamourpuss. She wore her hair short and bleached to within an inch of its life and never left the house without full make-up, though the foundation was two shades too dark, her pillar box red lipstick smeared on her teeth and her false lashes hanging loose. Her clothes were always skin tight, displaying every ripple and dimple on her body.

'Is he in?' She jabbed a finger towards Kelvin's closed door.

'He's in a meeting.' I tried to keep my voice calm as my eyes darted to the door. Kelvin was in there with Angelina. 'Would you like to come with me to get a coffee? I shouldn't imagine they'll be much longer.'

'I'll pass. I've tried the coffee here and it tastes like cheap crap.' I held my breath as Susan moved but she simply sank into the chair opposite me. I let my breath out slowly, not wanting to display the immense relief I felt. I wasn't keen on having Susan so close, but if she was sitting at my desk, she wasn't barging into her husband's office and finding him with his pants around his ankles. 'I'm not actually here to see Kelvin. I've come to make sure all the arrangements are in place.'

'They are.' I'd assured her over the phone half a dozen times already. How difficult did she think it was to phone a caterer, order a buffet and organise a bit of bunting?

'Yes, well, I hope so.' She jutted her chin at me. 'I'd hate to think what would happen to your employment here if you made a balls of this party.'

I doubted 'making a balls of a party', particularly one of a personal and not a business nature, was a sacking offence but I kept my mouth shut. I could wind Susan up on the phone but she was far too scary in person. 'The party will be fine. Better than fine. It'll be *fantastic*.'

'Don't go overboard, dear. It's just a little get together in that grotty little pub every damn party has to take place in.' She flung her handbag over her shoulder and rose from the seat, though there wasn't much of a height increase. I could barely see Susan over my desk. 'Tell Kelvin I popped in. And make sure he wears the clean shirt and tie.' She jabbed a finger at the plastic cover hanging off my office door. She weebled her way out without another word and within a minute, Angelina emerged from Kelvin's office, unaware of how close she'd come to being rumbled.

Kelvin's party took place at The Bonnie Dundee straight after work and the place was packed with H. Wood employees, who had turned up for a free feed rather than to wish Kelvin a happy birthday. There was little I could do about the scruffiness of the pub that sat on the edge of the business park but I'd done my best with the bunting and balloons. You can't polish a turd but you can throw a load of multi-coloured streamers at it.

'One day, H. Woods will pay for a decent party venue,' Erin said as we hovered at the bar. She caught my eye and we both sniggered.

'Yeah, right. And one day I'll be on the cover of *Vogue*.'

'Uh-oh. There he is. Shit.' Erin ducked behind me as Richard Shuttleworth came into view, craning his neck this way and that. 'Don't meet his eye. He'll come over to ask you where I am and then he'll spot me. Is he still there?'

I scanned the room but instead of spotting the ginger one, I spotted Jared and gave a gasp. He looked even more gorgeous than usual, having ditched his suit jacket and tie, undone his top button and rolled up his sleeves, flashing tanned forearms with the palest blond hairs.

'What is it? Is he coming over? I'm making a run for it. Tell him I've gone home. With Stuart.' Erin bolted from behind me and charged into the ladies while I gazed across the room at Jared. He really was lovely.

'Is Erin about?' My view was spoiled by Richard, his hands on his hips, head still swivelling around the room.

'I saw her leave a few minutes ago.'

'A few minutes?' Richard lifted his wrist to check the time, gauging whether he had time to catch up with her.

'She was with Stuart from Accounts.'

Richard's wrist dropped back down again. 'You're joking. Shit!' With his chest heaving with the effort of a huge sigh, Richard stalked away and when he shifted, Jared took his place.

'Can I get you a drink? To say thank you for all your help with my lunches?'

I hadn't helped much at all but I didn't point that out, not being one to turn down a free drink. 'That's very kind of you. I'll have a diet coke please.' As Jared moved away towards the bar, I was rewarded with a wonderful view of his bottom and I wondered what it would feel like beneath my hands.

'Mind if I join you?'

'You've just bought me a drink. I can hardly say no.' We weaved our way through the crowds and found an empty table, and when Jared sat down his knee brushed mine due to his long legs. I'd never experienced a galloping pulse or flushed cheeks when Gideon made contact with me, but I did with Jared, despite the briefest of touch, and it took my breath away for a moment.

'So did you have lunch here yesterday?' I asked because my muddled brain couldn't compose another set of words.

'I did and you were right.' Jared lowered his voice and had to lean towards me to be heard over the music. 'It *was* rubbery.'

I couldn't respond, my body too preoccupied with making swooning gestures from my closeness to Jared. He smelled citrusy and fresh yet manly and my face was on fire as I imagined being even closer to him, unfastening the next button on his shirt. And the next.

'Has he gone?'

I jumped at the sound of Erin's sudden voice, the image of undressing Jared cruelly snatched away. 'Who?'

'The Ginger Dickhead of course.' She scowled down at me until she caught sight of Jared and her features softened, a coy smile playing on her lips. 'Oh, *hello*. I don't believe we've met.'

I made the introductions before excusing myself. I had no chance of chatting to Jared with Erin around and I didn't fancy playing gooseberry. Disappearing under her shadow was one of the only flaws of being friends with Erin. She couldn't help it; men were drawn to her beauty and easy-going nature and if Erin was there, to men at least, I was not. I totted up my Weight Watchers points while wandering over to the buffet and calculated that I had twelve left to stretch over the remainder of the week. I looked back towards Erin and Jared and my heart sank when I saw Jared's head thrown back in laughter. He leant in close, resting his hand on Erin's shoulder as he whispered in her ear. Erin was obviously working her magic and no man could resist.

Oh, sod it. I grabbed a sausage roll and a pork pie. It wouldn't matter if I went over by a point or two.

NINE

Jared

Angelina stepped into the office, closing the door behind her before she sauntered towards Jared's desk, her hips swaying so much they almost bounced off the walls either side. Instead of sitting in the chair opposite, Angelina perched her pert bottom on the edge of the desk, her long thighs inches away from Jared.

'How can I help you, Angelina?'

Jared was starting to settle into his new role as purchasing manager at H. Wood Vehicles and was getting to know the other members of staff. He suspected the office junior had developed a bit of a crush on him, which was evident in the eyelash fluttering whenever she was in his presence and her skirt shortening by the minute, and it may have been quite exciting had Sammy not looked and acted like a twelve-year-old playing grown-ups with her orange foundation and overdone eye shadow. Jared had witnessed her having an actual tantrum over a missing stapler a couple of days ago.

Jared only suspected Sammy had a thing for him, but he knew, without a doubt, that Angelina did. She bit her cranberry red lip and leant back on the desk, flashing the tops of her stockings and the hint of a suspender belt as she crossed one leg over the other. Her arms pressed into the sides of her bosom, shoving her cleavage up to her chin as she peeped at Jared through thick Bambi-like lashes.

'Isn't that a novel question? I'm usually asking men how I can help them. Is there anything you need help with, Jared?'

Jared held back a sigh as she flicked her thick mane of hair over her shoulder. He didn't have time for this. 'No thank you, Angelina.' He wheeled himself an inch away from Angelina, as close to his computer as he could manage without the desk cutting into his torso. Undeterred, Angelina hooked a stilettoed foot into the armrest of the chair and wheeled him back again. Jared snapped his eyes away as the movement gave him full view of Angelina's gusset.

'Are you coming to Kelvin's birthday bash? You did get the email, didn't you?'

Jared had received the email but he wasn't planning on attending the party, finding Kelvin Shuttleworth to be slimy and condescending. He'd shaken his hand once and Jared could still feel Kelvin's sweat seeping into his pores. 'I don't think I can make it.'

'And why not?' Jared couldn't conjure a lie quick enough and Angelina gave a nod, her lips spreading into a smile. 'I see.' Slipping off the desk, she hopped onto the armrest of Jared's chair and ran a blood red tipped finger along his cheek. 'Don't worry, babe. We can show our faces for ten minutes and then sneak off to somewhere more intimate.'

Jared was not a wimp by any standard but Angelina terrified him and he felt trapped, pinned to the chair by a woman possessed. No man had ever turned Angelina down – not since her second boob job – and she wasn't about to let Jared slip through her fingers.

Jared's mind whirred but he somehow managed to claw an excuse and was about to tell Angelina about his poor, sick granny who needed his attention more than Kelvin Shuttleworth when Angelina spoke again.

'Everyone will be there, especially all the other managers. It won't look good if you're not there.'

Crap. Angelina was right. He'd only been working at H. Woods for a few weeks so he should socialise and get to know people beyond Purchasing.

Seeing the resignation on Jared's face, Angelina clapped her hands. 'We need to sort you out before you go.' She almost toppled off the armrest as Jared leapt from his chair and she giggled once she'd righted herself. 'I didn't mean like that, you naughty boy. I meant that.' She pointed at Jared's throat before reaching for his tie. She'd whipped it off and unfastened his top button before Jared could even blink. 'That's better. You don't look quite so stuffy. Perhaps we should undo another one.' Or two.

Jared clapped a hand to his throat. 'One is enough, thank you.'

Angelina gave a shrug. 'Suit yourself. Shall we go?'

The Bonnie Dundee was plonked at the exit of the business park and was small, dark and dingy with dust covering most surfaces and the floor was grubby and sticky. Caterers had provided a huge buffet spanning the whole of the back wall and every other available space was taken up by bodies. With barely room to draw breath, it was proving more difficult for Jared to ditch Angelina than anticipated, but when she coerced him into a corner and grabbed his arse, he knew he had to escape. Fleeing to the loo, he waited until she'd moved on, chatting up the ancient maintenance manager, before he sneaked back into the crowd. He planned to snake his way to the exit when he spotted Ruth, the lovely girl from the kitchen. She was the most genuine person he'd met at H. Woods and while he couldn't wait to break free and go home, he found himself approaching her for a quick chat.

'Can I get you a drink? To say thank you for all your help with my lunches?' It wasn't the best opener but he couldn't think of anything else to say and thankfully she accepted. Jared fought his way to the bar and somehow caught the attention of the barmaid. She had to be approaching her pension and, being hard of hearing, coupled with the din of too many bodies packed into a small space, it made it difficult to order the drinks, but she got it after the fourth attempt.

'Mind if I join you?' Jared hadn't anticipated staying longer but he'd bought himself a drink now.

'You've just bought me a drink. I can hardly say no.' Ruth smiled, and it was a warm smile, not devilish like Angelina's. He sat down on a vacant stool next to Ruth's and took a sip of his drink while he tried to think of something witty or vaguely interesting to say but his mind was blank.

Speaking to Ruth about his missing lunch wasn't the first time Jared had noticed her. It was around six weeks earlier that he'd spotted Ruth in reception as he waited for his interview slot, her laugh grabbing his attention as she chatted to the receptionist. The warm, booming laugh bubbled from her throat and it had made Jared smile as he wondered what they'd been chatting about to provoke such a reaction.

'So did you have lunch here yesterday?' Jared had failed to find an opening topic and was feeling like a bit of an imbecile until Ruth took the lead.

'I did and you were right.' The music blared so Jared leant towards Ruth to make sure she could hear him. Her sweet, floral perfume hit him full force and scrambled his brain. 'It *was* rubbery.'

Smooth, Jared. Real smooth.

'Has he gone?'

Jared followed Ruth's gaze and took in the pretty girl with Cher-like hair, her hands planted on her hips.

'Who?' Ruth asked her.

Jared couldn't quite catch the girl's response over the noise but he couldn't miss her scowl, which vanished as she turned her head towards him. She smiled then, which was more Angelina-like than Ruth-like and made Jared nervous. 'Oh, *hello*. I don't believe we've met.'

'Sorry, this is Jared Williams, the new purchasing manager. Jared, this is Erin. She works in Sales and Marketing and is my very best friend.'

'Hello, Erin.' Jared extended a hand, which Erin took in a dainty hold.

'Pleased to meet you, Jared. Very pleased.' She winked at him and Jared wished he'd followed his instincts earlier. He could have been half way home by now.

'Will you excuse me? I won't be a minute.' Ruth rose from her seat, which Erin plonked herself down in immediately. She placed a hand on Jared's bare forearm, running her fingers over the pale hairs.

'So you've been hiding away in Purchasing then?'

Jared snatched his arm away and was about to excuse himself when he spotted Angelina out of the corner of his eye, sashaying towards him, her face set in determination. To try and put her off, Jared threw back his head and laughed in uproar. Erin's brow, quite understandably, furrowed so he leant in close to whisper his plea. 'Angelina Littleman is on her way over. She won't leave me alone. Please help me.'

Erin gave a slight nod of her head. 'That woman's like a bitch on heat. Leave it to me.' Placing her hand on Jared's chest, she too threw her head back and laughed and when she righted herself, still giggling, she leaned in close, her lips brushing Jared's ear. 'Do you want me to sit on your lap?'

'That won't be necessary. I think she's got the picture.' Angelina's face barely acknowledged Jared as she passed the table and kept on going until she was out of sight. 'Thank you.'

Erin flicked her long mane of hair over her shoulder as she gave a shrug. 'No problem. I'll use any excuse to get Angelina's back up.'

Jared had managed to avoid Angelina for the remainder of the party and all through the following Monday, and he thought he'd got away with it as the office began to empty. He let out a puff of air but soon sucked it back in again as Angelina stepped into his office, closing the door behind her. Jared's eyes flicked to the open blinds of his office and was alarmed to see that the entire department had filed away for the evening. They were very alone.

'Finally. I didn't think I'd get the chance to speak to

you today.' Angelina's tone wasn't angry as she moved towards the desk but instead of giving him a lap dance, she placed herself in the chair on the other side of his desk. She didn't seem cross at being sidestepped on Friday. In fact, she was eerily calm. 'I thought I should give you a little warning, about Erin. I really think you ought to stay away from her.' Despite, or perhaps because of the pleasant tone, Jared checked his scissors and letter opener weren't within reaching distance. 'I know she's young and reasonably pretty, but she has a bit of a reputation. She's slept with most of the male employees here and she never goes back for seconds.' Angelina flicked her hair over her shoulder and the sudden movement caused Jared to jump in fright. 'I don't like to label people personally but she's known as the office bike.'

'Thank you for the advice.' Jared opened his drawer and tried to think of a way of slipping the sharp stationery inside without drawing attention to them. 'I appreciate it.'

'I hope you do. And I hope you take my word for it.' Angelina rose from the chair and thankfully she strolled out of Jared's office without a backward glance or the use of any violence.

TEN

Ruth

'What's this?' Erin jabbed at the food in front of her with her fork, her top lip curled and nose wrinkled.

'It's a butternut squash and feta salad.'

Erin's body gave a sudden jolt and I thought she was going to heave. 'It looks like spew.'

'It does not. It's too chunky for vomit.' I took a forkful and forced myself to eat it without gagging. I'd never eaten butternut squash before and I doubted I ever would again willingly. The smell alone as Billy chopped it ready to roast for me was enough to put me off, but I'd committed to this Weight Watchers malarkey and was determined to lose the weight and if that meant eating new things that I didn't particularly like, then so be it.

'What are these little seedy bits?'

'Seeds.' I didn't even need to look at what Erin was poking now and was quite saddened that she'd had to ask.

'*Seeds*? As in *seeds*?'

'Yep.'

'*Seeds*? Do I look like a bird?'

I wasn't so keen on eating seeds myself, but if it helped me shed the weight, I'd give them a go. I had a meeting that evening and I was quietly confident about the loss I was about to achieve. I'd been good all week, getting Billy to cook nutritional meals from scratch and only partaking in healthy snacks. Not one crisp had passed my lips and I hadn't so much as sniffed a chocolate bar. This week was going to be a tremendous week, I could tell. The previous week, after my spectacular fail at Kelvin's party, I'd lost a pound and while it wasn't an amazing loss, I was grateful not to have put back on the six pounds I'd lost over the last two weeks. I'd really gone for it at the buffet, stuffing my cheeks with sausage rolls and scotch eggs like a hamster in an attempt to block out the searing disappointment that Erin had muscled in on Jared. I'd never for a minute thought I stood a chance with him, but it was nice chatting to him and being paid attention to. So it was gutting to become invisible the moment Erin wandered into his line of vision. I'd only been gone thirty seconds before Erin was practically nibbling his ear.

Lucky cow. The thought of nibbling any part of Jared's anatomy filled my stomach with bubbles that fizzled downwards and made me moan with pleasure.

'Don't pretend they taste delicious, Ruth. They're seeds. Birds eat seeds – people don't.'

'Birds are skinny. Maybe they're getting it right.'

Erin spluttered. 'Are you kidding me? Have you seen the fat bastard pigeons in Manchester? I was in

Piccadilly Gardens last weekend and nearly got knocked out by one. It was like a boulder.'

'Ok, maybe not pigeons...' I tucked into my meal while Erin pushed hers into the middle of the table, refusing to even try it. The old Ruth would have cleared Erin's plate too, whether it tasted like chunky spew or not, but this brand new Ruth was much stronger and wiser than that. I scraped the leftovers into the bin immediately before temptation could take hold and dumped the plates in the sink.

The front door opened and closed, followed by footsteps heading for the kitchen. I knew it wouldn't be Billy as he was out with Clare again. Which left only one other possibility. I closed my eyes in preparation before Theo crashed into the room, kicking the door open and slinging his jacket on the back of a chair.

'I didn't think you'd be in. Aren't you supposed to be at Chub Club?'

My housemate Theo, as charming as ever. Erin's mouth gaped open, disgusted on my behalf. 'Chub Club? Do you have to be an insensitive prick twenty-four hours a day?'

Theo put a hand to his heart and took a little skip backwards. 'Oh, Erin, it's you. Sorry, I didn't recognise you with your clothes on.'

Erin narrowed her eyes and gave a slow shake of her head. 'You have never seen me without my clothes on. *And you never will.*'

'Then aren't I the lucky one?' Theo moved over to the fridge for a rummage but, seeing all my healthy stuff in there, quickly closed it again. 'What time are you off out? I've got a friend coming over.' He winked at Erin, who pulled the same face she'd used while observing her butternut squash.

'We're going now.' It was a little early but I grabbed Erin's hand and tugged her out of the kitchen, away from the vast supply of deadly weapons. The kitchen was the worst place to wind up Erin, what with all the knives, frying pans and rolling pins hanging around, ready to inflict damage. Erin and Theo had never got along, probably because they were both so similar. Both were persistently young, free and single and all too willing to drop their pants, although, thankfully, not for each other. That really would be unbearable.

'I don't know how you put up with him,' Erin grumbled as we wandered along Oak Road.

'He's not all bad.'

'No?'

I shook my head, though I couldn't pinpoint any good qualities at such short notice. 'Anyway, enough about Theo. I'm about to weigh in so I need thin, fabulous thoughts.'

'And not arrogant, knobhead thoughts. Yes, I see your point.' Erin linked her arm through mine as we turned onto the main road, discussing the kind of dress I would wear to the reunion. I wasn't sure of the exact details but I knew it had to be gorgeous and slinky and not a hint of sack-of-potatoes about it.

The church hall was just past the bus stop and a bus was pulling up, so we said a quick goodbye before Erin jumped on board, blowing me a kiss and wishing me luck. I waved until she disappeared from view and continued on my way, crossing over to the hall. I was the first one there, even beating Thin Lizzie (not her actual name, obviously, but I didn't know what she was called. It had to be something morbid – Morticia, perhaps) and so I was saved the repeated tale of her miraculous weight loss. The door to the hall was locked so I perched on a low wall while I waited, checking the time every twenty seconds or so. I couldn't wait to get inside and hop on the scales, already celebrating my loss inside. It had to be quite high, beating my four pound record by far.

'You're early.'

I jumped as Morticia appeared from behind the thick bushes surrounding the church hall and shuffled her way towards me.

'You must be keen.'

'I suppose I am, yes.' I couldn't help my great mood displaying itself on my face, my smile so wide I was sure my tonsils were on display. Morticia didn't appear to be in a great mood, her lips downturned, her eyes dull behind thick lashes. She took a seat next to me on the wall and we couldn't have looked more different; her in brown tracksuit bottoms and a black padded jacket, her face blank and immobile while I wore a turquoise wrap around dress and a pink denim jacket, grinning like a loon.

'You've lost so much weight and can't have much more to go. Why do you still come to the meetings?'

Morticia's dark eyes focused on mine and narrowed slightly but otherwise her face remained the same. 'This.' She indicated the church hall. 'Is for life. It isn't a quick fix. If I stopped coming to meetings, I'd end up back like you within weeks.'

'Oh.' Thanks.

Morticia's words took the edge off my good mood. Could I face a lifetime of butternut squash and seeds? I'd only focused on the reunion but what happened after that? Did I go back to gorging on crap and ballooning to my original size? It was a horrible thought but eating salad for the rest of my days wasn't any more appealing.

'Wendy's here.' Morticia rose from the wall and shuffled towards our leader, who was separating the church hall key from a huge set. The hall was cold but it soon warmed up after Wendy turned the heating on. Morticia and I helped set out the chairs while we waited for the others to arrive. The room suddenly filled up with bodies and chatter until Wendy quietened us all down and began her talk for the evening before the weigh in began. My feet were jittery as I waited for my turn, eager to step on the scales so the celebrations could begin. I daydreamed about how much I'd lost – five pounds? Six? Maybe even seven. Imagine that. *Half a stone.*

'Ruth?' Wendy motioned for me to join her at the scales, partitioned off for privacy and humiliation reduction. I wanted to drag the scales out into the open so everybody could see how well I'd done.

'Ready?' Wendy smiled at me and gave me some room. I stepped onto the scales and my eyes widened at the display. That couldn't be right. It wasn't possible.

'It's the same as last week.'

Wendy put a hand on my arm. 'It happens, I'm afraid.' She continued to talk but none of the words made it through to my brain. I'd behaved so well. I'd stuck to my points. I'd eaten seeds, for fuck's sake. And it was the same!

'You're doing great, Ruth. Really you are.'

Funny, I didn't feel so great as I stepped off the scales at the exact same weight as I'd been a week ago. How had I lost weight after stuffing myself with calories but failed to lose anything while restricting myself? It didn't make sense. Perhaps I should go over my points every week and see where that took me.

*   *   *

I'd had a pretty rough day at work, with Kelvin being more rude and demanding than usual, piling my in-tray with crap until it was overflowing onto my desk and leaving it until quarter to five to let me know that there were urgent files that needed photocopying and distributing to various departments. To top it off, the bus hadn't bothered to turn up and I'd been forced to wait in the rain for the next one, which was packed due to the backlog. But the day withered away as I sank into the sofa in my pyjamas and the theme tune to *A Beginner's Guide To You* started up. The lives of Meg and Tom never failed to cheer me up and Billy and I were soon clutching our stomachs and wiping away tears at their antics.

'Snack time,' Billy announced as the adverts came on and my mouth watered as he disappeared into the kitchen. I'd behaved impeccably and was looking forward to rewarding myself with a couple of blocks of chocolate.

'Fruit salad?' I couldn't help the disgust oozing from my voice, despite the effort Billy had gone to yet again. I craved chocolate. I *needed* chocolate. 'Haven't you got a massive bar of chocolate?' I *deserved* it.

'Is that wise? With your diet and everything?'

I gave a wave of my hand, imagining it was swiping away the bowl of fruit. 'I have enough points left to cover it.' It was a lie – but only a little white one and it was worth it when Billy disappeared with the fruit and returned with a giant Galaxy Caramel.

'You're a star.' I tore into the paper, my fingers working overtime. The glorious scent of creamy chocolate hit my nostrils immediately and the delirious feeling it generated was almost enough. Almost but not quite. Snapping the bar in half, I handed Billy his chunk as he settled himself back on the sofa. 'This is nice, isn't it? We haven't hung out in ages.'

'We watched *A Beginner's Guide* together last week.'

'Exactly.' Billy and I used to hang out most nights but lately we'd been reduced to only our weekly *Beginner's* ritual. Billy even prepared my meals in advance as he was too busy to cook after work and while I appreciated what he was doing for me, I would have liked to have had at least a brief daily conversation with him.

'Sorry,' Billy said because it was due to him that we no longer slobbed in front of the telly together night after night. Apart from my Weight Watchers meetings, I still slobbed in front of the telly most nights but had been forced to do so on my own since Billy was out most nights with Clare.

'It's okay. I sort of remember what being in a relationship is like. How is Clare?' I popped a square of chocolate into my mouth and closed my eyes, savouring the sensation as it began to melt on my tongue. I'd missed chocolate almost as much as I'd missed Billy.

'She's great. Really great.' Billy blushed and I giggled, nudging him in the ribs.

'Is it luuurve?'

'Sod off. And no it isn't. We haven't even, you know, yet.' Billy's face took on the appearance of an open fire, his blush seeping way beyond his face and neck, dipping into his T-shirt.

'You haven't had sex yet?' I blew out my cheeks. 'Blimey. What's gone wrong?' It had looked as though they were about to go at it when I caught them on the sofa and that was ages ago.

'Nothing has gone wrong.' Billy sat up straight and

jutted out his chin. 'There's no rush. We're getting to know each other properly.'

'Speaking of getting to know each other, we should all go out for a drink.' I didn't really know Clare, having only met her briefly in passing since the groping on the sofa event. We'd never sat in the same room as one another, let alone had a proper conversation. 'How about Friday?'

'I can't. We have plans for Friday.'

I bit back a giggle. 'Ooh, is Friday *the* night? Will you know each other well enough by then?'

'Bog off.' Billy threw a cushion at me and the conversation ended as *A Beginner's Guide* came back on.

Morticia eyed me from the low wall surrounding the church hall, raising her bushy eyebrows at me as I approached, as if gloating that she'd beat me. I think she liked being the first to arrive at the meetings and felt important as she set the chairs out in the hall. It was a bit sad really.

'Hello.' I still didn't know her name as she preferred to be weighed last and so I never caught Wendy calling out her name as I was either caught up in my own celebrations or commiserations by then. 'How do you think you've done this week?'

Morticia's eyebrows knitted together, creating a mega monobrow. They really did need a good plucking. 'I'm at my ideal weight. I maintain my weight now, and don't strive to lose any.'

Oh. I see. 'I hope I've lost a fair bit, to make up for last week.' I'd stuck to my buffet experiment, going slightly over my points to see if I could replicate the results after gorging myself at Kelvin's party.

'Of course you want to lose a fair bit. Why else would you be here?'

I gaped at Morticia. Did she have to be so rude? She'd been a fatty once upon a time so she should know how much it hurt to be sneered at. Not that Morticia was sneering exactly – sneering would require more facial movement than she could manage. Thankfully, Wendy's car turned into the small car park before Morticia could start taunting me with Mr Blobby and Free Willy jibes.

The meeting trickled past, Wendy's talk seeming to go on for an eternity while I waited to see how much I'd lost that week. I was itching to step on the scales and see a lower number displayed, to show I was heading in the right direction.

'Ruth, are you ready?' Wendy popped her head around the partition and waved her hand for me to join her. I slipped behind the partition, took a deep breath and stepped onto the scales. I exhaled quickly once I saw the numbers, thinking that perhaps it was the extra oxygen filling my lungs that had inched my weight higher. The display didn't flicker. I'd put on two pounds. Wendy was nice and comforting towards me, suggesting we go over my food diary to see if I could make any changes, but I knew that wouldn't help. My food diary looked perfect. Because I'd lied to keep my points on track.

I couldn't win. If I stuck to the plan, I didn't lose weight. If I deviated from the plan, I put on weight.

'How did it go?' Morticia cornered me as I grabbed my rose-printed jacket from the back of my chair. Having somehow endured the rest of the meeting I wanted nothing more than to get the hell out of that church hall. Chatting to Morticia was the last thing I wanted to do.

'Not too bad.' It could have been worse, right? Two pounds was very little in the grand scheme of things.

'Did you put on?' Morticia didn't even attempt to sound sympathetic. Or lower her voice and I felt every eye turn to me.

'No, I didn't. I lost two pounds, okay?' It was a great big fib, but so what? Morticia didn't know that and I'd never have to see her again. As I left the hall, my head held as high as I could manage, I knew I wouldn't be returning.

ELEVEN

Billy

The night was going to be perfect. Billy had ensured the house would be empty, with Theo out on the pull and Ruth out with Erin, and he was going to cook Clare a romantic meal. Well, perhaps cook wasn't the correct word. He was going to *provide* Clare with a romantic meal and pass it off as his own, so it was almost cooking. He could manage the basics and he'd been pushing his culinary abilities lately, but if he wanted to woo Clare – and he desperately wanted to woo her – some sort of grilled fish and a salad was not the way to go.

'That's everything – starter, main and dessert. Put the food in the oven to keep it warm and the cake in the fridge. All you need to do is provide the coffee and good conversation.' Cosmo patted Billy on the arm. 'Oh well, at least you've got the coffee.'

'I'll have you know Clare thinks my conversational

skills are second to none.' It was a pity she had yet to experience any of his other skills, but he was hoping all that would change tonight. They'd been seeing each other for five weeks and they had yet to do the deed. Why did Billy have to be such a loser with women? Theo only had to glance in a woman's direction and she dropped her knickers.

'Good luck, mate.' Cosmo slapped Billy on the back before he ducked back into the kitchen. Billy crept out of the little yard at the back of the restaurant and scurried home, the tubs of food warming his hands. After following Cosmo's instructions for the food, he galloped up the stairs to shower and change before Clare arrived. He had just enough time to lay the table with a cleanish tablecloth and light the candles before Clare rang the doorbell.

'Wow.' Clare wore a pleated, burgundy halterneck dress, a gold belt cinching in her waist and nude strappy sandals encrusted with diamantes to match the dress. 'You look amazing. You know we're staying in, right?'

Clare smiled, her already glowing face radiating. 'There's no harm in dressing up. It is our five-week anniversary.'

Billy stepped aside, still gawking at Clare as she made her way into the sitting room. She really was stunning and he had to wonder what she saw in him.

'Can I get you a glass of wine?' he asked as Clare draped herself on the sofa, somehow making the sagging furniture appear lavish.

'That would be lovely. Thank you.'

Billy took a moment to compose himself in the kitchen. There was a beautiful woman in his sitting room and she was here to spend the evening with him and not Theo. Several deep breaths later and two glasses of wine in hand, Billy returned to the sitting room, amazed that Clare was in fact in there and not an image he'd conjured to wank over.

Clare took a sip of wine and nodded towards the kitchen. 'Something smells delicious.'

'Thank you. It should be ready soon.' Billy perched awkwardly on the arm of the sofa, his glass of wine untouched in his hands. He didn't even like wine but wanted to appear sophisticated for Clare's benefit.

'What are we having?'

Billy's mind went into blind panic as he tried to remember what Cosmo had prepared for them. Was it clams for starters or were they having linguine with clam sauce for their main course? He knew there were clams in there somewhere, but he couldn't be sure where exactly.

'You'll just have to wait and see, Miss Impatient.'

'Impatient? Me?' Clare put a hand to her chest. 'I've waited five weeks for tonight. I have lots of patience.'

Was she referring to the food or something else? Billy crossed his fingers. Please let it be something else.

It turned out the meal consisted of clams in white wine sauce followed by linguine with roasted peppers, sweet Italian sausage and a spicy tomato sauce.

'And what's for dessert?' Clare dropped her gaze to the tablecloth before glancing back up at Billy with flushed cheeks.

Innuendo, Billy thought. She was definitely hinting at something more than cake. 'I have a limoncello mascarpone cake in the fridge but if there's something else you'd rather have, I'd be happy to oblige.'

Clare's lips twitched for a few seconds before she spluttered, biting her lip as she giggled. Billy kicked himself for being too cheesy but it wasn't the 'happy to oblige' comment that had tickled Clare.

'I *knew* you hadn't cooked all this.' She swept her hand across the table full of dirty dishes. 'Pasta, maybe. The clams in white wine sauce was pushing it, but limoncello mascarpone cake? Come off it.' She placed her arms across her chest and tilted her head to one side. 'Come on, own up. Who cooked it?'

Billy scratched his unruly curls. Shit, busted. 'My mate Cosmo.'

'From the restaurant?'

Billy nodded and averted his gaze. The fridge magnets were surprisingly interesting at that moment in time. 'You're not mad, are you?'

'Mad? Why would I be mad? That meal was divine. Who cares where it came from?' She rose from her seat and took Billy's hand, tugging him to his feet. 'Come on, it's time for dessert. I'm sure you'll be happy to oblige.'

Billy allowed himself to be led upstairs, thankful that he'd remembered to change the bedding earlier. His two-year dry spell was finally shattered, and it was possibly one of the most incredible moments of his life so far.

TWELVE

Ruth

My feet were burning. No, that doesn't quite describe the excruciating pain advancing from the very tips of my toenails, scorching the balls of my feet, slicing along the soles and up my ankles, settling on my calves. Each step produced a whimper from my lips, my face scrunched up and making me look like Miss Piggy's evil twin. Spotting a tree ahead, I was desperate to lean against it for a short reprieve, but I knew it would only prolong my agony and so I proceeded towards H. Woods, desperate to reach my desk for the first time ever.

'What's wrong?' Quinn flew from behind the reception desk as I hobbled into the building, bent at the knees and gasping with each fairy step that brought me towards the relief of sitting down.

'I want to cut off my feet. Can I borrow your scissors?'

'What's happened to you?'

I held up the tall, thin plastic bag in my hands, still shuffling towards the stairs. I couldn't stop. I had to reach my desk. I'd crawl if I had to.

'Subway did this to you?'

'New diet.' It was the only information I could give at that moment, blinded by the pain and only a step or two from openly weeping. I'd discovered the diet late the previous night. I'd been scouring the internet for almost two hours – though the majority of that time was taken up by Ebay – and I was weary and mole-eyed by the time I stumbled upon it so only skimmed through the details but how hard could it be? The Subway Diet sounded like heaven. I adored Subway and there was a shop a fifteen-minute walk away from work. Unfortunately, it wasn't on my bus route so I'd walked the whole way there and then onto H. Woods, which wouldn't have been so bad if I wasn't sporting five-inch heels.

Clinging onto the rail, I dragged myself up to the first floor and was barely able to stand when I reached the top, but at least my office, particularly my chair, was in view. With renewed strength, I shuffled to my desk and sank into the fake leather chair. I had never felt such comfort in my entire life as the blood returned to my toes.

I didn't have much time to rest as I had to get Kelvin's office ready for his arrival, but I did slip off my shoes before scurrying through to his office, switching on his computer and opening his blinds, only wincing very slightly with each step. The morning had been such an ordeal but it would be worth it when I lost the weight and arrived at the reunion looking fabulous.

'Why aren't you wearing shoes?' Kelvin was filling the doorway when I turned from the window.

'I just took them off for a minute.'

'Get them back on and please remember you're at a place of business.' Kelvin strode into his office and plonked himself into his real leather chair. I had never hated the man more as I slipped my bruised feet back into my shoes. The python skin stilettos were no longer a thing of beauty but a thing of torture and forgiving them would take time.

'Did I ask you to get me a coffee?' Kelvin called through the open door of his office.

'Nope, but I'm on it.' Taking deep breaths, I lifted myself up from my chair. White light flashed before my eyes and my stomach gave a worrying swirl. I was going to vomit through the pain.

'Are you sure you want a coffee now, Kelvin? It's a bit early.'

'Then it'll wake me up.'

Shit.

'What was that?'

'Nothing.' Clutching the desk, I took my first step. The back of my neck prickled and a bead of sweat rolled from my temple. It was going to be a long day.

It took over half an hour to make the coffee, including a break from my shoes and a weep in the kitchen before I forced my unwilling feet back into the evil footwear and continued with my duties.

'What took you so long? Did you take yourself off to Brazil for the coffee beans?' Kelvin chortled to himself while I imagined thrusting a sharp object up his fat arse. Didn't he realise what torment I had gone through for that cup of coffee? How much blood had seeped from my toes?

'You forgot my biscuits.'

I left his office as quickly as my mangled feet could

manage before the sharp object fantasy became reality.

With Kelvin out of the office for most of the morning, I managed to remain at my desk until lunchtime. I'd have eaten my sandwich at my desk too had Erin not begged – literally *begged* – me to meet her for lunch.

'I have to get out of Sales and Marketing, even for half an hour. Ginger Pubes is doing my head in. He's been hovering around my desk all morning and I swear he *growled* when Stuart from Accounts walked past. He claims he was clearing his throat but I don't believe him. Please, Ruth. Get me out of here. Please, please, please, please, please, ple –'

'Alright, alright. I'll meet you at the bench.'

There was a rusty old bench at the very far corner of H. Woods' car park where Erin and I would often meet as it was the furthest away you could be from the building without leaving the site. I was sitting on the bench, shoes kicked off, when Erin approached.

'Don't tell me you've given up on the ridiculous notion of losing weight for that moron Zack.' Erin eyed my foot long sandwich as she dropped onto the bench. 'I knew you'd come to your senses eventually.'

I finished chewing and swallowed before answering, holding up my index finger for emphasis. 'First of all, dieting isn't ridiculous.'

'It is when it's for a man.'

Possibly true, but I ignored the comment. 'And second of all, I am still on a diet. The Subway Diet. How fantastic is that?'

Erin paused the unclipping of her box of sushi, twisting in her seat to look at me properly. 'Is that a... *real* diet? Or did you... I'm not suggesting you made it up. Not at all. But did you perhaps... dream it up?'

'No! It's a real diet.'

'According to who?'

'The internet.'

'Oh.' Erin, losing interest slightly, opened the box and twisted the cap off the tiny bottle of soy sauce.

'Apparently, some guy lost shit loads of weight doing it.'

Erin lifted a California roll to her mouth but didn't pop it inside. 'By just eating Subway?'

'Yep. How great is that? This is going to be a piece of piss.'

Almost a week had passed and I still adored my new diet. It was so refreshing to be eating things I enjoyed for a change. I wished I'd spotted the Subway Diet first and not wasted time and guilt on the others. I felt fantastic and had even started to take pleasure in the walk to and from work. With my iPod blasting Girls Aloud or early Madonna and Kylie, I'd lose myself in the music and arrive at work happy and awake and looking forward to lunch. Walking to and from work also had the added bonus of not having to fight the little old ladies for a seat on the bus and the money saved from bus fares came in handy for funding my diet.

'See you in the morning.' I turned to give Quinn a cheery wave and in doing so, collided with another body also on their way out. 'Sorry. I wasn't looking where I was going.' The smell was familiar and my heart gave a jolly bounce when I looked up at Jared's smiling face.

'Sorry, Ruth, I didn't see you down there. You've shrunk.'

I poked out a foot to explain. Walking in heels had proved far too painful and so I had taken to wearing trainers for my walks, changing into heels once I was at the office.

'That explains it.' Jared pushed open the door, allowing me to leave first before following me into the car park.

'Can I give you a lift home?' Jared nodded towards his car and the temptation was high. It was chilly that evening, spring still reluctant to show itself fully, but I shook my head.

'Thanks, but I need to pick something up on the way.'

'Ok.' Jared smiled at me again and I had the urge to sprint across the car park and throw myself into his car. 'I'll see you tomorrow.'

'Bye.' I gave a little wave before forcing myself forward, thinking only of the reunion and not how hot Jared was.

THIRTEEN

Jared

The sight of his parents' home held a jumble of memories and emotions for Jared. It was the home he'd grown up in with his younger sisters, his bedroom a shrine to Jennifer Aniston, Baby Spice and Neve Campbell, with dirty socks strewn about the floor. The three-bedroomed house had been crowded with the six of them, particularly Jared's room, which was little more than a matchbox, but he remembered his childhood home being filled with love and laughter, Monopoly tournaments and thousand-piece jigsaws taking up the kitchen table. Jared couldn't help smiling when he thought back over his childhood. He'd had dreams that had never been fulfilled and though it had hurt like hell at the time, it didn't overshadow the joy that had filled the house.

Jared reached for the gate, willing his brain to focus on those memories, of playing swingball in the back garden with Ally and Freya, of playing rounders and marbles in the street and the smell of baking on a Saturday afternoon as his mum jigged along to the Bee Gees in the kitchen. He wanted those memories, needed them to keep him moving towards the front door but he was tormented as the bad thoughts filtered through, clouding the good. He'd moved out of this house, lugging boxes and bags into his dad's work van, hopeful for the future that lay ahead of him, only to return five years later with seemingly no future at all. He'd returned to his bedroom, now clear of the posters and dirty socks, kitted out in cream and sunshine yellow, now a generic guest room. He'd wept into the floral pillowcase every night, never believing the tears would end.

But here he was now, standing on his own two feet, feeling stronger than he had in a long time. He'd moved out of his parents' house again a year ago and had settled into his flat.

'Are you coming in or not?'

Jared looked up, his hand still resting on the iron gate. His mum was standing on the doorstep, her cupcake-print apron tied around her waist. She beckoned to Jared and her familiar smile urged him on and he managed to push through his dark thoughts as well as the gate and was enveloped in a tight hug.

'Come in. Everybody's already here.' Linda ushered her son into the house, taking his coat and hanging it in the hallway while Jared went through to the sitting room to join the rest of the family. Bob rose from his armchair to clap his son on the back while Freya patted the empty seat next to her on the sofa.

'We didn't think you were coming,' Ally said from the beanbag by the window.

'Do you want a beer?' Ally's husband lifted his own bottle but Jared shook his head. Besides driving, Jared didn't tend to drink much anymore. He'd drunk himself stupid far too much over the past few years in an attempt to block out his shitty life, but he'd knocked it on the head eighteen months ago. He hadn't been an alcoholic but he knew how easy it was to slip into the habit, how soothing it was to forget everything for a little while.

Linda crossed the room and gave her youngest daughter a nudge. 'Aren't you going to say hello to your brother?' Jimmy was sprawled across an armchair, her legs dangling over the edge, mobile in hand while she tapped away at the screen.

'Hey, bruv.'

'How's school?'

Jimmy continued to tap away at her phone. 'It's okay.' She finished typing out her text message, sent it and slipped the phone into her pocket, swinging her legs around into a normal sitting position as she did so. 'I got an A for my history project and I'm getting an award for my maths.'

'Brilliant.'

Jimmy gave a shrug of her shoulders, taking her achievements in her stride. She'd always been studious and popular at school, unlike Jared, who had found school hellish. He'd been an easy target for the bullies and they'd been relentless.

Sunday was a family day for the Williams's, a day when they all gathered around the table for a good old-fashioned roast. Linda relished having all of her family under one roof again and she was dreading the day when Jimmy, the tiniest bird in the nest, grew wings and fluttered away like the others. Their small house would seem ginormous when it was only herself and Bob rattling about the place.

'So then.' Linda had seen to everybody else's needs and was now sitting at the table, pouring gravy over her lamb. 'I was talking to Jillian Dean – do you remember Jillian? No? Anyway, I bumped into her at the market and you'll never guess who's returned from Australia?' She glanced around the table, beaming at her family while they shot blank looks in return. 'Her daughter, Marie. You remember Marie, don't you, Jared? You went to primary school with her. Lovely girl. Very pretty.'

Jared groaned to himself as he dropped his gaze to his roast potatoes. He vaguely remembered Marie Dean from school and knew exactly where this conversation was heading. They had the same conversation week after week.

'And she's single. Can you believe it?'

'Yes, I can. If I remember rightly she had buck teeth, a great big hairy mole on her chin and a hunchback. It's a wonder she got through border control.'

Jimmy sniggered while Linda shot Jared 'the look' they'd all feared as children. 'That isn't true and you know it. Why do you have to make this so difficult?'

'Because I don't want to date Marie Dean.' Jared speared a piece of potato and wedged it into his mouth. It was too big and he struggled to chew, let alone speak up, as Linda addressed the rest of the table.

'Well then, what else do we have?'

Ally and Freya reached into their pockets and pulled out scraps of paper. Ally read from hers first. 'Nancy Hunter has been dumped by her boyfriend. She's gorgeous. Long blonde hair, legs to die for and she isn't needy or anything.' She looked at Jared, who shook his head, still chomping on the potato. 'How about Keira Poole? I know you said no to her last week but I can't see why. She's stunning. I took a photo on my phone. It doesn't really do her justice but –'

Jared swallowed hard, bruising his gullet. 'Put your phone away. I don't want to see her photo.'

'I don't have a photo, but my friend Dee's sister's neighbour is single and very cute,' Freya jumped in.

'Not interested.'

'Clara Ross from the florist?'

'Not interested.'

'Judith Gold's granddaughter?' Linda this time. 'She's only twenty-two but very mature.'

'Not interested.'

'Kelly Smith is looking well.' Jared gaped at his father. He expected all this matchmaking nonsense from his mother and sisters but now his father was in on the act? The females of the family were constantly trying to set him up with friends, neighbours, colleagues and nice-looking strangers behind them in the queue at Asda, but Bob had always left them to it and while he had never actually claimed to be on Jared's side, he'd always remained silent on the matter.

'Don't look at me like that. I'm not asking you to marry the girl.' Bob cringed as he heard the words and tried to apologise to Jared.

'It's fine, Dad. But I'm not interested in Kelly Smith or Marie Dean or any of the other women.'

Ally put her fork down and placed her hand over Jared's. 'But you can't stay single forever.'

'Why not?' Gavin asked. 'What if Jared doesn't want to get back into dating? He's not doing any of you lot any harm by staying single.'

Ally gave her husband her own version of 'the look'

and Gavin shrank in his seat. Jared was on his own.

'I appreciate you looking out for me, really I do.' And Jared meant it. He knew they were worried about him and were trying to help him in their own special and frustrating way. 'But I don't want to date any of these random women.'

Linda spotted a weakness in Jared. He usually claimed he wasn't ready to date any woman at all but, to her trained motherly ear, she detected the difference. 'So you *are* ready to date again?'

'No.' He wasn't, was he? It was too soon to be even thinking about another woman.

'It's been five years, Jared. It's time to move on.' Ally felt her brother's fingers tighten on his cutlery beneath her hand. 'Or at least think about it.'

'He *is* thinking about it. Look at his ears.' Linda pointed across the table, her face alight with triumph and a dash of relief. 'They're pink and his eye is twitching. He's got his eye on somebody already, the sly old dog.'

Freya sat forward in her seat, her chest landing in a pool of gravy in her eagerness. 'Who is she?'

Ally swivelled round in her seat. 'Where did you meet her?'

'And when do *we* get to meet her?' Linda clasped her hands together, already planning the cosy little get-together. She'd bake something, a Victoria sponge or a cheesecake and they'd eat it over tea and coffee, less formal than a meal for a first meeting.

'I do not have my eye on anybody.' Jared snatched his hand away from Ally's and threw his knife and fork onto his plate, splashing gravy onto the tablecloth. 'I keep telling you it's too soon. Why won't you listen to me?' Scraping back his chair, he left the table, grabbing a beer from the fridge and taking it out into the cool back garden where he slung himself onto the wonky bench his father had crafted years ago. He could hear his family chattering from within the kitchen, but they allowed him to stew for a while and it was Gavin who was eventually pushed outside to talk to him.

'They mean well, you know.' Gavin lowered himself onto the bench, steeling himself for its collapse but it held tight.

'I know, but it pisses me off. They've been going on at me for months now. Why can't they wait until I'm ready? It still hurts.'

'I know.' But Gavin didn't, not really. He'd been with Ally pretty much since they were teenagers, had lived across the road from the family since he was thirteen. He'd never suffered like Jared, had never had his heart crushed in the same way. 'But one day you'll be ready to get out there again, I'm sure. You'll meet someone else.'

'I think I already have.' Jared hung his head, the words he never thought he would utter disgusting him. He'd loved Frances so much – still did – so how could he even contemplate being with another woman?

'That's fantastic.' Gavin clapped Jared on the back, a grin plastered across his face. He wasn't a blood relative of Jared's, but they may as well have been brothers and Gavin, like the rest of the Williams clan, had been worried about Jared over the past five years. Gavin had never seen anybody so utterly defeated as Jared had been as he'd sloped back home, unshaven and stinking of alcohol and BO. He couldn't take care of himself after Frances and so Linda had taken him in.

'Who is she?' Gavin was curious about the woman who had cracked through Jared's hardened heart.

'I don't really want to go into detail.'

'Of course not.'

'You won't tell them, will you?' Jared pointed his bottle towards the closed back door where the family was clearing away the dirty dishes.

'Are you kidding? They'd be on you like a pack of wolves. I'll keep it to myself, don't worry. And you know where I am if you need to talk, yeah?'

Jared managed a small smile. 'Thanks, Gavin.'

Gavin gave a shrug. 'Are you ready to go in? Linda's about to serve apple crumble and I'm not allowed any until I talk you into coming back inside.'

FOURTEEN

Ruth

I could hear Kelvin rummaging around in his office, the filing cabinets swishing and clunking open and shut followed by the hiss of swear words as he failed to locate the file he needed. As quietly as the tiniest mouse wearing cotton wool slippers, I crept to my desk and slipped off my shoes, sneaking them into my oversized handbag while easing my trainers onto my feet. My computer had already been shut down at five on the dot so all I needed to do was make it over the threshold without being summoned.

'Ruth! Where have you put the sodding Hartman file?'

I paused my creeping, my hand still on the corner of my desk, breath held steady in my chest. The door to Kelvin's office was closed. If he couldn't see or hear me, how would he know whether I was still there or not?

'*Ruth*! Are you out there? Get in here now!'

My eyes darted from Kelvin's door to the open office door, the stairwell enticingly within view, and decided to make a run for it. With my trainers on, my feet barely made a sound as I scurried along the corridor, down the staircase, collapsing against the reception desk for only a moment as I wheezed a goodbye to Quinn before propelling myself out of the building. I was in the car park! I was free! Digging inside my handbag I located my iPod and my shoulders relaxed as Olly Murs serenaded me in his own cheeky chappy way.

Normally I would leave work and head for Subway to pick up something for my tea, but not that day. The Subway Diet had lasted for a valiant week and a half but I'd officially thrown the towel in that afternoon after sinking my teeth into my millionth sandwich and realising that I was *sick to fucking death of fucking Subway*. It wasn't as though the diet was even working – mainly because I'd been eating a Mega Melt for breakfast on the way to work, a 12-inch sub and a cookie for lunch and another 12-inch sub and a cookie, plus a packet of crisps (from the basket at the till so still technically 'Subway food') for tea. Deep down I was aware that I was supposed to choose the healthier subs rather than the sandwiches laden with cheese and sauce, particularly since I'd re-read the website I'd found the diet on a couple of days earlier. I wasn't supposed to even *sniff* the crisps and biscuits, never mind ingest them.

But, despite giving up the diet, I decided to continue to walk to and from work because, shockingly, I quite enjoyed it and it was a relief to give up the stress of the bus journeys. I turned up the volume on my iPod as I left the car park and set off towards home. I didn't think I could face another diet. I'd tried several with little to no results so what was the point? I was going home via the chippy to gorge on chips and curry sauce with a jumbo sausage and perhaps a meat pie on the side. My mouth watered at the thought and my step quickened. I'd missed chips with a passion and couldn't wait to sink my teeth into their greasy goodness.

But wait.

My feet shuffled to a halt as I gazed into the window of the shop I was passing. My body turned towards a dress displayed on a bald-headed mannequin and my hands reached out to touch it, resting on the glass as my mouth gaped open. It was a strapless fuchsia dress, its satin shining and cascading down to the floor, pooling around the mannequin's feet. Intricate beading in silver, pink and the palest blue ran across the top of the dress, meeting in the middle and continuing down the dress in a V shape to the nipped-in waist. This was it. I was in love. Or perhaps just randy with lust but either way, this exquisite creation was the dress I would wear to the reunion. I *would* slim down and when I did, I would fit into my dream dress and knock Zack's arrogant little socks off.

Inspired, I turned up the volume even louder and set off at a brisk pace, my arms pumping in my effort to squeeze as much exercise out of my walk home as possible. My breath was ragged and my calves burning but it didn't matter as I pictured Zack's gobsmacked face as I arrived at the school wearing That Dress. It would be an amazing feeling to see his jaw drop, his eyes widening first in surprise and then lust. I could see him falling to his knees, begging my forgiveness while I sneered down at him. I was better than Zack – and *he* was about to realise it.

Somewhere in the back of my mind I was aware of a

car beeping its horn, but I ignored it, too caught up in my fantasy of turning Zack down in front of a packed hall, of humiliating him the way he had humiliated me. I heard the car horn again and this time the car pulled up at the side of me and a voice yelled out my name. Tugging out my earphones, I turned and saw Jared poking his head out of the window. Sweet Jesus, he was divine. I'd forgotten quite how hot he was and I almost wet myself at the heavenly sight of him.

'Can I give you a lift home?'

I looked back down the street towards The Dress but the boutique was no longer in view. I'd had no idea I'd walked so far so surely that was enough exercise for the day? Besides, how could I not climb into the seat beside Jared? I was drawn to him, my body moving towards him without my permission. The fact that had my body requested action I'd have replied in the affirmative was beside the point.

'That would be great. Thanks.' I shoved my iPod into my handbag and climbed into the car, concentrating on gliding into the seat and not tangling myself in the seatbelt and/or whacking my head against the roof. I felt my cheeks grow warm at being so close to Jared and silently cursed my face and its inability to remain calm in situations such as these.

'Where are we going then?'

Had I been Erin, I'd have instructed Jared to take us to his place and ravish me till dawn, but I wasn't Erin. I was Ruth Lynch, dumpy and unfanciable. 'Oak Road? Do you know it?' Jared nodded and we set off, the radio playing softly in the background.

'I haven't seen you around lately,' Jared said after a few minutes. I hadn't seen much of Jared since he practically copped off with Erin at Kelvin's party and I

was both disappointed and relieved by our lack of
contact. I couldn't help feeling jealous towards Erin.
Why couldn't men fancy me for a change? Why did I
always end up with blokes like Gideon, whose favourite
pastimes were scratching their arses and marking their
farts out of ten?

'No, we haven't bumped into each other, have we?'

'I suppose it's my fault. I haven't been keeping my
lunch in the kitchen. I've learned my lesson.'

'Sorry about Kelvin.'

Jared stopped at a red light and turned to me. 'It's
not your fault. He's a grown man. He should know
what's his and what isn't. He's a rude arsehole if you ask
me.'

'And arrogant. But don't tell him I said that.'

Jared grinned at me. 'I won't tell him you called him
arrogant if you don't mention I called him an arsehole.'

'Deal.' Like a moron, I stuck out my hand but Jared
humoured me and shook it, his fingers snug over my
hand. It was almost like holding hands, I thought, my
treacherous cheeks glaring again.

'So how long have you worked at H. Woods?'

'Too long.' I gave a shrug as I threw my eyes
heavenwards. 'It's been three years. I'm sure I must
have done something terrible in a former life. But there
are worst jobs, I suppose.' And I wouldn't be chatting to
Jared if I'd never worked for Kelvin so I suppose I should
have been grateful to him for that.

'And why have you started walking home?'

The question silenced me for a moment. I didn't
want to tell Jared about my weight loss bid. I'd only told
Erin, Billy, Quinn and Theo so far (although I didn't
technically tell Theo, the nosy bastard was earwigging
on my *private* conversation with Billy) and I didn't want

to broadcast it. Imagine the sniggers – *'Ha ha, the fatty is trying to lose weight. As if!'* And the laughter would only increase if I failed.

'Money's been a bit tight this month. I'm too skint to catch the bus.' Better Jared thought I was poor than deluded. 'It's just on the right, in front of the camper van.' We'd reached Oak Road too quickly. I'd been enjoying the drive and my cheeks had finally started to behave themselves. 'Thanks for the lift.'

'Anytime. Just give me a shout if you need a ride home again.'

'Thanks.' I climbed out of the car and gave a little wave before closing the door behind me. Jared waited until I reached my front door and had successfully unlocked it before he gave a wave and drove away. Grinning, I skipped inside and leant against the closed door. Had that really just happened?

'What's up with you?' Theo wandered out of the kitchen, scratching himself. 'You look happy for a change.'

I let it go. I was in too good a mood for even Theo to wind me up. 'It must be the sight of you. You're a very handsome man, you know. There's no need to look so alarmed, Theo. I'm not coming on to you.' I skipped up the stairs, running through my conversation with Jared. My mind switched to The Dress as I flopped onto my bed, trying to recreate its beauty in my head. I reached under my bed and pulled out my laptop, untying my trainers and kicking them off while I waited for it to load. I checked my emails first, replying to one from my brother and deleting the junk before beginning yet another search for diets. I was running out of time and now I'd found The Dress, I was looking for instant results so this time I searched for crash diets. Bingo! My eyes lingered on the classic Cabbage Soup Diet before I clicked for more details. It promised to help me lose weight fast – as much as ten pounds in a week, which would be a huge amount and may even counteract the damage I'd done by not following the Subway Diet correctly. I set the recipe to print and knocked on Billy's bedroom door where his wireless printer was housed. There was no answer so I prayed he wasn't in there with Clare as I eased the door open and peeked inside. The room was thankfully empty, so I snatched up the document from the printer on top of Billy's chest of drawers and had turned to leave when something caught my eye. It wasn't as though I'd never seen a box of condoms before – I had a box gathering dust in the drawer beside my bed – but this particular box gave me a jolt and I felt my skin prickle. The box was open and had fallen over, spilling the lone condom packet onto the bedside cabinet. My mind wandered to the missing condoms and the back of my neck grew warm at the thought of their use. I'd never imagined Billy having sex before, not in any graphic form, and I wasn't sure I wanted to begin now. Clutching my printout tighter, I hurried back to my own room where I elbowed all thoughts of a naked, sweaty Billy out of my mind and made up a shopping list. I had a good feeling about the Cabbage Soup Diet. A very good feeling indeed.

FIFTEEN

Billy

'You work too hard.' Billy could detect Clare's weariness even over the phone. 'You should take a few days off.'
'I've got a couple of days booked off in a few weeks to go on my cousin's hen night.'

Billy swapped the phone to his other ear and sank further into the sofa, resting his bare feet on the coffee table. 'That's hardly going to be a restful break, is it? Going clubbing with a bunch of rowdy women waving plastic willies around.'

'It's not going to be that kind of hen night. We're far too mature for that kind of thing.'

'Really?' Billy thought it was the law that women had to turn into shrieking harlots before their mate/relative walked down the aisle.

'No, not really. There will definitely be plastic willies. And a condom veil.' Billy had no idea what a condom veil was but he wasn't sure he was brave enough to ask and Clare didn't elaborate. 'Are you free tonight? Becki and a few of the girls and their fellas are meeting up in the pub if you want to come along.'

Billy cringed. He didn't want to turn down Clare's offer but... 'I can't. It's *A Beginner's Guide To You* night. It's a sort of tradition for me and Ruth to watch it together. Why don't you come round? We can all watch it together. You don't really know Ruth that well so you can hang out and get to know her better.'

'You don't really know my friends either. You could hang out with them and get to know them.'

'And I will. Another night, I promise.'

Billy held his breath while Clare mulled over his suggestion. Was he screwing up the first relationship he'd had in two years over a sitcom? Should he jump in quickly and agree to the meet up in the pub?

'Ok. Give me half an hour.'

Billy allowed his breath to rush out. 'Great. Ruth will be really pleased and you'll love her, I promise.'

After saying goodbye, Billy raced up the stairs and showered before dousing himself in Theo's aftershave. He raced back down the stairs and almost vomited on the bottom step. It was the second day of Ruth's Cabbage Soup Diet and the house was filled with a thick green smog, the aftereffects of the diet. He found Ruth in the kitchen, forcing down another bowl of the repulsive soup.

'I've had enough of this diet, Ruth. I can't take it any more.'

'I'm not asking you to eat the soup, am I?' Ruth spooned more into her mouth and pretended it was delicious. 'I'm not even asking you to make it any more. I nailed the last batch.'

'No, but you're making me smell it. Clare's going to

be here in fifteen minutes. What if she thinks it's *me* who's farting?'

'Will you relax?'

'Relax? My girlfriend is coming round and the place reeks. I know you don't want her to come round tonight, but –'

'I never said I didn't want her to come round.'

Billy tried not to gag as another wave of cabbage hit his nostrils. 'You may as well have.'

It was true that Ruth hadn't been too pleased when Billy mentioned that Clare would be joining them for that evening's telly entertainment.

'But we always watch it together,' she'd pointed out, pout in place. 'Just us. Even Erin knows that Thursday evenings are *our* night.' But what could she do? Billy had already invited Clare along and he was right, Ruth did want to get to know her better, so she decided to get a grip and stop sulking.

Ruth's spoon clattered into the bowl as she rose out of her seat. 'You're overreacting. I don't mind Clare joining us. It was just a surprise, that's all. And we'll open the windows so it'll be fine.' Billy and Ruth tore around the house, opening every window and, to be on the safe side, Billy wafted the front door, trying to dispel the stench further.

'What are you doing?' Clare stood by the gate, catching Billy mid-swing.

'Just checking the hinges. They've been sticking but they seem fine now. Come in.' Billy took a quick sniff of the hallway as Clare made her way across the short path to the house. He could hear Ruth spraying the sitting room liberally with citrus fruit air freshener.

'I've never actually watched *A Beginner's Guide To You* before. Is it any good?'

Billy took Clare's jacket and hung it over the banister with the rest of the coats. 'Any good? It's brilliant. You'll really enjoy it. We've got the first two seasons on DVD if you want to borrow them.' He froze as Clare sniffed the air.

'What's that smell?'

Billy decided to play dumb. It wasn't a great stretch of his acting abilities. 'What smell?'

Clare gave another long sniff. 'Have you been chopping lemons or something?'

Billy's breath rushed out. 'Oh, that smell.'

'Yes, it's lovely.' Clare sniffed the air again. 'Mmm. Lemony and... something else. Limes?'

Billy didn't care what the smell was as long as it wasn't cabbage or farts. He led Clare into the sitting room, where Ruth whipped the can of air freshener behind her back.

'Hi, Ruth. It's nice to see you again.'

'You too.' Ruth stepped forward, extending her hand to shake Clare's. As their hands met, a fog erupted from behind Ruth's back and it wasn't citrus fruit scented.

'Oh, God. I am so sorry.' Billy sank onto his bed, his head in his hands. It had happened a couple of hours ago and yet he was still mortified. They'd all somehow managed to sit through *A Beginner's Guide* but Billy had been too tense to enjoy it and hadn't laughed once. Instead, he'd sat next to Clare on the sofa while Ruth sat in the furthermost chair, both waiting for the ground to swallow them whole.

'It's this stupid diet she's on. She's trying to lose weight for a reunion we're going to in August but I don't know why she's putting herself through all these diets, making herself hungry and miserable for a bunch of idiots who made her life hell at school. She's fine the way she is and shouldn't change for anybody.'

'No, she shouldn't.' Billy felt the bed dip behind him as Clare climbed into bed.

'She's pretty, isn't she?'

'Hmm.'

'And funny and a great mate.'

'Billy?' He turned as Clare tugged at his arm. 'I'm in your bed, naked. Why are you wittering on about your housemate?'

'Because I'm a complete moron?' Billy grinned as he peeled his T-shirt over his head, clumsily hopping out of his jeans before joining Clare in bed. She was indeed gloriously naked.

Clare woke early and left to go home to get ready for work, leaving Billy sleeping, his hair a mass of curls on the pillow and his mouth puckered like a baby's. She stooped to kiss his warm cheek before creeping out of the bedroom and relishing the fresh air as she stepped out of the front door.

An hour or so later, Billy stirred and headed downstairs for breakfast. Ruth was already up and about in the kitchen, stacking containers of soup on the counter.

'Please tell me you're shoving them in the wheelie bin.' Billy was aware that his tone was pleading but if begging was what it took for Ruth to quit the Cabbage Soup Diet, he'd get down on his knees.

'Don't be silly. I'm taking these to work with me. Kelvin might steal one tub but he won't come back for seconds, trust me.'

Billy groaned as he grabbed a bowl from the draining board. 'So you're carrying on with it? Even though you smell like a dodgy drain?'

'Billy, I weighed myself this morning. Do you know how much I've lost?' Billy had no idea how much weight she'd shed, but she was about to lose a friend. 'Five pounds, Billy. Five beautiful pounds. If I carry on like this, I won't have to buy The Dress in the biggest size.'

'If you carry on like this, I'm going to have to move out.'

Ruth gave Billy's hair a ruffle. 'If I'd have known a few cabbages would get rid of you, I'd have stocked up years ago. Could you be a doll and take Theo with you?' She picked up the stack of soup and left Billy alone in the kitchen. No longer hungry after the stench lingering around his bowl, he headed upstairs to get ready for work.

Theo was up late as usual and no matter how much Billy chivvied him along, they left the house at the very last minute and had to run for the bus. It was one of the many cons of both living and working with Theo.
'I'm buying you an alarm clock for Christmas,' Billy grumbled as they searched the upper deck for a non-existent vacant seat.

'You bought me an alarm clock last year. It's still in the box.'

'So why don't you use it?' Billy grabbed hold of a pole as the bus swerved, sending his feet shuffling along the floor. He felt like a tit as a couple of teenage girls ineffectually muffled their giggles behind their hands.

'I don't need an alarm clock with you nagging like an old woman for me to get up. You should chill out. When are we ever late for work?'

'Every day? You do realise we start at nine, don't you?'

'You might start at nine but I don't. I need my breakfast and my morning dump before I can even think of working. Speaking of taking a dump, what the hell is going on with Ruth? I was scared of using the oven last night in case the spark ignited the whole house.'

'It's her new diet for the reunion.'

Theo shook his head. 'It's a waste of time. Why doesn't she just sit on the tossers who teased her? That'd teach them more of a lesson than showing up skinny.'

'I think it's more about her own self-worth than teaching them a lesson. And they didn't just tease her. They tortured the poor girl. The only time anybody ever spoke to her was to call her disgusting names.'

'Whatever. She should still sit on them.'

The bus trundled along, depositing people at every stop but none from the upper deck so Billy and Theo had to remain standing for the entire journey. They arrived at the office a mere twelve minutes late.

'I'm off to the canteen. Coming?' Theo asked, but Billy shook his head and went straight to his desk and switched on his computer. He got straight to work, only pausing at lunchtime to grab a sandwich and check his emails.

```
To: billy.worth
From: s.lynch
Subject: Girlfriend???

What's this I hear about you having a
girlfriend? Ruth has just emailed me
and assumed I knew who 'Clare' was.
Come on, matey, spill!
```

Billy was sure he'd told Stephen about Clare, even if it

was only a vague email back in the beginning. He wasn't sure why he hadn't mentioned her since – he probably didn't want to jinx their relationship or something.

To: s.lynch
From: billy.worth
Subject: Re: Girlfriend???

I have been seeing somebody. I guess you could call her my girlfriend. She's really cool. You'd like her. She's pretty and funny and has somehow found herself with me.

Anyway, how are you, Aubrey and the little ones?

To: billy.worth
From: s.lynch
Subject: Re: Re: Girlfriend???

We're all good. Austin's looking forward to coming to England again. He wants to watch a soccer match while we're there and Riley wants to meet the Queen. She's planning on bringing her plastic tea set with us. Ryder couldn't care less. He's eighteen months and doesn't know what England is yet. I've tried teaching him but it doesn't seem to be going in. He did master 'square' yesterday so I'm sure England will be his next triumph.

To: s.lynch
From: billy.worth
Subject: Re: Re: Re: Girlfriend???

You could start by teaching Austin
it's football and not soccer. Repeat
after me: Foot. Ball. Football. Not
soccer. Don't go all American on me

To: billy.worth
From: s.lynch
Subject: Re: Re: Re: Girlfriend???

Sorry, sorry, sorry. You're right.

Football.
Football.
Football.
Football.
Football.

Is that better?

To: billy.worth
From: theo.logan
Subject: Canteen Jo

She's wearing a low-cut top and one of
them pushy up bras. Her tits are up to
her eyeballs. Go and have a look!

To: theo.logan
From: billy.worth
Subject: Re: Canteen Jo

I'm seeing Clare, remember?

To: billy.worth
From: theo.logan
Subject: Re: Re: Canteen Jo

You're not married.

To: theo.logan
From: billy.worth
Subject: Re: Re: Re: Canteen Jo

I'm here to work, not ogle women.

To: billy.worth
From: theo.logan
Subject: Re: Re: Re: Re: Canteen Jo

Pussy.

To: billy.worth
From: ruthlynch01
Subject: Cabbage Soup Diet

You win. The diet's off.

Ruth x

SIXTEEN

Ruth

I had a fantastic start to the morning, waking early and refreshed after a fabulous night's sleep. Instead of groaning and pulling the covers over my head and wishing I could pause time for another hour or three, I leapt out of bed, eager to start the day. And I hadn't even weighed myself by that point. That glorious moment came five minutes later, about three seconds before I began a silent squeal and dance around the bathroom, not wanting to wake the others in the house. Five pounds! I'd lost *five bloody pounds*! Happy doesn't come close to describing the way I felt in that moment as I stepped off the scales and stepped on again to double check. Nope, I was right the first time. Five bloody pounds! Cabbage soup wasn't the most appetising meal but it was working and that was all that mattered.

I showered and dressed in a yellow daisy print dress,

so the outside represented my cheerful mood inside and skipped down the stairs for breakfast. I was humming to myself as I gathered a few tubs of soup in the kitchen when Billy shuffled into the room, stopping dead in the doorway.

'Please tell me you're shoving them in the wheelie bin.'

'Don't be silly.' Why would I throw them away? I should have been building a shrine to the wondrous foodstuff. 'I'm taking these to work with me. Kelvin might steal one tub but he won't come back for seconds, trust me.' I'd have paid good money to see his face as he took a sneaky sip of the nauseating soup.

'So you're carrying on with it? Even though you smell like a dodgy drain?'

'Billy, I weighed myself this morning. Do you know how much I've lost?' Placing my hands on my hips (had they shrunk? They felt smaller), I awaited an answer that never materialised. 'Five pounds, Billy. Five beautiful pounds. If I carry on like this, I won't have to buy The Dress in the biggest size.'

'If you carry on like this I'm going to have to move out.'

I gave Billy's hair a ruffle, my mood so great I almost stooped to kiss his chaotic curls. 'If I'd have known a few cabbages would get rid of you, I'd have stocked up years ago. Could you be a doll and take Theo with you?' Giggling to myself, I grabbed the stack of soup and popped them into my fabric bag for life along with my heels and headed out to work.

My mood was further lifted as I felt the first weak rays of the sun on my face as I stepped outside. Spring, like my diet, had given itself a kick up the arse and was out in full force with daisies and crocuses popping up in gardens and grass verges. The air was approaching warm and was certainly more comfortable than the biting frost we'd had lately. I was now truly grateful that I was walking to work in the fresh air instead of catching the stuffy bus because at least while I was out in the open, I was no longer engulfed in a cloud of cabbagey farts, the only downside of my diet.

I made it to H. Woods slightly out of puff but with a feeling of exhilaration and pride. A few weeks ago I would have laughed in your face if you'd suggested I walked to work, but I'd done it yet again and it was getting easier every day.

'You look lovely and bright this morning.' Quinn smiled at me as I headed towards her desk for our usual morning catch up.

'I feel lovely and bright this morning.' I paused to add a bit of suspense and mystery to our ritual gossip as I leant forward on the desk and lowered my voice. 'I've lost five pounds.'

'*Five*?' Quinn's mouth gaped, her eyes practically popping out of her head. 'Wow, that's fantastic. Let's have a look at you.'

I took a couple of steps back from the desk and gave a twirl while Quinn applauded.

'You look wonderful, Ruth. Well done.'

'Thank you.' I flicked my wrist to check the time. As much as I was enjoying being praised and admired, I didn't want Kelvin to catch me chatting away instead of being chained to my desk.

Quinn saw me checking the time. 'There's no rush. Kelvin's just phoned. There's a bit of a crisis so he's got back-to-back meetings at Westerly's all morning. He asked me to let you know so you can cancel his appointment with Angelina at eleven and he said his wife might call about a plumber or something.'

Yes! A whole morning of skiving. 'In that case, would you like a coffee?'

I was having a fabulous morning. Not only had I lost five pounds, Kelvin would be out of the office all morning, leaving me to sit back, feet up on the desk, leafing through the stack of magazines Quinn had finished with. I'd tried to convince Erin to pop over for half an hour but she was adamant she couldn't leave her office.

'I'm sorry, Ruth. I can't get away. We're really busy over here.'

'Busy? But you're never too busy for a skive and we need to celebrate my weight loss.'

'And we will, I promise.' I heard Erin cover the mouthpiece, followed by muffled voices. 'I'm really sorry. Richard needs me. It's urgent. I'll call you later.'

Fine. I'd celebrate by myself. I'd pretend my cup of vending machine water was champagne. Raising the plastic cup, I toasted myself before taking a delicate sip.

'It's no use. It's just crappy old water.'

'It's the first sign of madness, you know, talking to yourself.' My water nearly flew in the air as I jumped in fright, swinging my feet back down to the floor and sweeping the magazines under the desk. Jared strode into the office looking as gorgeous as ever in a grey tailored suit.

'I think it's too late for me. I lost my marbles years ago.' I chortled as I kicked the magazines further under the desk.

'You're not the only one.' Jared gave a small smile and perched on the corner of my desk, his arse mere inches away from my hands. I could easily reach out and stroke his leg. But I wouldn't.

'I think most of H. Woods' employees have lost it. They must have to still be working here.'

Jared laughed but stopped suddenly, his brow creasing. He sniffed the air, his nose wrinkling in response.

'What is that smell?'

Oh bugger. It was me. Being the only one in the office that morning, I'd been free to do whatever I pleased. Including polluting the air with cabbageness.

'It's Kelvin,' I whispered, nodding my head towards the empty office next to mine. Luckily the door was shut so Jared wouldn't know whether he was in there or not. 'I think he had something dodgy for his tea last night. He's been hiding in there all morning, stinking the place out. I told him he should be at home, tucked up in bed but he refuses. He's a martyr to this business. And he's a stubborn git.'

Jared hopped off the desk and my hand, completely of its own accord, flew out in a last ditch attempt to caress him so I hid the gesture by reaching for my hole punch.

'I've got some forms that I need him to sign.' Jared waved the stack of papers in his hand while I jumped out of my seat, dropping the hole punch onto the desk with a clatter.

'Don't go in there!' I had to stop him before he discovered the empty room and figured out that I was the foul-smelling beast. 'He's so embarrassed, you see. He doesn't want anybody to see him while he has his upset stomach. If you leave the forms with me, I'll get Kelvin to sign them and bring them back to you later.'

I held my breath, willing Jared to hand over the papers and leave. My breath came out in a rush as the papers were lifted towards me and my fingers made contact. Phew! Disaster averted.

'That company couldn't find their arse with both hands and a map. Coffee, Ruth, quick as you can.'

I squeezed my eyes shut as Kelvin strode into the office, stomach in full working order and his body odour free. The papers were snatched out of my reach as Jared turned towards the voice.

'Hello, Kelvin. You're looking well.'

'I don't feel it.' Kelvin gave a shake of his head, his jowls flapping in rhythm. 'I've been stuck at Westerly's since eight. I didn't think I was ever going to get into the office today.'

'Is that so?'

'It's been a bloody nightmare.' Kelvin turned to me, unaware of what he had done. 'Did Susan call about the plumber? And what is that smell? It smells like someone's died in here.'

The only thing that had died was any scrap of self-respect I'd ever possessed – and the Cabbage Soup Diet.

I felt like James Bond over the next few days, sneaking around corners, peering up and down corridors before revealing myself in case Jared Williams happened to be there. I avoided the kitchen, the place we had conversed most frequently, making Kelvin's cups of coffee in a flash before scurrying back to the office, eyes darting left and right at all times. It was exhausting.

'You look like you could do with a sit down.' Quinn patted the vacant seat next to her behind the reception desk. 'Have you got five minutes?'

Taking furtive glances around the general area, I assessed the risk was low and sank into the seat.

'What's up with you? You've been really jumpy lately

and I saw you sprint across the car park when you left last night.'

I *had* sprinted across the car park. And thought I was suffering from a heart attack as a consequence. It turned out to be a stitch but it had been a truly terrifying experience for those five breathless minutes.

'Who are you avoiding?'

'Avoiding? Nobody.' I laughed off the very idea. I couldn't tell her the truth, could I?

'Is it Erin? Have you had a falling out?' I hung my head, giving it a bob up and down. I hoped my nose didn't start to grow. 'Oh, that's a shame. You two are so close. I bet it's over something silly, isn't it? I'm sure you can sort it out.'

'Thanks.' I lifted my head to smile at Quinn but my face froze as I saw Jared through the small window in the door leading to reception. 'Shit! I'm not here, okay?' Quinn didn't have time to respond before I flung myself under the desk, curling up as tight as I could. I squeezed my eyes shut, trying to pretend I was somewhere else as I heard Jared's footsteps approaching. He exchanged pleasantries with Quinn and then he was gone.

'That wasn't Erin.'

I unfurled and rose to my feet, smoothing down my skirt. 'No, it wasn't.'

'What's going on, Ruth?'

I cringed. 'I can't tell you. It's too embarrassing.'

Quinn smiled as she placed a hand on my arm. 'Do you fancy him? Is that it? It's okay, you know. I think every woman in the building fancies the pants off him.' She patted my arm, problem solved.

'Thanks, Quinn.' I attempted a smile as I backed away. 'I'd better be getting back up to my desk.' Making sure the coast was clear, I made my way out of reception and up the stairs, surveying the corridor before continuing to my office.

'Ruth!' I'd barely got my toes over the threshold before Kelvin started barking. 'Where have you been? I've been looking everywhere for you.' He was sat behind his desk, arse welded to his leather chair. He hadn't moved an inch since I'd left the office, the lying toad. 'I've got a meeting at half past eleven. I need you to take minutes.'

My head snapped up, my interest piqued. I didn't usually get given the opportunity to take minutes, mainly because I was a bit crap at keeping up and my notes may as well have been made by little green men from Jupiter for all the sense they made. One of the HR assistants usually carried out the role, so I was excited. Taking minutes was the best way to hear all the gossip first hand. When the L. M. Brown contract went tits up because Mr Brown was a raging alcoholic who'd accidently set fire to his warehouse, I'd been sitting at the table as Kelvin and co discussed the fallout, too engrossed and itching to share it with Erin to make proper notes. But now I was being given the opportunity to redeem myself.

'Cheryl's on holiday so you'll have to do it.' I was sure Kelvin rolled his eyes at me beneath his thick glasses. 'You'll need to order lunch for...' He held up a hand to count, muttering the names to himself as he went. 'Five. Or six if you're hungry too.'

'Thanks but my lunch is sorted.' I had a couple of grapefruit sitting in my bottom drawer. I wasn't keen on that particular fruit but the Grapefruit Diet was similar to the Cabbage Soup Diet without all the nasty side effects, so I was hoping it would have similar results.

'Hmm, whatever.' Kelvin tapped his watch and sent

me on my way. I organised a lunchtime banquet to be delivered from a local sandwich shop and hurried to the kitchen to make pots of tea and coffee, setting them up in the meeting room just before it was due to begin. All was going well until the attendees started to filter into the room. Sally from HR, Production Manager Hugh Gunner, Glenn from Accounts and Purchasing Manager Jared Williams.

Shit! My eyes flew about the room in search of a hiding place but it was too late. He'd seen me. Kelvin waddled into the room and I flew at him, my eyes wild.

'I can't take the minutes.'

'I know. You're crap at it but we've got no choice.'

'No, I *really* can't take the minutes. I'm not feeling well.'

Kelvin narrowed his eyes at me, hunting for any signs of bullshit. 'What's up with you?'

I only had one shot at this so I had to be convincing. I clutched my stomach, letting out a howl. 'It's my stomach. It's, you know...' I lowered my voice. '*Women's trouble.*'

Kelvin's nostrils flared and he stood up straight, clearing his throat and averting his gaze. 'Yes, yes. Go. Sally will have to take the minutes.' I scurried away before he could change his mind, but he called me back before I could reach the door. 'You did order lunch, didn't you?'

SEVENTEEN

Jared

Sammy was wearing more make-up than usual, her face a strange orange colour that ended at her jawline and tinged her thin eyebrows. The apples of her cheeks shone brightly with a deep pink and, coupled with thick, spider-leg-like eyelashes, gave the impression of a doll. Jared wondered whether she would close her eyes if he tipped her backwards but he quickly pushed the thought away. Any contact with Sammy, especially of the horizontal kind, would only encourage her crush.

'So that's two black pens and a pack of post-its?' The office junior was sitting opposite Jared in his office, a notepad on her lap while she sucked suggestively on the end of a biro. Sammy could have taken his stationery order via email as she had with the rest of the department, but she'd made an exception for Jared. He was beginning to think the poor girl had been taking lessons from Angelina. Speaking of which, Jared glanced above Sammy's head and noted that the vamp was still there, hovering on the other side of his window, segmented by the half open blinds.

'Yep, that's it. Thanks, Sammy.'

'Are you sure there isn't anything else you want from me?' Sammy gave a girlish giggle and batted her eyelashes, which must have taken great strength given the three million coats of mascara she'd applied that morning.

She *had* been taking lessons from Angelina.

'No thank you. The pens and post its will be fine.'

'I'm not just offering stationery, you know.'

Jared was appalled. Sammy was just a kid, barely out of school. He thought of his sister, a year or two younger than Sammy, and felt his gut clench. He'd kill anybody who touched Jimmy, let alone a thirty-odd-year-old man in authority.

'There's nothing else I need, Sammy.' Jared's tone was brisk with no hint of friendliness in case she mistook it for flirtation. 'Now, I really must get on. I have a meeting in ten minutes.'

'Oh. Okay.' Sammy rose from her seat and tugged down her skirt, attempting to cover a little more of her thighs. She scuttled out of the room on her stilt-like heels, but there wasn't even a split second of reprieve as Angelina strode into the office in her place. They were like a bloody tag team.

'What can I do for you, Angelina?' Jared kept his head down as he scribbled on his notepad. If he made eye contact, she would pounce.

'Are you busy?'

'Extremely.' Thank God. 'I have a meeting with Kelvin in a few minutes.'

'Oh.' Angelina pouted her glossy red lips but she

took it upon herself to glide into Sammy's vacated seat. She was wearing a short, low-cut black dress that displayed both her lacy bra and suspender belt when she sat down. Jared held back a sigh. Some days it felt like he was working on a porn shoot.

'Is that the time? Sorry, I really must get to my meeting. I hope it wasn't anything urgent you needed me for.' Swiping his jacket off the back of his chair, Jared fled from his office, not even bothering to save or close his work on the computer. He was aware of Angelina watching him as he dashed away, her red lips parted in shock. Still, she'd survive.

Despite leaving earlier than he needed to, Jared was still almost the last to arrive at the meeting room, with only Kelvin trundling along the corridor behind him. Jared slipped into the room and a smile crept onto his face as he spotted Ruth laying out the tea and coffee cups. It was a relief to be able to talk to a woman who didn't throw herself at him, desperate to undo his trousers at a mere 'good morning'. Not that Ruth was talking to him any more. She'd been avoiding him at all costs over the last few days, even throwing herself under the reception desk at one point. Of course he'd seen her, but he didn't want to embarrass her further by pointing it out.

Ruth turned and froze when she spotted Jared. His smile widened, wanting to show that they were still friends, but the smile wasn't returned. Ruth leapt at Kelvin, babbled at him and ran from the room. Jared wished she would get over her embarrassment. He missed chatting to her in the kitchen, which he frequented far more than he should in an attempt to bump into her. He liked Ruth and enjoyed her company. She was down to earth and natural and didn't feel the need to shove her cleavage in his face. An image of Ruth's cleavage popped into Jared's head and it both pleased and repulsed him. He hadn't thought about a woman like that since Frances.

'Jared? Are you going to sit down then?'

Jared blinked away the image. The others were all sitting around the table, looking up at him as he daydreamed by the door.

'Yes. Yes, of course.' He sat down at the table and poured himself a coffee, determined not to think about Ruth until after the meeting.

He thought about Ruth for the duration of the meeting. How could he not? She had, after all, prepared the coffee and the towering plate of fancy biscuits. She'd ordered their lunch and so he thought of her with every bite of his sandwich and vanilla slice. He wasn't sure what it was about Ruth, but he felt drawn to her. Perhaps it was her laugh or her vibrant mood, from her colourful clothes to her radiant smile. Perhaps it was simply because she was a happy person and Jared hadn't felt anything close to happy since his heart was broken. He hadn't felt particularly *unhappy* for the past year or so, not like in the beginning, but he hadn't felt light and free and so perhaps he was hoping Ruth's jovial energy would somehow transfer itself onto him and remind him what being content felt like.

'I think that's it then.' Kelvin glanced around the table, ensuring there hadn't been any neglected points. 'I'll be off for a late lunch then.'

Jared looked from Kelvin, struggling out of his seat, to the empty plates. Hadn't they had lunch? What were the sandwiches and pies and quiches? The cakes and pastries?

Kelvin managed to heave himself to his feet before addressing Sally. 'Pass those notes onto Ruth. She'll type them up and circulate this afternoon.'

'I'll take them up to Ruth.' Sally blinked in surprise as the sheath of papers was tugged from her fingers. 'I'm going up that way anyway.' Jared moved quickly before anybody could argue and hopped up the stairs towards Ruth's office. He wasn't sure what he was going to say to her, but he had to say *something* otherwise their friendship, however brief, would crumble into nothingness.

Jared paused in the doorway but Ruth's office was empty. He tried Kelvin's office but the door was locked. His shoulders sank. Picking up Ruth's stack of pink post-it notes, he tore the top sheet off and stuck it to the minutes before scribbling a note.

Kelvin wants you to type up and circulate these this afternoon.

Jared

Did he leave an *x*? Or leave it at that?

He left it and wandered back towards the stairwell, passing the kitchen en route. As he did so, he spotted a familiar frame within and his spirits lifted. Ruth was holding a pair of grapefruit in her hands, which made Jared think of her cleavage once again. He pushed the thought away. It wasn't right and made him feel sordid.

'Ah, there you are.' He strode into the kitchen, his friendliest smile plastered onto his face. 'I've just been to your office. Kelvin asked me to leave the minutes on your desk. He's gone out for lunch.'

'Oh. Thanks.' Ruth juggled the grapefruit into the crook of one arm, yanked open the little drawer above the cupboard and grabbed the first knife she could lay her hands on. It was a butter knife, which Jared didn't think would be much use with the grapefruit. Flashing Jared an almost-smile, Ruth legged it from the kitchen.

'Ruth, wait!' She acted as though she hadn't heard as Jared called after her, but he knew she probably had so there was no point in going after her. Instead, he made his way back to his own office, shutting himself away so he could think. He wasn't permitted thirty seconds before Angelina popped her head around the door.

'Not now, Angelina. I'm busy.' Jared hadn't meant to snap but perhaps it was for the best. Perhaps that was what Angelina needed to back off. Glistening lips pouting, she retreated, closing the door softly behind her.

Jared picked up his phone and, before he could think himself out of it, he had dialled Ruth's extension. He couldn't explain it, but he had to talk to her.

'Hi, Ruth. It's Jared. I was just wondering if you found the minutes.' Should he have put an *x*?

'Yes. They're in my in tray. Thank you.'

'Would you like to come to the pub with me for lunch?' He spoke quickly, before she could hang up on him. He'd already eaten, but if Kelvin could have two lunches, why couldn't he?

Jared waited an age for Ruth to answer. He assumed she would say no, still too mortified after the smelly office incident. But Jared didn't care about that and he'd never mention it again.

'Yes, I suppose so.'

Jared was stunned. He'd been prepared for rejection. 'Oh, right. Yes. Fantastic. Do you want to meet me in reception? Five minutes?'

'Ok.' Ruth was still hesitant, but she hadn't retracted her acceptance.

Yes, yes, yes! Lovely Ruth was meeting him for lunch.

Perhaps their friendship could be salvaged after all.

'Great. See you in five minutes then. Bye.' Jared put the phone down and found himself drumming his fingers on the desk, his own little private happy dance. Checking he had his wallet, he floated out of the purchasing department, skipping along the corridor until he was greeted by Erin.

'Hi. It's Jared, right?' They hadn't spoken since Kelvin's birthday bash, the night when Erin had helped him avoid Angelina's clutches.

'Yep and you're Ruth's friend, Erin.'

'Good memory. I'm just on my way to see Ruth, actually.'

'Oh, she won't be there.' It took great effort for Jared to stop himself from tapping his fingers along the pale blue wall of the corridor in another celebration. 'I'm meeting her for lunch.'

'Really?' Jared was taken aback as Erin looped her arm through his. 'I haven't eaten lunch yet. It's been manic up in Sales and Marketing and I'm starving. Where are we going?'

'Ruth and I are going to The Bonnie Dundee.' Jared was too nice – and weak – to tell Erin that she wasn't invited but he hoped that by reiterating that it was his and Ruth's plan, she may have got the picture.

'The Bonnie Dundee?' Erin pulled a face. 'It's a dive but better than nothing, I suppose. At least they serve alcohol.'

Erin hadn't got the picture and by the way she tugged Jared along the corridor by his arm, it seemed she had taken over the whole lunch date.

EIGHTEEN

Ruth

Why did I ever think the Grapefruit Diet was a good idea? The Cabbage Soup Diet had been one of the most mortifying experiences of my life – yes, even more mortifying than the time Zack and two of his friends swiped my PE top from my bag and all squeezed into it before parading around the school grounds – but at least I could *eat* the bloody soup. I'd been hacking away at my grapefruit for ten minutes without success. Granted, I'd grabbed a butter knife in my haste to run away from Jared, but this was ridiculous. I threw the knife down onto my desk as the phone rang and snatched up the receiver. My face was aflame as soon as I heard Jared speak on the other end, the Green Fog Incident instantly flashing before me. He asked me to meet him for lunch and my immediate reaction was a big fat *no*. I couldn't bear to be in the same room as Jared, never mind sit with him to eat. Oh, God, it was so embarrassing. Not only had I farted so much that I'd filled the room with a retch-inducing stench, I'd lied about it and blamed it on Kelvin, only to be caught out. I'd never be able to look Jared in the eye again.

But then I looked at the grapefruit, stabbed and grazed, and I knew that even if I did manage to penetrate the skin, it wouldn't be worth it. I'd be left hungry and the bitterness would cause a twitch in my eye for at least quarter of an hour afterwards. The idea of going out to lunch, even to the humble Bonnie Dundee, was tempting despite my shame. I found myself agreeing to meet Jared in reception, already wincing at the discomfort I would feel throughout the lunch break. Hanging up the phone, I grabbed my handbag and flew along the corridor, catapulting myself into the ladies' to touch up my make-up. Jared wouldn't fancy me, especially after the Green Fog Incident, but there was no harm in looking my best. A quick smear of lipstick and a fresh coat of mascara and I was as ready to face Jared as I was ever going to be. I tried to hold my head up high as I slowed my pace and headed down to reception, but it was difficult with the fog still lingering in my mind.

'Where are you off to?' Quinn asked when she saw my coat slung over my arm.

'Out to lunch. I'm meeting...' My words clogged in my mouth as Jared came into view, arm in arm with Erin. She was giggling, her eyes shining as she gazed up at Jared, her body leaning into his as they walked with their arms linked together. With my heart sinking to my knees, I realised what a gorgeous couple they made – Jared tall and lean with shorn blond hair and Erin petite with dark, heavy hair. Opposites, but utterly perfect together.

'Hi, Ruth. Are you ready?'

Part of me had been hoping that Erin was simply walking with Jared while on her way to somewhere else in the building, but it seemed we were off out to lunch as a threesome. I wondered how the arrangement had come about; had Jared asked me or Erin first? Was I gate-crashing a date?

'I'm not really that hungry, actually. I think I'll leave you to it.' I backed away, but Erin loosened her grip on Jared to grab me by the arm.

'Don't be silly. Come for a drink if nothing else.' She looked at Jared, who nodded in agreement. 'I hope you don't mind me tagging along. I ran into Jared and he invited me along too.'

It wasn't that I minded Erin coming as such. She was my best friend, I adored the girl. But with Erin there, I'd become invisible and – Oh God – become a gooseberry. It wouldn't be Erin tagging along to lunch, it'd be *me*.

'Come on, before they unplug the microwave for the day.' Erin tightened her grip and I found myself being pulled out of the building. With Erin in the middle, the three of us walked across to the pub, Erin chatting away as we went.

'So do you have a girlfriend then, Jared?'

'No.'

Erin's smile seeped up into her cheeks. Correct answer. Not that having a girlfriend would have stopped her homing in. 'A wife? Any kids?'

Jared laughed. 'I thought we were having lunch, not an interrogation.'

'I'm just getting to know you. You can ask me questions too. Go on. Ask me anything.'

'What are you having to drink?' We'd reached the pub and Jared broke away from our trio to open the door.

The pub was deserted, with just the landlord propped up against the bar watching daytime TV on the tiny, dusty television in the corner of the room. He stood up straight as we walked in, his bushy eyebrows jumping up to his hairline. I don't think many customers frequented The Bonnie Dundee in the afternoon. Perhaps they would have had a booming trade from H. Woods and the other units of the business park if they served decent food, but it wasn't to be.

Jared went to the bar while Erin and I chose a table. The least grubby was by the window and it also had the added bonus of being as far away from *Loose Women* on the telly as possible.

'He's gorgeous, isn't he?'

'Who? Timothy?' The landlord was greying and the wrong side of fifty, and he was no George Clooney who could pull off the look.

Erin gave me a nudge with her elbow. 'Don't be daft. I'm talking about Jared. Do you fancy him?'

Did I fancy Jared? I had eyes and a libido. Of course I fancied the man. 'No. He's not my type.'

'Good. Because I fancy the pants off him.' She rubbed her hands together, already gleeful and confident that she would bag him. I felt a little bit sick. It was so easy for Erin.

'Do you want me to leave the two of you alone?'

'Don't be silly.' Erin gave my hand a squeeze. 'The drinks are here now, anyway.'

Jared placed our drinks on the table and sat opposite us. 'The ploughman's is off the menu today. They haven't got any cheese. So I've ordered us the spaghetti bolognese.'

'Yum.' Erin rubbed her stomach before pulling a

face. 'This place is seriously depressing. We should go on a proper night out. How about this Friday?'

Jared bobbed his head up and down. 'Sounds good. I'm in. Ruth?'

I shook my head. 'I can't. I have plans.' It was Billy's birthday on Monday so Billy, Clare, Theo and I were going for a meal at Cosmo's to celebrate, and Friday was the only evening we could all get together.

'How about Saturday then?'

Erin shook her head this time. 'I can't. It has to be Friday, I'm afraid.' She placed a hand on Jared's arm, her raspberry-painted nails bright against the pub's dull interior. 'Don't worry, I'll take care of you. Let's swap numbers.'

With the Grapefruit Diet out, I needed to find another diet. Yet another search on the internet came up with the Israeli Army Diet and while it was restrictive, it did offer variety throughout the week. On days one and two I would eat just apples. Days three and four would then be cheese, followed by chicken for days five and six, and salad for days seven and eight, with black tea and coffee permitted throughout. I was sick of the sight of apples by lunchtime of day one, so I was more than happy to switch to cheese on Friday, just in time for Billy's birthday celebration. I'd bought a pale blue tunic dress with a deep pink rose design for the occasion, which I teamed with thick white tights and caramel suede tasselled boots.

'You look lovely,' Clare told me when she arrived. Billy was still getting ready upstairs, having left it until the last minute, so I led Clare into the sitting room.

'Thank you. You look gorgeous. I love your dress.' Clare had dressed up for the occasion, wearing an emerald, beaded halterneck dress that hugged her waist before flowing down her thighs and calves and grazing the floor.

'Thanks. It cost a fortune but it was worth it.' Clare didn't seem to mind that Billy had dressed in a pair of jeans (albeit his least scruffy pair) and a T-shirt. She gazed at him with utter adoration and I felt my stomach tighten momentarily, a feeling I was familiar with. It was the same feeling I'd had when Zack O'Connell flirted with the popular girls at school, laughing and joking, slinging his arm around their shoulders and ruffling their hair. I wanted to be like those girls, to have the attention of somebody like Zack. To be desired.

'Wow, look at you.' Billy paused to take in Clare before kissing her cheek while she beamed. The knot tightened in my stomach again and for the first time in a decade, I doubted that I could manage to eat a meal. But it was too late to back out now as Billy was leading us out of the house. I hung back a few paces with Theo while Billy and Clare walked ahead, hand in hand.

'Sickening, isn't it?' Theo nodded at their entwined hands and pulled a face.

'Don't you want that?' I did, very much so. I wanted somebody to gaze at me with adoration as I gazed back equally enthralled. I wanted to walk hand in hand, to have a companion and friend as well as a lover.

'I can't think of anything worse. Commitment is for losers.' Theo sounded exactly like Erin. 'Why would I want to stick with one bird when I can have them all?'

Theo didn't see the point of a loving relationship, of a partnership that went beyond sexual gratification and I didn't have the energy to try to explain. He wouldn't have listened and I would have felt that gut-tightening need again.

Ahead, Billy and Clare paused on the pavement and Billy stooped to kiss Clare, cupping her chin in such a tender way I couldn't bear to look. An image of Jared cupping Erin's chin in a similar manner popped into my head and my appetite was wiped out completely. They were going out on their date that evening and I knew exactly how that would end – the same way all of Erin's dates ended. The only saving grace was Erin's inability to commit. She'd sleep with Jared and then toss him aside, which was a relief because I didn't think I could have stomached seeing them together, hand in hand, stares of adoration radiating between them. For once, Erin's sluttish tendencies were a godsend.

Unless... My mind went into overdrive, throwing up alternate outcomes. Erin might find a man to tame her one day, a man who would convince her of the benefits of settling down into a proper relationship and who better to do that than Jared? What if they got together? Dated on a regular basis, gave each other pet names, perhaps even moving in together one day? I'd have no choice but to watch their love blossom before me. Erin was my best friend and I would never let a man come between us, so I would have to endure her relationship with Jared on a sickening daily basis.

I kicked a large stone, not caring if I damaged my suede boots, sending it soaring along the pavement before it collided with a fence, pinging off the wood panel before falling to the ground. It wasn't fair. Why was it so easy for other people? For Billy and Clare and even Erin, who didn't even *want* a boyfriend?

'Cut it out you two.' We'd caught up with Billy and Clare, Theo nudging Billy with his elbow as we passed. Giggling, they broke apart and ambled after us, still hand in hand. We reached the restaurant where Cosmo greeted us with his usual enthusiasm, shaking hands with Theo, patting Billy on the back and pulling Clare and me into warm hugs. I thought back to the time I'd turned up on Stephen's doorstep, sleeping on the sofa until Cosmo moved out and I could claim his vacated bedroom, and I realised I was no better off now than I was back then. I was still fat and I still had no boyfriend.

Cosmo led us to our table and pulled out my chair. 'You look glum, *tesorino*.'

'Do I?' I tried to laugh it off but couldn't pull it off. I looked glum and I felt glum, which wasn't right. It was supposed to be a birthday celebration and I didn't want to spoil Billy's evening.

'Want to chat?'

I smiled, genuinely this time. 'Thanks, but I'm fine, really.'

'Are you sure?' Cosmo placed a hand on my shoulder and I had to fight the urge to burst into tears. I'd barely had the chance to get to know Cosmo when we'd lived together briefly, but he was a good friend of Stephen's and he'd taken on a brotherly role since Stephen decided to stay in New York permanently. Suddenly I wanted my brother to be there, to give me a hug and tell me everything would be okay.

'I'm sure,' I lied, picking up the menu to distract myself. I didn't need to see the list of delicious food as there was only one thing I could eat on my diet – the cheese platter. At that thought, my mood lifted and I made a determined effort not to let thoughts of Erin and Jared filter into the evening again.

I somehow managed to enjoy myself for the remainder of the evening, helped by the selection of delicious cheeses and a sneaky glass of champagne, which wasn't strictly in my diet plan but that only made it taste even more divine. My good humour, however, was short-lived, ending at the exact moment Erin called me the next morning to fill me in on her date. She skipped the beginning of the evening and, in true Erin style, went straight to the nitty gritty.

'I don't think I can walk properly after last night and I have a love bite. A love bite! The bastard. Do I look thirteen?' Erin had giggled while I shrivelled to nothing on the other end of the line. He'd slept with her. Jared had actually had sex with Erin, and while I knew I'd never stood a chance with him myself, the knowledge caused a sharp pain in my gut. I was alone in the house, as Theo was off gallivanting with some woman or other while Billy was visiting his father and wouldn't be back until late, so I spent the day in my pyjamas, curled up on the sofa watching repeats of *A Beginner's Guide To You*. It was while Meg was receiving a makeover from her best friend that I decided to stop moping about my crappy life. Meg was undergoing a makeover (which Tom went nuts for) as were my life and I. Men would look at me differently once I was thin – they'd look at me like they looked at Erin.

I awoke with renewed energy and determination the next morning, Meg's fabulous makeover still fresh in my mind. I was going to visit my parents, in the house I'd grown up in and which held the ghosts of my painful childhood, but even that wasn't enough to dampen my mood. Even still, I was grateful when Billy offered to come with me. I felt more secure travelling back to the town that contained every bad memory I possessed with Billy by my side, chatting to me the whole way to keep my mind off it all. I knew it was difficult for Billy too, with memories of his mum, particularly her death, still raw. I think it had been a relief when his dad had moved to Liverpool to make a fresh start with his new wife as it meant he no longer had to face his haunting memories on a regular basis. I gave Billy's hand a squeeze as we turned the corner onto Poplar Avenue, the houses familiar but strange with new windows, low brick walls bordering the gardens instead of unruly privets, some gardens now non-existent, as a driveway stood in their place. Billy's old house had changed most of all with pale grey rendering now covering the orange bricks, shuttered windows in place of the old, peeling frames and an immaculate lawn to the front instead of the overgrown jungle Billy's father had left behind. Billy looked up at the house, at the new shuttered bedroom window at the front, his mum and dad's old bedroom and the room in which she had passed away. I gave his hand another squeeze and he dropped his gaze, staring straight ahead as we moved towards Mum and Dad's.

From the front, our house hadn't changed much since I was a kid. The same patch of grass lay at the front, bordered by pansies and the wooden wishing well decoration standing in the middle. The old uneven path had been replaced with a patchwork of various-coloured brick but other than that, it was the same. Even the front door, solid wood with a stained glass window depicting yellow roses, hadn't changed. I lifted the brass knocker and rapped it three times. Mum answered, dressed in a knee-length black skirt with silver flowers stitched on the hem and a cream top with a pleated neck instead of her usual jeans and a jumper combo. Her hair was sleek and she smelled of expensive perfume as she pulled me into a hug.

'I thought you were bringing someone,' she hissed into my hair.

'I have.'

Mum raised her eyebrows at me and pursed her lips before she turned to Billy, beaming smile now in place. 'Ah, William. How nice to see you. Come in. I'll put the kettle on.'

I tried not to giggle as I stepped into the house. Poor Mum. I'd phoned before we left, letting her know there would be two of us for lunch and she'd obviously misunderstood and thought I was bringing a new boyfriend home.

'Alright, son.' Dad nodded at Billy as we stepped into the blazing hot sitting room, the gas fire on full as well as the central heating. 'I didn't know you were coming. Vee, why didn't you tell me our Billy was coming? I'd have got some beers in.'

'I didn't know myself.' Mum glared at me as she passed through to the kitchen.

'How's Brian?' Dad asked as Billy and I plonked ourselves on the sofa.

'He's alright. I went to see him yesterday.'

'That's good. I haven't seen your dad since...' Dad sucked in his breath, trying to recall. 'Ooh, must be a good eighteen months. Do you want to come out the back and see what I've done to the place?' Dad heaved himself out of his armchair and Billy followed out of politeness. I'd already seen the monstrous back garden, which Dad had transformed into a mini-golf course. Mum hated it, complaining that she nearly broke her ankle tripping over obstacles every time she pegged the washing out.

'And,' she'd told me tearfully during my last visit. 'He's even thinking of inviting the local youths to play. Says it'll give them something better to do than smash up telephone boxes and hang out on the streets, intimidating folk. So they're going to intimidate me and smash up my garden instead.'

Luckily he'd been talked out of inviting the local yobs over, but the mini-golf course remained.

'Have you heard his latest scheme?' Mum asked later as we sat down to eat. I was up to the chicken part of the Israeli Army Diet so Mum had cooked me a small chicken for lunch. 'He wants to transform the loft room into a cinema. A bloody cinema! It isn't enough that he converted it into a fourth bedroom. Now he wants to butcher it all over again. Where will the grandkids sleep when they visit?'

Dad gave a tut. 'We've already got two spare bedrooms for when they come to stay and the cinema will provide enjoyment all year round.'

'For who? I don't have time to be sitting down watching films.' She jabbed a carrot-laden fork in Dad's direction. 'And don't even *think* of opening it up to the public, Louie.' Having underlined the point, Mum turned to me, pursing her lips at my plate. 'Are you sure you won't have some vegetables? Vegetables are good for you. Or even a bit of gravy?'

If only. It had soon become apparent that chicken on its own was in no way appetising. I'd rather have been back on the apples. They didn't fill me up, but at least they weren't dry. Still, I thought as I forced a chunk into my mouth and chewed and chewed, I was one step closer to my makeover.

NINETEEN

Billy

It had to be Billy's best birthday to date. Not only had he been woken by a frisky Clare, she had brought him breakfast in bed: bacon, eggs, beans and a tower of toast, along with a cup of strong coffee. Clare was perfect in every single way and Billy felt like a very lucky boy indeed.

'It's a good job you gave me my breakfast in bed.'

'Why's that?' Clare slipped beneath the covers again, despite being fully dressed, wrapping her arms around Billy's waist and nestling herself against his body.

'I couldn't eat this downstairs. It wouldn't be fair on Ruth.' Ruth was still on her stupid apples-cheese-chicken diet, so it wouldn't have been fair to rub her nose in the delicious cooked breakfast.

'No, I suppose not.' Clare pushed herself back into a sitting position and checked the time. She didn't have long to celebrate Billy's birthday as she was going away for a couple of days for a work conference and needed to set off for the station in half an hour.

'Shall we go and have a quick shower together?'

'But you're already dressed.'

Clare gave a shrug of her shoulders, already unbuttoning her blouse. 'So I'll get undressed again. It's easy. See?' She slipped the blouse off her shoulders and let it slide onto the floor. Billy shoved one last corner of toast into his mouth, licked the melting butter from his fingers before taking a swig of coffee and racing into the bathroom. Clare really was the best girlfriend in the world.

Clare's hair was damp as she dressed again but she didn't have time to do anything other than gather it into a ponytail as Billy tore into the wrapping paper of his present. She had to leave for the station in two minutes at a push.

'Oh wow, thanks.' Billy grinned as he pulled the wii game out of the paper along with a pair of Zelda socks. 'I'm already dressed so I'll save these for tomorrow if that's okay.'

'Of course.' Clare stooped to kiss Billy before checking her watch. 'I really have to go. Have a great birthday.'

'Thanks. You're the best, do you know that?'

'I do try to be.' Clare kissed Billy one last time before she flew from the bedroom, grabbing her coat and handbag from the bottom of the stairs. She paused only long enough to blow Billy a kiss as he stood at the top of the stairs. He waved as she threw herself out of the door before he wandered down the stairs himself at a more leisurely pace. He found Ruth in the kitchen, chicken leg in hand, and she pulled him into a slightly greasy hug.

'Happy birthday, old man. How does it feel to be a pensioner?'

He'd had sex twice that morning so pretty good so far. 'You're only a couple of years behind me, don't forget.'

'Yeah, yeah.' Ruth stuck her tongue out at Billy. 'Carry on like that and you won't get your pressie.' She left the kitchen, chicken leg still in hand, and returned a moment later with a card and gift bag. Inside was a pair of Fozzy Bear boxers.

'I love them. Thanks, Ruth.' Billy gave her a quick peck on the cheek before rushing upstairs to change into them. When he returned to the kitchen, Ruth put on an act of disappointment at the sight of his trousers.

'I thought you were going to model the boxers for me.'

'It's my birthday, not yours. I get the treats today.' Billy winked at Ruth while she pretended to gag.

Billy had a fantastic birthday, buying a stack of cupcakes on the way to work, which he was sure bumped up his birthday collection by a quid or two. People who he had never even spoken to before stopped by his desk to wish him a happy birthday and grab a cupcake. He went for a quick drink with his team after work and when he returned home he spent the evening in front of the telly with Theo, Ruth, a fridge full of beer and a takeaway. Ruth even relaxed her diet for the occasion and ordered a chicken curry.

To: billy.worth
From: s.lynch
Subject: Happy Birthday!

Happy Birthday mate! Sorry I'm not there to celebrate with you but have a

drink for me! I posted you a card last
week – I hope it's arrived. Riley
wrote it out in case you were
wondering about the handwriting.

To: s.lynch
From: billy.worth
Subject: Re: Happy Birthday!

I did get the card – thanks mate. I
wondered why the handwriting was much
more legible than usual (ha ha).

To: billy.worth
From: sunshine_clare
Subject: Hi

Hi babe. God, this conference is so
boring and I'm stuck sharing a room
with Val. I've told you about Val,
haven't I? Her heart is in the right
place but she *does not* shut up. I
swear she doesn't even pause for
breath! I'm sick of hearing about her
nieces and nephews (she has twelve and
she's told me the life story for each)
and I could go on Mastermind with the
specialist subject of Val's Husband.

Anyway, I hope you had a nice
birthday. Miss you loads.

Love, Clare xxx

To: sunshine_clare
From: billy.worth
Subject: Re: Hi

Birthday was good. Miss you too. Can't you go to bed early? That way you won't have to listen to her any more!

Billy

To: billy.worth
From: sunshine_clare
Subject: Re: Re: Hi

Morning babe!

Sleeping was even worse! Val doesn't talk in her sleep, but she snores like a bear with a blocked nose. I swear she took all the tiles off the roof!

Oh well, only one more night and then I can come home. Can't wait to see you!

Lots of Love, Clare xxx

TWENTY

Ruth

I'd been dieting for two months and had ended up coming full circle, back to eating salad again. Except this time I didn't have the luxury of snacking on apples and carrot sticks. I was permitted to eat only salad for the next two days, which I somehow endured. Kicking off my slippers, I stepped onto the bathroom scales and watched the display, an eager smile waiting to jump out should the numbers be good.

They weren't.

After eight days on the Israeli Army Diet I'd lost a lousy pound. After eight days of stomach cramps, hysteria-inducing cravings and sheer boredom, I'd lost one sodding pound. Disappointment made my chest tight and, with frustration joining the party, I found it difficult to breathe. The backs of my eyes started to sting, but I blinked away the tears. I would not cry. I would not.

'Hurry up in there. I need a dump.' Theo's banging on the door brought me out of my self-pitying slump and I shoved my feet into my slippers.

'Alright, alright. Give me a minute. I just need to wash my face.'

I emerged from the bathroom feeling much more composed and headed into my bedroom to dress for work. I needed cheering up so I chose my red belted dress with giant white spots that reminded me of ladybirds and summer. It did the trick and I was much lighter on my feet as I left the house. I paused, as I did most days, in front of the boutique on my way to work and was relieved to see it was still there. The Dress beamed at me, encouraging me to keep going. I had lost a grand total of five pounds over the course of two months, which meant I'd only have lost a stone by the reunion if I continued on the same path. Losing a stone would be amazing, but it wasn't enough to wow my old classmates *and* it wasn't enough to fit into The Dress. I needed to up my game and fast. With renewed determination, I picked up my pace and powered my way to work, my hair slicked to the back of my neck with the effort by the time I pushed my way into H. Woods' reception. I attempted to have a chat with Quinn, but the puffs and wheezes that emerged from my mouth couldn't be translated and so I gave up and dragged myself up the stairs where I collapsed at my desk to recover. I was still panting by the time Kelvin thumped his way into the office.

'Coffee. Now.'

With what was amazing effort, I jumped to my feet and saluted. 'Yes, sir!'

'I could do without the sarcasm, thank you very

much. Just the coffee will do.' Kelvin strode towards his office and kicked open the door. 'And if that bitch phones tell her I'm not here.' Uh-oh. Sounded like a domestic. I rubbed my hands together, planning to pass the gossip on to Erin at the first opportunity.

The kitchen was occupied when I arrived, and I paused in the doorway when I saw that it was Jared inside. I hadn't spoken to Jared since his date with Erin. He'd been up to the office a few times to see Kelvin but I'd always pretended to be too busy to chat. I knew it wasn't Jared's fault that he was gorgeous and I wasn't but I couldn't help backing away from him. My crush was ridiculous, I know, but I couldn't help it and the thought of him with Erin was too much.

Jared hadn't noticed me hovering by the door and I considered shooting away until he'd finished but then I remembered his lovely, tight arse and lean body (but particularly the lovely arse) and The Dress came to mind. We could never be friends with my boulder of a crush blocking the way but there was no harm in asking for a bit of advice from a work colleague.

'Hi, Jared. You're pretty fit, aren't you?' I decided to get straight to the point before I chickened out.

Jared turned to face me, a smile on his face. Oh Lord, why did he have to be so gorgeous? It really wasn't fair. 'Are you flirting with me?'

I laughed as I strode into the kitchen, flicking my hair over my shoulder in a manner that I hoped portrayed confidence. 'God, no. You should be so lucky!' I laughed again as I shook my head. 'No, I'm afraid I don't like you that way, especially since you've already slept with my best friend.' As though I could afford to be that fussy!

'Are you talking about Erin?' Jared narrowed his eyes and even though there was only a hint of vivid blue through the slits, they were still breathtaking. 'Did she tell you that?'

She had. I remembered too clearly the phone call in which she had told me she could barely walk, and how could I forget the love bite? But the look on Jared's face told me I shouldn't admit that.

'No, of course she didn't. I just assumed that the two of you went out and...'

'And I jumped into bed with her?' His eyes narrowed further, his lips a thin, mean line. I stepped back, sorry that I had offended him. 'I don't jump into bed with women.' His face softened suddenly and he winked at me. 'I'm not that sort of boy.' Grabbing his cup of coffee, he marched out of the room, leaving behind a strange air. I stood for a moment, trying to figure out what had happened and how I had angered him over a simple assumption. Giving a shrug of my shoulders, I made Kelvin's coffee, filled a plate with chocolate digestives and returned to my office. The phone was ringing so I dumped the coffee and biscuits on my desk to answer it.

'Is my dumpy bastard of a husband there?'

It was Susan Shuttleworth and, from her tone and language, I didn't dare wind her up that day. 'I'm afraid he isn't, Susan. He had to go out for a meeting with Barnsley and Grotton. Can I pass on a message?'

'Yes. You can tell the podgy prick that I'll have the divorce papers ready by the end of the week.'

I squealed with delight at the unexpected nugget of gossip, but luckily Susan had already slammed down the phone and didn't hear. Picking up the coffee and biscuits, I skipped into Kelvin's office and placed them carefully on his desk.

'Susan just phoned.' I kept my tone light, as though it

was nothing important.

'Oh, right. I hope you told her where to go.' Kelvin snatched a chocolate digestive, sinking his teeth into it and sending crumbs cascading down his tie.

'She asked me to pass on a message.' The corners of my mouth itched, dying to spread their wings and display my delight across my face.

'Come on then, spit it out.' To demonstrate, Kelvin showered me with damp biscuit crumbs.

'She said she'll have the divorce papers ready by the end of the week.'

I took a couple of steps back, expecting fireworks to fly, but Kelvin dropped his half-eaten biscuit onto the paperwork on his desk and threw back his head, his round stomach and jowls wobbling as he roared with laughter.

'Divorce? Is that what she said?' Kelvin removed his glasses and wiped tears of mirth from his eyes. 'I should be so bloody lucky.'

I left Kelvin tittering to himself, easing the door closed behind me before I rang Erin. 'I have gossip.'

'Work or home?'

'Work.'

Erin gave a gasp. 'Sounds like skive o'clock to me. Meet me on the bench. You bring the coffee, I'll bring the chocolate.'

I was supposed to be dieting but I hadn't worked out a new plan yet and this was a special occasion, so I tore into the Snickers and took two huge bites while Erin waited patiently. I took my time, dislodging a nut from my back tooth with my tongue as Erin's patience wore thin. Her foot tapped and she arched her thin eyebrows at me as I took a gulp of coffee.

'Kelvin and Susan are getting divorced.'

Erin's eyebrows drooped and she leant in towards me, looking more concerned than delighted. 'Are you sure?'

'I heard it from the donkey's mouth. Susan told me herself. She says the divorce papers will be ready by the end of the week.'

'And she wasn't kidding?'

I gave a tut. 'When has Susan Shuttleworth ever cracked a joke?'

Erin nodded and gave a sigh as I finished off my Snickers. 'It's a shame, really, if you think about it.'

'Is it?' They were both vile people, and Kelvin was knocking off Angelina and probably any old slapper he could get his paws on. It was hardly a marriage to aspire to.

'Well, you know me. I'm never getting married, but if I did, it may as well be for life. What's the point otherwise?'

'That's way too deep for this time in the morning.' Draining my coffee, I rose from the bench, about to return to the office. Spreading gossip wasn't nearly as much fun when it turned serious. Remembering my conversation with Jared, I sat back down, pulling Erin with me. 'Did you sleep with Jared?'

'Why? Are you interested in him after all?' Erin grinned at me while I sent a silent plea to my cheeks to behave.

'No. I told you I wasn't.'

'Good. Because he's gay.'

It took a moment for Erin's words to sink in. 'But you said you'd slept with him.'

'Did I? When?'

'When the two of you had that night out.' She'd clearly said they'd had sex and quite rampant too by the sound of the aftereffects.

'I had sex that night, yes. But not with Jared. I obviously gave it a go – who wouldn't? – but it turns out he's not into girls.'

Jared's words in the kitchen floated back into my mind. *I don't jump into bed with women* and *I'm not that sort of boy.* No, clearly he wasn't. He was the kind of boy who jumped into bed with other boys.

'He's gay.' Strangely, the revelation was a relief rather than a disappointment. I never stood a chance with Jared, gay or straight, but at least now my crush wouldn't get in the way of our friendship. Jealousy would no longer blacken my mood – and think of the shopping trips!

'Yes but he isn't a feather-boa-wearing, shout-it-from-the-rooftops gay, so keep it quiet. I'm not even sure if he's out or not.'

I mimed zipping my lips closed. 'I won't say a word.'

My new-found knowledge gave me the confidence to ring Jared as soon as I was back in my office to invite him out for a drink after work. We met down in reception and walked across to The Bonnie Dundee, which was as empty as ever. We sat by the window and I decided to get straight to the point.

'I'm trying to lose weight.' Jared looked taken aback by my sudden admission but I kept going, explaining about the reunion and the bullying I'd suffered while at school. For some reason, I kept Zack to myself, not wanting to admit I was doing this for a man. I no longer felt embarrassed about pointing out my figure with neon fat signs to Jared, as there was no possibility of him finding me attractive whether I was fat or thin.

'I was bullied at school too.'

I choked on my diet coke, snorting bubbles out of my nose. Jared wasn't the kind of person I expected to be a victim of bullying. He was gorgeous and in fantastic shape. Had he been really ugly as a child? But then I remembered his sexual orientation. Kids could be cruel little shits and would use any slight 'difference' to pick out a kid to torment.

'I was into ballet. It's all I wanted to do when I grew up. I was pretty good too, but I broke my ankle when I was seventeen. It was a bad break and it weakened my ankle and destroyed my career.'

I found myself reaching across to give Jared's hand a squeeze. 'I'm so sorry. That must have been hard to deal with.'

'It was. The worse thing was, I almost gave up myself, a few years before. The bullying got so bad that I was going to give up dancing. I was battered on an almost daily basis, always outside of school and with a crowd watching and laughing. I just wanted it to stop. I loved ballet, loved how it made me feel when I performed and I'd worked so hard since I was little, but I couldn't take it any more. It was the humiliation more than the actual punches and kicks.'

'What made you decide to keep going?'

Jared smiled, his whole face lighting up despite his story. 'I couldn't do it. I couldn't give up something I loved so much. I wanted to dance more than anything and so that's what I did.'

I stared at Jared with renewed awe, more out of admiration of his strength and commitment than his beauty this time. I wished I was as strong as Jared, that I could be who I was no matter what other people thought of me. I also wished that Jared wasn't gay because right at that moment, more so now that I knew him a little better, I wanted to throw my arms around Jared and kiss him.

TWENTY-ONE

Jared

Jared had been a member of the Roxy Fitness Centre since he'd started working at H. Woods. The multi-storey gym was located at the entrance of the business park, meaning Jared could fit a workout in before or after work without going out of his way. Despite the ankle injury destroying his dancing career, Jared had kept up his fitness regime ever since. It had been strange discussing his old aspirations with Ruth as he never really dwelled on them anymore. He'd had tougher heartache to deal with in recent years so his love of dance had been put to the back of his mind, along with the taunts he'd endured throughout his childhood. The other kids didn't understand his passion and had assumed he was gay and they'd tried to take away their disgust by beating him repeatedly. They'd perceived Jared as being weak, but he was far from it. His love of dance was so strong that he wouldn't let them win, although in his most bitter moments after his injury he'd thought he may as well have given up back then and saved himself the bruises.

Jared had felt a connection as he'd sat chatting to Ruth in the pub, which was strange as he'd started off the morning full of anger towards her after she'd suggested he slept around. He hadn't slept with anyone since Frances – how could he when he still loved her and would do anything to get her back? But they'd shared something that evening and Jared felt a bond forming. He understood Ruth's pain and she understood his and so when she had asked for his help, he'd been happy to assist.

'I'd been praying it wouldn't come to this.' Ruth's usual cheerful demeanour had vanished, replaced by slumped shoulders, a glum expression and shuffled steps as they headed towards the entrance of the gym. A few days had passed since Jared suggested she join but Ruth had yet to come round to the idea.

'You'll be fine. You might even enjoy it.'

Ruth pulled a face as Jared opened the door and allowed herself to shuffle into the reception area. A blonde woman with a swishy ponytail and gleaming white teeth greeted them.

'Hi. I'm here to...' Ruth swallowed hard. She couldn't even bring herself to say the words out loud.

'She'd like to join the gym.' Jared stepped forward to help, fearing Ruth would bolt from the building if it were left to her.

'Fantastic! If you could fill out this form, making sure you enter your bank details carefully, I'll see if we have a trainer available to show you around and give you a fitness assessment.'

Ruth's face had drained of colour as soon as the

fitness assessment was mentioned and she was barely able to breathe, let alone speak, so Jared thanked the receptionist and grabbed the clipboard and pen before guiding Ruth to the set of chairs beneath the noticeboard. She filled the form in with shaking hands before the receptionist took her photo and handed her a membership card.

'If you'd like to follow Courtney, he'll explain how everything works.'

Courtney was sickeningly gorgeous; tall and broad with smooth brown skin and a wide, dazzling smile but while he was muscly, he wasn't overly Hulk-like. Jared noticed Ruth's enthusiasm leap up a notch as the trainer shook her hand and introduced himself. She could barely spit out her name as she gawped up at the man and Jared felt himself turning away, unable to witness the adoration on her face.

'How about a tour of the place?' Ruth nodded, mouth agape, at Courtney's suggestion and duly followed him around the premises. Jared had seen it all before, of course, but it was new to Ruth and her enthusiasm waned with every room they entered. She turned a deeper shade of green with every piece of equipment she spotted and looked terrified by the time they made it back down to the ground floor.

'Are you okay?' Jared gave her hand a squeeze as she nodded, her wide eyes telling a different story. 'You'll be alright. I'll be with you.'

'Shall we pop in here for your fitness assessment? It shouldn't take too long.' Courtney opened one of the doors close to the reception desk, holding it open while Ruth plodded inside as though she were being led to her execution.

'Is your boyfriend coming in with us or would you

rather he waited out here?'

Ruth snorted, the noise jabbing Jared in the gut. 'He's not my boyfriend.' She giggled at Jared while he tried hard not to appear wounded. Was it so ridiculous that she would be attracted to him? She hesitated a moment, trying to weigh up the pros and cons of having Jared witness the humiliation of her fitness assessment. 'Would you mind waiting out here?'

'No. Of course not.' Jared took a step back and the door was closed behind them. He wandered to the chairs in reception, sitting down and returning the receptionist's smile. She wiggled her fingers in a wave and gave a giggle before she busied herself with work. Jared swivelled in his seat and read the notices above him two or three times and then Ruth and Courtney emerged from the room.

'So we'll repeat the assessment in six weeks to see how you're getting on. I'll take you through to the women's gym and go through some warm ups and show you how to use the equipment.'

Jared had risen from his seat as the door opened but he sat back down again at Courtney's words. 'I'll meet you back out here then,' he told Ruth and she gave a wobbly smile in reply.

'We'll be about an hour or so,' Courtney told him, so Jared decided to head to the weights room in the meantime. He'd sometimes pop into one of the equipment rooms to have a run on the treadmill, but the weights room was where he spent most of his time while at the gym. He'd barely begun his workout before he was back in reception and found Ruth waiting for him, her pink sports bag by her feet as she sat on one of the chairs.

'How was it?' he asked as they made their way out

of the building.

Ruth gave a shrug. 'It was okay, I guess. Not as bad as I thought it was going to be. And how hot is Courtney?'

Jared felt his lips twitching but he stopped them before they pulled up into a sneer. 'I can't say he's my type. Do you want a lift home?'

'Thanks. That'd be great.'

They wandered across to H. Woods' car park and climbed into Jared's car, Ruth chatting about the fitness assessment and the scary looking equipment, mentioning Courtney's calves on more than one occasion. Jared felt that jab in the gut again. He prided himself on his calves. She continued to chatter for the duration of the drive, only stopping as Jared pulled up outside her house.

'So we're going for our first session at the gym tomorrow then?'

Ruth nodded, the colour draining from her face. 'I suppose so, yes.'

'What do you fancy doing first?'

Ruth unbuckled her seatbelt and grabbed her sports bag. 'The sauna?'

'I was thinking more along the lines of a workout.'

'I think I'll stick with the safety of the women's gym. I don't want any menfolk catching a glimpse of my tree-trunk thighs.'

'Don't be daft.'

'I'm not being daft. I'm being realistic.' She opened the door and swung her legs round to step onto the pavement. 'Thanks for the lift. I'll see you in reception at five tomorrow.'

Jared waved as Ruth backed away from the car, waiting until she was inside her house before he let his face fall. He couldn't help feeling disappointed. He'd been looking forward to spending time with Ruth without work or Erin as distractions, but it didn't look like that was going to happen with Ruth holed up in the women-only gym.

His sister lived quite close to Ruth, so Jared decided to pop by on a whim, not feeling up to spending the evening alone with his memories. Being in Ruth's company left him confused. He liked her more than he'd liked any woman since Frances and he enjoyed spending time with her. She was fun and laid back, and when he was with her Jared felt the old spark of happiness beginning to ignite. Although his feelings for Ruth were nothing compared to his feelings for Frances, he couldn't deny that he'd been jealous as she'd rattled on about Courtney and his manly calves. *He* had manly calves! He'd been a dancer for years and he'd kept his body in top condition ever since, but it seemed Ruth wasn't attracted to him in the slightest. It shouldn't have bothered him. He wasn't supposed to be interested in other women. But it did. It bothered him quite a bit, which only made him feel bad about Frances. She was the love of his life and even though he knew she would never come back to him, he felt disloyal.

Ally and Gavin lived in a little flat above a hairdressers on the main road. He rang the bell and was buzzed up by his brother-in-law.

'Ally's not in. She's over at Freya's. Man trouble or something.'

'Again?' Jared followed Gavin through to the tiny sitting room and flopped onto the old leather sofa.

'She's broken up with the latest. Mick? Josh?' Gavin

gave a shrug. 'I can't keep up. Beer or coffee?'

'Coffee, please.' In the mood he was in, Jared knew one beer wouldn't be enough. It wouldn't be enough until he was passed out, all thoughts of Frances banished through his drunkenness.

'So what's up?' Gavin placed the coffees on the little side table squeezed under the window and joined Jared on the sofa.

'Nothing. Why?'

'I've known you long enough to know when there's something bothering you.'

He was right, of course. Jared and Gavin had always got along well, more like proper brothers really. When he and Frances had become engaged, he'd asked Gavin to be his best man. Not that he'd needed Gavin's services in the end.

Jared threw back his head with a sigh, covering his eyes with his hands. 'It's that girl I was telling you about. Do you remember?'

Of course Gavin remembered. It warmed him to know there was a glimmer of light for Jared, that losing Frances hadn't destroyed his mate completely, and it had taken every ounce of restraint not to tell his wife. Ally worried about Jared – the whole family did – but he'd promised not to say a word, and he hadn't.

'I remember.'

Jared shook his head. 'I can't explain it, but there's something about her.'

'You fancy her.'

Jared laughed. If only it were that simple. 'She's beautiful, yes, but it's not just that.'

Could it be that Jared was developing feelings for this girl? Gavin tried to keep the grin off his face. 'You like her.'

'A lot. She's great.' Jared didn't realise it, but his face began to glow and flashes of the old Jared appeared. 'But I don't think she likes me. Not like that.' The glow dimmed. 'In fact, I know she doesn't. She told me so.'

'Oh.' What else could Gavin say?

'I think she wants to be friends though.'

'That's good then.'

Jared nodded. 'Yeah. I don't think I'm ready for more than that anyway.'

'Then be friends. Have fun, no pressure.'

Jared nodded. He could do that. He could be friends with Ruth without his messed-up head complicating things.

'Thanks, Gavin. I can't talk to the others. They'd go nuts if they got a sniff of me liking a woman, even as a friend.'

'I know, mate. And don't worry, I won't say a word.'

Jared left the flat an hour later feeling much lighter and his head clearer. Friends. He could handle that.

TWENTY-TWO

Ruth

I never thought I would find myself willingly inside a gym, but there I was, pink gym bag slung over my shoulder, a concrete block of dread in the pit of my stomach at the thought of the workout ahead. It wasn't getting any easier, even though I had been using the gym every day after work. I still dreaded five o'clock when I would have to switch off my computer and meet Jared in reception for my daily torture. I'd even begged Kelvin for extra work that evening – surely he had some urgent filing or photocopying that needed doing – but the lousy bastard had let me go home on time.

'I guess I'll meet you out here. Seven again?' Jared paused by the women's gym and I gave myself a stern talking to inside as I contemplated making a run for it – hey, at least running would be exercise.

'Yep, seven.' I nodded, trying to convince myself this was a good idea and that while seven o'clock seemed a long time away, it wasn't too bad. It'd take me a good while to change into my gym gear, and then I'd have to fanny about with my warm-up before I started my workout. Then, before I knew it, it would be time for a leisurely shower. I'd be lucky if my workout lasted half an hour.

I pushed my way through the door of the women's gym while Jared continued on towards the weights room. The women's gym had its own changing room so I didn't have to risk the humiliation of passing a hot male in the corridor in my shorts and T-shirt. After years of hiding myself away and trying to disguise my figure, I now usually dressed in bright colours and prints, doing my best to stand out in the crowd while sticking two fingers up to my figure. Just because I was fat didn't mean I should shy away from the world, but I felt the opposite at the gym. My shorts were black while my T-shirts were plain and mostly dark in colour. I wanted to blend into the background, away from the beautiful, fit women who belonged in the gym. This was their territory and I felt like I didn't belong there, though I needed it far more than they did. I didn't make conversation or even eye contact with any of the women at the gym apart from the perky receptionist, and I only allowed her a simple hello and goodbye as I passed through. In fact, the only person, other than Jared, who I'd had a conversation with while at the gym had been with Courtney.

Ah, Courtney. I gave a sigh as I sank onto the bench and slipped off my heels. Beautiful Courtney. It was almost worth the mortification of the fitness assessment to get a good ogle at the man. The assessment would be repeated after six weeks and, while I didn't relish the idea of stepping on the scales in front of another human being ever again, I couldn't wait to have Courtney's undivided attention. He really was lovely, both in body and mind, and if I couldn't lust after Jared anymore, I would have to focus my attention elsewhere.

I changed into a pair of ugly, black shorts and a sage green T-shirt and pulled my short curls back into something that resembled a ponytail before heading out into the gym to stretch as Courtney had demonstrated. Funny, *he* didn't look like a tit as he stretched and lunged.

I started off on the bike before moving on to the rowing machine and finished with a gentle stroll on the treadmill. I was beginning to think all the people who claimed to love exercise were great big fibbers. I was bored, utterly fed up of cycling and walking towards nothing and rowing away from the computer image of a crocodile. But I had a vast amount of weight to lose before the reunion so I had no choice but to keep at it.

After running through my cool-down exercises, I showered and changed, feeling more like myself in my navy wraparound dress with tiny brown and turquoise owl print and massive heels. Jared was waiting for me by the noticeboard and we wandered over to H. Woods' car park together.

'Do you fancy going for a drink?'

Jared usually gave me a lift home after the gym, but this was the first time he'd suggested we do anything afterwards.

'Yeah. Why not?' I could do with a drink after my dull workout and I enjoyed spending time with Jared, more so since my silly crush had been put aside.

The Bonnie Dundee was as dead as ever, with only one other patron, sitting at the bar and playing crib with the landlord. We carried our drinks to what was becoming 'our' table by the window.

'So how's it going at the gym?'

I took a sip of my diet coke – Jared was driving and I didn't want to get plastered on my own – and pulled a face. 'OK, I guess.'

'That doesn't sound very encouraging.'

'I don't feel very encouraged.' I gave a shrug of my shoulders, allowing a long sigh to whistle through my lips. 'It's just so boring, isn't it?'

'It doesn't have to be. Why don't you try something different? It's bound to get boring if you do the same thing over and over again. Why don't you try the weights room with me tomorrow? You can work on toning up while you lose the weight.'

Toning up did sound like a good idea and it couldn't be boring if Jared spent most of his time in there. He must love it, surrounded by all those sweaty men rippling with muscles.

Actually, maybe lifting weights wasn't such a bad idea.

'Ok. You're on.'

'Really?'

I nodded, picking up my glass to clink against Jared's. 'Really.'

We remained in the pub for a couple of drinks and discovered a dusty old juke box tucked away in a corner. We poured money into it, taking turns to choose songs. It seemed the music hadn't been updated since the glorious age of The Spice Girls, Boyzone and B*Witched, so I was in heaven. Unfortunately Jared didn't have the same taste in music as I did and I was both disappointed and surprised – I'd have thought he would have been a huge Spice Girls fan.

'You don't even like "Livin' La Vida Loca"?' Disgust fogged my voice and I selected it anyway.

Jared ran his finger down the list of tracks. 'How about "Don't Look Back In Anger"?' I gave a shrug and he selected it. 'Your turn. No way. Please tell me you're kidding.'

'I never kid about S Club 7, doll.'

We took our drinks back to our table by the window, Jared continuing to tease me about my taste in music while I maintained there was nothing at all wrong with a bit of cheese or eighties pop.

'Do you not even like early Madonna?'

Jared almost spat his drink over the grubby table. 'Not even a little bit.'

'Kylie then. When she was frizzy.' I took Jared's eye rolling as a no and felt offended on behalf of Ms Minogue. What kind of gay man dissed Kylie? She was like their queen.

We waited until our songs had finished before we headed back out to H. Woods' car park and Jared's car. We were still debating music when we pulled up outside my house.

'So you're definitely coming with me to the weights room tomorrow?'

'Yes. Definitely.' Anything had to be better than the computerised croc.

'Great. I'll see you tomorrow then.'

'See you tomorrow. Thanks for the lift.' I levered myself out of the car and gave a little wave before letting myself into the house. The smile I'd been wearing throughout the evening slipped as soon as I stepped into the sitting room and felt the frosty glower emitting from Clare. Billy looked annoyed, but not quite as pissed off as his girlfriend.

'Where have you been?'

Who was he, my dad? 'I've been to the gym. Why?'

'*A Beginner's Guide* was on tonight.'

Was that all? I thought I'd actually done something wrong. 'Didn't you record it?'

'Yes. You know I always record it.'

'What's the problem then?' I flopped down on the sofa and stretched my aching calves. If I didn't end up with gorgeous pins after all this exercise I was going to be miffed.

'That's what I said.' Clare raised her eyebrows at Billy before she rose to her feet. 'And now I'm going home. Goodbye, Ruth.'

'Bye,' I returned, but Clare had already vacated the room. Billy ran out into the hallway after her while I slipped off my shoes and propped my feet up on the coffee table, giving my toes a well-deserved wriggle.

'Thanks for that.' Billy returned to the sitting room and flopped onto the sofa beside me, folding his arms across his chest.

'What have I done?' I didn't understand. Billy knew I was desperate to lose weight and needed to go to the gym. So what if we watched *A Beginner's Guide* an hour later than the rest of the UK?

'Clare's going away for a hen weekend tomorrow. She wanted to go out to the pub tonight but I said we had to stay in because we always watch *A Beginner's Guide* together. Except you never turned up and now we've wasted our last night together.'

Jeez, talk about a couple of drama queens. Clare was going away for a hen weekend not a gap year. Besides, I wasn't psychic. How was I supposed to know?

'She'll calm down.' I picked up the remote from the arm of the sofa. 'So shall we watch *A Beginner's Guide* then?'

'You're doing *what*?' Erin paused, a Malteser hovering between the packet and her gaping mouth. The weather had made a sudden change, deciding to be kind and emitting warmth from the sky instead of the drizzle that had plagued us for the past couple of weeks, so Erin and I had decided to take a break from the office and were sitting on our bench in the furthest corner of the car park.

'Lifting weights.'

Erin crumpled at the middle, her curtain of black hair obliterating her face, but it couldn't mask the sound of laughter. I snatched the Malteser that was still between her fingers and popped it into my mouth. Well, if she wasn't going to eat it, I may as well. Even I could work off a Malteser.

'I thought that was what you said.' Erin straightened, wiping smudged mascara from beneath her eyes with her fingers.

'It's not that funny.' Miffed, I snatched another Malteser from the bag and shoved it into my gob. Erin turned to face me, her lips still twitching.

'Ruth, you struggle to lift a tin of beans with both hands.'

'I do not.' I did. 'And anyway, that's one of the reasons I'm doing it, to build up my strength.'

'And what's the other reason?'

'To tone up.' My own lips twitched into a grin as I nudged Erin with my elbow. 'And to ogle all the fit men. The weights room will be full of them.'

Erin gasped and all the mirth drained from her face, replaced by admiration. I thought she was going to give me a round of applause. 'That is a brilliant plan. I wish I could come with you.'

'Why don't you?' It would have been great having Erin there to compare notes with. Jared would be with me but he was pretty shy and closed off about men. He never spoke about them or eyed them up and I knew nothing about his past relationships. I knew Courtney wasn't his type, but that was the extent of my knowledge. Being shy – and possibly firmly in the closet – I didn't think Jared would make a great ogling partner.

'I can't tonight. I have plans.'

'Doing what? Can't you cancel?' I couldn't imagine anything Erin would prefer than a room full of sweaty, burly men, probably with their tops off.

'I have a date.' Erin flicked her hair over her shoulder, feigning nonchalance, but I knew my friend and instantly picked up on the brief but definite pink tinge to her cheeks. She was blushing. Erin didn't blush, ever.

'Who with? Someone I know, obviously.'

Erin shook her head, her eyes a little too wide to be telling the truth. 'No, it's nobody you know. I met him at my salsa class.'

'Liar.' I giggled as I popped the last Malteser into my mouth. 'Who is it? And don't forget I'm your very best friend. I can tell when you're telling porkies.'

Erin crumpled the empty Malteser bag and turned to drop it into the bin next to the bench. 'It's Stuart from Accounts. But don't say anything, will you? I don't want it being spread around.'

'Stuart from Accounts?' Wow, this was big news. Not only had Erin slept with him on more than one occasion, she was going on an actual date with him. Erin never dated once the deed had been done – she didn't see the point. Perhaps this was it, the one who could change Erin and show her how wonderful it was to fall in love. My little Erin was growing up.

'Ssh!' Erin's eyes darted around us, but we were far from civilisation in the outer depths of the car park. 'Please don't say anything to anyone.'

'I won't. I swear.' I made a little cross over my heart and mimed zipping my lips. 'So where's he taking you?'

Erin pulled a face. 'The theatre.'

'Stuart from Accounts is a fan of *the theatre*?'

Erin clamped a hand over my supposedly zipped up chops. 'Will you stop saying his name? What if someone hears you? Please don't say anything, not even to Stuart. I don't want him getting a big head, thinking I've been talking about him.'

I peeled Erin's hand away from my mouth. 'Sorry. I won't say another word. I promise.'

With Erin out on her date with you know who, the ogling was left to just Jared and me but, to be honest, it wasn't worth the effort. The men were undoubtedly fit and sculpted and I imagined doing some very naughty things with each and every one of them, but they were more interested in their own reflections than anything else. I wasn't expecting them to swoon when I rocked up in my baggy sweat pants (no shorts in front of the blokes), but they didn't even converse with one another or lift their eyes away from the mirrors. I was bored after five minutes but tried to keep going for Jared's sake. Finally he'd had enough and, after taking a couple of sneaky photos on my phone for Erin, we went to the changing rooms to shower and change.

'Well? What did you think?'

We'd met back in reception after our showers, clean and appropriately dressed. I thought about lying to Jared, but couldn't bring myself to do so, mostly because if I did, I would have to endure the whole experience again.

'I was bored senseless. Sorry.'

'Really?'

I nodded. 'I think I'll stick with my own gym from now on. There's some weightlifting-type equipment in there. Enough for me to be getting on with. I don't want to end up looking like Jodie Marsh.'

'Why don't we try one of the classes? It'll give your workouts a bit of variety and stop you getting bored and demotivated.'

I hadn't really thought about taking part in any of the classes. Although I was aware that there were many on offer, I didn't want to look like a pleb, so I'd dismissed the idea. But if Jared was willing to have a go with me, it didn't seem so bad.

'Alright then.' We wandered over to the noticeboard where a timetable displayed the various classes. The spinning class caught my eye straight away, conjuring up images of when I was young and carefree, twirling in the back garden with Stephen and Billy until we all fell over into a giggling heap on the grass. The class took place every Monday and I found myself looking forward to a gym session for the first time.

TWENTY-THREE

Billy

Billy and Clare had barely spoken since she'd stormed out of the house the previous night. They usually exchanged a gazillion texts and emails throughout the day, but apart from a terse 'good morning' in reply to Billy's text there had been silence. Billy didn't want Clare to go away for the weekend while still angry with him so he decided to take action. Instead of sending an apologetic email, he took an extended lunch break, planning to make up the time later, and headed to Clare's office.

'What are you doing here?' Clare's tone was harsh as Billy stood beside her desk but he could see her features were already beginning to soften. And he hadn't even produced the bouquet of flowers from behind his back yet.

'I thought I could take you to lunch. To make up for last night.'

'Oh. Maybe.' Clare gave a non-committed shrug but her face lit up as Billy swept the blooms from behind his back. 'Oh, Billy, they're gorgeous. Thank you. Let me put these in water and then we'll get going.' Clutching the flowers to her chest, Clare dipped her face into the bouquet and breathed in deeply, sighing at the scent. Billy made a mental note to email his thanks to Ruth as soon as he got back to the office. Her suggestion was working a treat.

'What time are you off tonight?' Billy and Clare were seated in a café close to her office, waiting for their food to arrive.

'Straight after work. I have my suitcase in the boot of my car and I'm picking a couple of the girls up on the way.'

Billy reached across the table and took Clare's warm hand in his. Everything about Clare was warm, so she must have been pretty annoyed to go off on one. 'I'm sorry about last night.'

'Me too. I may have overreacted.' Clare screwed up her nose and Billy couldn't help smiling. She looked so cute when she did that. 'I just wanted to spend a bit of time with you before I go away. I'll really miss you.'

'I'll miss you too.' Billy wasn't sure he'd actually have time to miss Clare – it was only a weekend apart, after all – but he knew it would make Clare feel better if he said it.

'Will you? Will you really?'

Billy gave her hand a squeeze. 'Of course I will.'

Clare flashed him a smile and he knew in that moment that he was safe.

Billy worked late that evening to make up for the time he'd spent with Clare at lunchtime and decided to treat himself to a pint on the way home. It felt weird to be sitting in the pub on his own as he was usually with Clare these days. Making the most of his short reprieve, he stayed at the pub for a little longer, feeling quite merry by the time his rumbling stomach sent him home. He was making his way along Oak Road and nearing his house when he spotted Ruth climbing out of a car, her pink gym bag slung over her shoulder. He admired her determination to lose weight, even though he thought she was doing it for all the wrong reasons. Why put herself through all these diets and exercise for some little prick she went to school with?

'Oi, Ruthie!' He staggered towards his friend and threw his arms around her, pressing his beer-tinged lips onto hers. Ruth giggled and ruffled his hair.

'Are you drunk?'

Billy gave a shrug. 'Maybe.'

She laughed, her signature boom filling the darkening street with happiness. 'You are. Come on, let's get you inside.' She turned to wave at the driver of the car before looping her arm through Billy's to keep him steady and leading him to their house.

Ruth helped Billy out of his jacket and deposited him on the sofa before she removed her own jacket and slipped off her shoes. She flung her gym gear into the wash before returning to the sitting room where she found Billy squinting at a stack of takeaway menus.

'I'm starving. What shall we have?'

Ruth shook her head. 'I'm not having a takeaway.' She was no longer on her strict diets but it seemed a shame to put all her hard work at the gym to waste. 'It'll take me ages to work it off.'

'Then don't.' Billy observed Ruth for a moment before emitting a short sigh. 'You don't need to lose weight. You're perfect the way you are. So pretty and lovely.'

'Jesus, Billy, how much have you had to drink?'

Billy jerked his body upright, sitting up straight on the sofa. 'Not that much. I'm not saying this because I'm pissed. It's true. Look at you.'

'You're pissed.'

Billy gave a lopsided shrug. 'Perhaps. But I'm also starving. Are you sure you don't want a takeaway?'

'Oh go on then.' Ruth snatched the sheaf of menus. 'As long as it's Chinese.'

Billy and Ruth didn't get the chance to hang out together very often any more as Ruth spent most evenings at the gym and Billy was usually with Clare, who Ruth didn't think liked her very much.

'It's just a vibe I get from her.'

Billy waved away her concern. 'She doesn't dislike you. She's a lovely girl. I don't think she has it in her to think badly of anyone.'

Ruth jabbed a mushroom and chewed it slowly, deep in thought. 'So is it love between you two then?'

Billy spluttered. 'Don't be daft. It's only been a couple of months.'

'More like three.'

'Whatever. It's too soon for love.'

Ruth fished a water chestnut out of her food and dumped it into an empty foil container with a shudder. 'Have you ever been in love?'

Billy shrugged his shoulders. 'Dunno. I thought I was in love with Louise but now I'm not so sure. I think I just thought that was how I was supposed to feel because we'd been together for eleven months. Did you love Gideon?'

'Honestly? No. I was only with him for so long because I was scared of being on my own.'

'And are you scared of being on your own now?'

Ruth thought about the question but shook her head in the end. 'I've been too busy plotting my spectacular entrance at the reunion and picturing Zack's jaw hitting the floor to even think about being single.'

'Did you love Zack? Proper love?'

Ruth wasn't so sure. She thought she'd been in love with him at the time and it had certainly felt like it, but she'd been little more than a kid who'd never been kissed. She'd had a massive crush on him for a couple of years and she'd built that up when Zack had feigned interest in her. 'I was young and naïve. I was probably just infatuated with him. A bit like you with Jess's knickers.'

Billy dumped his plate on the coffee table and turned to face Ruth, his face twisted in annoyance. 'I did not fondle her knickers. They fell off the radiator in the bathroom and I was simply picking them up when she barged into the room. If you think about it, it was damn rude of her not to knock first.'

'I believe you. The knickers fell off the radiator and that salt and pepper shredded duck simply fell into my mouth.' Ruth grinned at Billy but the smile soon vanished as Billy pounced, knowing exactly where to tickle her to have her squealing for mercy.

To: s.lynch
From: billy.worth
Subject: Ruth

Your sister is amazing. She is the greatest friend in the world. She beats you hands down.

To: billy.worth

From: s.lynch
Subject: Re: Ruth

Have you been drinking?

To: s.lynch
From: billy.worth
Subject: Re: Re: Ruth

A little bit. Head hurts now. Think I'm going to be sick.

TWENTY-FOUR

Ruth

My whole body felt as though it had been sledgehammered during the night. In the old days I would have woken up feeling sore and heavy after a fantastic night out on the sauce but these days the pain was down to the gym. At least when I had a hangover, I'd had a bloody good night beforehand.

Even my eyelids ached as I prised them open and squinted at the clock on my bedside table. At least it was Saturday so I'd had a decent lie in. My shoulder blades were on fire as I wrestled myself into a sitting position and my legs were dead weights as I lugged them out of bed, swinging them around and planting my aching feet on the soft rug. I should have got used to waking up like this by now, but I still felt like slumping back beneath the covers and shoving a pillow over my face and putting myself out of my misery. It took every single ounce of energy and a slideshow of images depicting Zack's shocked face to force me out of bed.

I hobbled my way into the bathroom, each tiny fairy step dulling the pain until I was feeling almost normal by the time I made it down to the kitchen. I made myself a slice of toast, using wholemeal bread and low fat spread. The toast was followed by a low fat yogurt and a slightly bruised apple to make up for the pig-out I'd had the night before. And because there was little food left in the house.

'We need to do a big shop,' I told Billy as he wandered into the kitchen to check the cupboards, shaking the near-empty cereal box. There was enough for one bowl, but there wasn't any milk left, so Billy ate his Coco Pops dry.

I showered and dressed after breakfast, my muscles no longer screaming out but simply murmuring their objection to my movements.

'Where are you off to?' Theo asked, having finally risen. He looked pretty fresh, considering his 4am return that morning, with only slightly bloodshot eyes giving any clue to the previous night's antics.

'Big shop.' I pulled a thin jacket on over my strawberry-print dress.

'Give me a minute and I'll come with you.'

I paused, one arm in the jacket, the other frozen half way in the sleeve. 'You're going to come shopping with us?' I caught Billy's eye and he was just as astounded as I was. Theo had never even bought a pint of milk since he'd moved in with us. He left his share of the shopping money on the kitchen table once a month and expected the shopping fairies to provide him with nourishment. There could only be one explanation.

'Who is she?' He had to have his eye on someone who worked there.

Theo placed a hand over his heart. 'She's an angel.' I shot my eyes up to the ceiling, having heard that little gem many times before. 'No, I mean it, she is. I saw her the other day when I popped in to stock up on beer. She's beautiful and sweet.'

'And totally unsuitable for you, obviously.'

Theo shook his head. 'No, I think this is it. I think I might be falling in love.'

'And I'm Scarlett Johansson's identical twin sister.'

Theo gave a shrug. 'Mock all you want. I'll marry Verity one day, you'll see.'

The Big Shop can be one of the most soul-destroying Saturday morning activities, with supermarkets filled with miserable, hungry people, snapping and grumbling and throwing things into their trollies. Fortunately, Billy and I didn't join in with those poor beasts. If you had to take part in the dreaded Big Shop, you may as well have a bit of fun with it.

'What the fuck are you doing?'

Theo backed away from the trolley park as I stepped up onto the bar running under the trolley, one leg slung over into the trolley while Billy used both hands to shove my fat arse.

'Give us a hand,' I panted, but Theo held his hands palm up, shaking his head. He glanced around the car park, ensuring he wasn't in view of anybody he knew. He wanted everybody to know he was Not Involved. 'That's it, Billy. Shove a bit harder.'

Theo had started to wander away, well and truly washing his hands of us, as I finally plopped over the edge and found myself fully inside the trolley.

'Ready?' Billy asked after I'd steadied myself onto my feet.

'Ready.' I held up my wrist so I could see my watch.

'On your marks, get set... Go!'

I'll never forget the startled look on Theo's face as the trolley whizzed past him, me stood in the middle of it, arms outstretched for balance while Billy pushed, his feet pummelling away at the ground. We made it into the store, dodging a little old lady and her basket and a kid eyeing up the loose grapes as we entered the fruit and veg aisle and had to swerve to avoid the security guard as he plodded towards us, his face as red as the beetroots to our left.

'Oi, pack that in now. Get out of the bloody trolley, you daft sod.'

It took almost as long for me to get out of the trolley as it had to get in. The security guard stood to one side, hands on hips, watching to make sure we didn't tear off again but he never offered any assistance, even when my foot got stuck.

'What the fuck was that?' Theo hissed, only able to join us once I was out of the trolley.

'Trolley surfing.' Billy turned to me. 'How did we do?'

I pulled a face. 'Pretty rubbish, actually. Fourteen seconds.'

Billy thumped the trolley's handle. 'Fourteen? You're pushing next time. You're better than me.'

Trolley surfing was my favourite part of the whole shopping experience. Our record was thirty-eight seconds before we were asked to use the trolley in an appropriate manner.

'Right.' Billy rubbed his hands together. 'Fruit salad juggling. What are we having today?' Billy strode off towards the fruit, selecting an apple and a banana.

'No, please not a grapefruit. Juggle a pineapple instead. I dare you.' I tried to stop Billy from picking up the fruit, but he ignored my pleas and grabbed one before tossing it into the air with the apple and banana. I dared Billy to juggle a pineapple every week but he had yet to take up the challenge.

'Ta-dah!' Billy caught the fruit before placing it into the trolley. Our rule was whatever was juggled went into the trolley, so, unfortunately, the grapefruit was coming home with us.

'Can you two act like normal human beings?' I suspected this would be Theo's first and final shopping trip with us. 'And can we go to the baby aisle now? It's a great place for picking up single mums.'

'What about Verity?' He'd been declaring undying love for the girl twenty minutes ago.

'I have to keep my options open. I haven't even got her number yet.'

'My heart is filling with joy at that sentiment. And no, we're not going picking up single mums. We're playing Cheese Bingo.'

Theo eagerly steered us towards Verity's checkout once we'd filled our trolley and I was surprised to see a wholesome looking girl with a short blonde ponytail and a sparkly pink clip. She was short and smiley with a dimple in her left cheek and not Theo's usual type at all. She didn't look like she carried a spare pair of knickers in her handbag. Nor did she seem the sort who didn't bother to wear knickers at all. Theo charmed the poor girl while Billy and I loaded the shopping onto the conveyor belt and packed it into bags.

'Well, what do you think?' We were walking home, weighed down with bags – even Theo, despite his protests.

'Sorry mate, but she's too sweet for you.' Billy shot Theo an apologetic look but I had to agree with him. Poor Verity would be heartbroken when Theo cast her aside. She wasn't hardened (or loose) like the others.

'Piss off. We'd be perfect for each other.'

'But for how long?'

Theo's mouth screwed up as he observed Billy, and I half expected him to dump his shopping bags on the pavement and punch him, but he simply turned away from us and increased his speed, striding home ahead of us. He'd cheered up by the time Billy and I had put the shopping away and suggested we spend the afternoon in the pub. He soon forgot about Verity and her phone number as he spotted the elusive Caitlin, the barmaid who had so far failed to fall for his charms.

'Shall we remind him he has a date with poor Verity on Friday night?'

I shook my head as Billy and I sat down with our drinks, watching Theo work his magic at the bar. 'It wouldn't stop him anyway.'

Billy and I left the pub after a couple of hours, leaving Romeo to work on Caitlin. Billy had an early start in the morning as it was his father's birthday and he was going to visit him. I had no plans so I offered to go with him. Billy had been ten when his mum died and Brian had done his best to take care of his son. It hadn't been easy as he'd had to work to provide for them, so Billy would spend a lot of time with us and became part of the family. Stephen and Billy had been best friends since a very young age and I couldn't recall a time when I hadn't known Billy. Brian had been on his own after Patricia's death until five years ago when he met Pearl. Brian had found it difficult to begin with and he struggled to move on, despite his growing feelings for Pearl. They were friends to begin with – the most Brian could offer at the time – but in the end even Brian couldn't hide his feelings. He and Pearl had married two years ago and moved to Liverpool, where Pearl had grown up, for a fresh start.

'You won't mention Clare, will you?' Billy and I had just stepped off the train at Lime Street, following the crowds towards the station's exit.

'Why not?'

Billy turned his gaze away from me. 'I haven't told them about her.'

'You haven't told them about Clare?' We stepped out of the station and my words were swept up by the noise of the traffic. We joined the queue for the taxis and I waited for Billy to elaborate. I couldn't understand why Billy wasn't shouting from the rooftops that he finally had a girlfriend – and one as beautiful as Clare. He still hadn't explained as we climbed into a cab.

'Why haven't you told them you've got a girlfriend?' My patience had worn thin so I was forced to repeat my question.

Billy shrugged his shoulders. 'You know what Pearl's like. She'll make a great big fuss and Dad will get his hopes up that I'm finally settling down. We've only been together a few months.'

'But they'd be happy for you.'

'Too happy and then what happens when we split up?'

'Who says you're going to split up?'

'Nobody.' Billy gave a sigh, steaming up the window next to him. 'But it's what happens, isn't it?'

'Not always. Not if you love each other.'

'I suppose.' A silence fell about the taxi until we pulled into Brian and Pearl's street. 'You won't say anything, will you? Not yet?'

I shook my head. 'Not if you don't want me to.'

'Thanks.'

Pearl was waiting for us on the doorstep and ushered us straight into the warmth of her home, taking our coats and generally making a fuss of us. 'Brian's just out in his greenhouse. I'll give him a shout and put the kettle on.'

I had vague memories of Patricia Worth – she was tall and slim with straight brown hair and a long fringe. She wore jeans and T-shirts and would offer us fruit juice and healthy snacks whenever we went round to play. Pearl was the complete opposite to Brian's first wife – short and plump with cropped greying hair and a liking for pencil skirts and pastel sweaters. She never allowed anyone to be without a cup of tea and a biscuit.

'He's just washing his hands. Won't be a minute.' Pearl bustled into the warm sitting room with a tea tray and a plate of Penguins. 'So, what's new with you two then?' Pearl sat in a roomy armchair as Brian stepped into the room, drying his hands on a tea towel. I wondered if Billy would use this opportunity to tell his dad about Clare.

'Nothing much,' Billy replied.

Pearl's shoulders sagged and she slumped against the cushions. 'No love in the air then?'

Billy reached for a Penguin and tore the wrapper while I held my breath. Now was the perfect time to tell them about his relationship. 'Afraid not. So, Dad. What are you growing this time?'

TWENTY-FIVE

Jared

The weekends were the worst time for Jared. While most people looked forward to the break, for Jared it meant he had more time to sit around and think of Frances, remembering the good times they'd had. And there *were* good times, many of them. He met Frances when he was seventeen and his dancing career, like his ankle, was shattered. Jared had slumped into depression because what had been the point of it all? The constant bullying, the training and arduous rehearsals had all been for nothing. He may as well have hung out on the streets with the other kids, getting pissed on cheap cider and copping off with girls. Girls hadn't featured much in Jared's life yet, partly because they all assumed he was a twinkled-toed poof but mostly because of his gruelling schedule. There was one girl, when he was fifteen, but she soon dumped him when the taunts about having a fairy for a boyfriend became too much. Jared didn't blame Janine – he knew what it was like to be on the receiving end of the taunts and at least she'd let him cop a feel during the three months they were together.

There had been a few girls at college, where it didn't matter how different you were. The girls at college thought it was cool that he was a bit 'out there' and didn't follow the crowd and in the end Jared lost his virginity at a house party. Several house parties followed with similar results, but he never found anybody special and then the accident happened, destroying his dance aspirations, and he didn't care about anything anymore, not even girls.

Frances changed all that in an instant. Jared first spotted her in the college canteen, laughing with a couple of other girls as they ate their lunch. The other girls hid their mouths with their hands as they giggled but Frances was unabashed, her head thrown back as the laughter pulsed from the very depths of her chest. Her brown curls shook and her mascara ran as she tittered, now clutching her aching stomach. Frances swept a finger under her eyes to remove the tears of mirth and stray mascara and she said something to her friends, setting herself off with the giggles once more. Jared was mesmerised. Here was a girl who loved life while he detested everything about it. She found such joy on a normal Tuesday afternoon that Jared began to wonder whether he was wrong and that there was more to life than ballet.

Jared had become quite confident with girls since starting college. They seemed to find him attractive and hung onto his every word, so it was easy to saunter over to the table and plonk himself on an empty seat opposite the curly haired girl. She was even prettier up close with pale skin and rosy cheeks and when she spoke Jared noticed a cute little gap between her front teeth.

'Can we help you?'

'Hi. I'm Jared.' He stuck his hand across the table and the girl eyed it for a moment before taking it and giving it a brief shake.

'Pleased to meet you, Jared. I'm Frances and this is Cara and Melody.' She indicated the other girls around the table. Jared had paid little attention to them so far, but he said hello out of politeness before leaning in towards Frances, watching her eyebrows rise ever so slightly and the corners of her lips twitch.

'I was wondering what was so funny.'

'Ah.' Frances folded her arms across her chest. 'I couldn't possibly share that with you.'

'Why not?'

'It was part of a private conversation.' Frances gathered up her tray, her friends following suit. 'Bye, Jared. See you around.'

Jared was hooked from that moment on and his obsession with dance was replaced with an obsession with Frances Bunton. He sought her out in the canteen, found out what classes she took and which pubs she frequented. Frances was in the first year of a childcare diploma and had a part-time job at a café in town. Jared drank more coffees than he would ever be able to count as he sat in that dingy café, hoping to catch a minute of Frances's time. Years later she would admit that she noticed every single visit Jared made to the café, though she did her best to avoid him, sending another waitress to his table whenever possible. Frances fancied the pants off Jared – all the girls did – but Frances had a boyfriend. She'd been with Martin since they were thirteen and although her feelings had thawed after the first flush of first love, she couldn't imagine ending their relationship and breaking Martin's heart. He was her first love and she cared about him a lot.

'You must be mad,' Cara told her on many occasions. 'Jared is *hot* and Martin is, well, *Martin*.'

'You don't know him like I do,' Frances would point out and Cara would thank a God she didn't quite believe in for that. Martin was freckled, a bit podgy and had about as much charisma as a soggy dishcloth. The thought of a naked Jared sent shivers up her spine while the thought of a naked Martin made her shudder. She doubted any girl other than Frances fancied Martin, but Cara was wrong. Dull, podgy Martin, loyal and faithful boyfriend and best friend to Frances, was caught with his hand up another girl's skirt at a party with no explanation other than he was drunk. Drunk or not, Frances was hurt, humiliated but most of all furious. How *dare* he do this to her? Temptation had been thrown at Frances from every direction since she'd started college, but she'd never even thought of acting on it.

'I'm sorry, babe. I am. But don't you think you're overreacting a bit? It's not like I had sex with her.'

'You would have if I hadn't caught you.'

'No, I wouldn't have, I swear.' Martin was a terrible liar, his glowing ears a dead giveaway and in that moment, as his ears lit up the room, Frances wondered whether he had always looked this ridiculous and unattractive.

'Go back to your little tart, Martin. You may as well finish the job because we're over.' Threading her way through the crowds in search of Cara or Melody, Frances bumped into Jared and a wicked thought crossed her mind. If Martin could have a fumble with some random girl, why couldn't she have a fumble with a random guy? Jared obviously liked her and she was no longer spoken for. Before she could change her mind, Frances acted on impulse for possibly the first time in her life and pulled Jared's lips towards her own. It was Frances who led them upstairs to find a vacant bedroom, who pushed Jared down onto the bed and climbed on top of him, her fingers undoing his jeans and sliding them down his thighs. Frances had never had a one night stand before but then sex with Jared was never to be a one-time thing. From that moment on they were inseparable, and Jared believed they would be together forever.

It pained Jared to remember his time with Frances but he also knew he could never let go completely. He had loved her so much and the feelings lingered on, caught in a time warp, refusing to abate. They were supposed to be married by now with a house full to the brim with children, but Jared lived alone in a one-bedroom flat, wishing his weekends away so he could be back at work with his mind occupied on anything other than painful memories. At least it was Sunday, which meant he would be visiting his family and there would only be a matter of hours where he was left to his own devices before he could head into work again.

Jared dragged himself out of bed and poured himself a bowl of cornflakes, which he ate in front of the television. He thought about heading to the gym to work his memories away but it was already late in the morning and his mum would be expecting him. She still worried about Jared, despite his life being back on track now, so he finished his cereal, jumped into the shower and changed into a pair of jeans and a T-shirt before climbing into the car. His parents lived on the other side of town, close to where he and Frances had lived, which brought yet more memories to the surface. Their first home together had been a shitty little bedsit riddled with damp and the odd mouse but it didn't matter. Frances didn't care that the curtains didn't quite meet in the middle and their sofa was old and lumpy and the central heating only worked every other day. It was their home and it felt like a palace.

Jared tried to push the thought away but it clung to him. They'd grown to love that shitty bedsit and it had been a wrench to leave it, even when they'd secured a mortgage on a lovely little two-bedroom house with a tiny patch of grass at the back that Frances planned to transform into a floral wonderland. Thinking about that house and the potential it proposed was one of the most painful memories he possessed. Instead, Jared concentrated on the radio, singing along to occupy his mind until he turned into his parents' street and pulled up outside the house. He was the last to arrive as usual, with Ally and Freya already gossiping in the kitchen while Gavin watched a football match with Bob, both on the edge of their seats, cans of lager in hand. Jimmy was sprawled on the sofa, earphones plugged in to drown out the cheers and jibes over the match while she concentrated on her homework. Jared lifted her feet and squeezed onto the sofa.

'I should warn you.' Bob leant even further over the edge of his armchair towards Jared, his voice barely above a whisper. 'Your mum's been to the bingo with your aunty Sheila this week.'

Jared closed his eyes with a groan. 'How long is the list?'

Bob gave a sad shake of his head. 'Longer than ever. Won't it be easier if you just said yes to one of them? It might get her off your back.'

'No, Dad. It'll only encourage her to keep setting me up with women. Can't you have a word? Tell her to stop?'

'I've tried son, I really have. Yes! You beauty!' Bob's eyes darted from his son's pleading face to the television screen where Manchester City had just scored. 'Did you see that, Gavin?'

Despite Jared's preparation, it was still torture as Linda rattled off a list of potential suitors over lunch. Jared let the names waft over his head, not interested in Mavis Longbottom's granddaughter or Nelly Winters' niece or the nice girl who works at the bar at bingo. He said no to every name, ignoring the disappointment clouding his mother's eyes. His sisters were next, reeling off their own lists but again Jared declined them all. Why couldn't they understand he wasn't ready? That he may never be ready to start dating again?

'How's it going with the girl from work?' Jared and Gavin were alone in the kitchen, washing and drying the dishes after lunch. 'The being friends thing?'

'It's going great.' Jared smiled as he thought of Ruth. She'd finally agreed to emerge from the women's gym, although she hadn't liked the weights room. She had agreed to try one of the classes though and Jared was looking forward to it. 'It turns out we can only be friends anyway. She's got a boyfriend. I had no idea as she's never mentioned him before, but they live together.' Jared had tried to ignore the searing pain in his gut when he'd dropped Ruth off at home and saw them kissing outside her house, arms thrown around each other as they laughed about something or other. It was good that she was happy and settled – something Jared could never offer her.

'I suppose it takes the pressure off then.'

Jared handed Gavin a plate to dry and nodded his head. 'I suppose it does, yeah.' Although it wasn't feeling the pressure Jared was struggling with at the moment – it was white hot jealousy.

TWENTY-SIX

Ruth

I arrived at H. Woods in record time, my cheeks flushed from the exertion of my walk but I felt happy and a sense of self-satisfaction. I no longer slumped against Quinn's desk, gasping for breath as I stumbled into the building and I had gradually picked up my pace, giving myself an extra few minutes in bed each morning. My calves no longer squealed and begged for mercy at the sight of my trainers as I slipped them on before leaving the house, and my thighs had come to terms with their extra use.

'You're looking well.' Quinn stood up behind her desk to get a proper look at me and I grinned back at her.

'I feel well.' In fact, I felt fantastic, the misery from the diets now completely flushed out of my system. 'Is Kelvin in yet?'

Quinn nodded and leaned across the desk, lowering

her voice. 'According to Pete on security, he's been here all weekend.'

'He's been working all weekend?' I couldn't believe it. Either Kelvin had been abducted by aliens and replaced by a non-lazy robotic Kelvin or he'd been hit over the head with a heavy object and forgotten he was a lazy arsehole.

'And sleeping here, apparently.'

'He hasn't been home at all?'

Quinn shook her head and I rubbed my hands together with glee. My fingers itched to text Erin to revel in the gossip but she hadn't been very receptive last time.

'Do you think his wife's kicked him out?'

'She must have.' It was the only explanation. I could quite easily imagine Kelvin turning into a raging alcoholic, but never a workaholic. 'I'd better get up there. I'll keep you updated if I hear anything.'

My feet skipped up the stairs but halted as I neared my office. It was quite clear Kelvin had spent the entire weekend in the office by the musty stench wafting out of the door. My nose wrinkled but I pressed on, heading straight to the window and shoving it open.

'Ruth? Is that you?'

The stench wasn't going away, so I eased the window open wider. 'Yes it's me. Do you need anything?' Like deodorant? A bar of soap?

'Can you come in here please?'

My eyebrows shot up at the word 'please', a word I didn't think Kelvin was aware of but I headed into his office, preparing myself for an attack of eau de unwashed man as I opened the door. I didn't, however, prepare myself for an almost naked Kelvin and my retinas burned at the image of my boss sat at his desk in a pair of too-small navy underpants.

Kelvin raised his chin, refusing to feel any scrap of embarrassment. 'The bitch has kicked me out of the house. Changed the locks and everything and she won't give me any of my things. But she won't win this battle.' Kelvin barked out a chortle. 'Oh no! She's locked me out of the house and I've locked her out of the bank account. Lazy cow hasn't worked a day since I proposed, so she isn't getting her hands on any more of my cash.'

'Were you in your undies when she locked you out?' I couldn't look at Kelvin as he sat there, hairy chest and bulging stomach on display so I asked the plant beside his desk the question instead.

'What? Oh no. I was fully clothed of course.' He pointed to the chair opposite him where a pile of clothes lay. 'I need you to take those to the dry cleaners and then go into town to buy me a couple more suits to tide me over until bitch-face gives in. Take the measurements from inside the garments. I'll need new underwear too.'

I grimaced as I stepped forwards to gather up the clothes. I wasn't paid enough to shop for Kelvin's underpants.

'Here, take my credit card.' He held it out and I was forced to take a step closer to his fleshy mass. 'Don't be getting any cheap crap.' He had the cheek to look me up and down, his lip curling at what he saw. I wanted to hurl the clothes at him (keeping a tight hold of the credit card, of course) and tell him where to go. How dare he judge me while he was sitting in a pair of crusty undies?

'And don't take too long. I can't sit here half naked all day.' *Half* naked? If only. My eyes could have coped with a flash of leg, but I'd seen practically everything.

'And lock the door on your way out. I can't risk anyone popping in and seeing me like this.'

'But what if there's a fire?'

'Look at me.' Kelvin rose, the movement rocking his chubby rolls, sending them into a flurry. I could no longer see his underpants as the rolls settled and drooped again. 'I'd rather burn to a crisp than step foot out of the office like this. Besides, I have a spare key.' Kelvin sneered at me as though I was the stupid one.

Locking the door, I headed downstairs, the clothes, which smelled even worse than the office, tucked under my arm. I wondered why Kelvin had waited until now to buy new clothes when he'd had all weekend to kit himself out and then it dawned on me. Susan may have been a lazy cow who hadn't worked since Kelvin proposed, but I doubted he'd shopped for a pair of socks since the ring slid onto her finger.

'He's up there in nothing but a pair of underpants.'

Quinn's eyes widened at the latest piece of gossip. 'You're kidding.'

'Nope. He wants me to get his clothes dry cleaned.' I held the clothes up and Quinn gagged as the stench hit her. 'And then I've got to go shopping for new clothes for him.'

'I dare you to buy him a clown suit.'

I laughed but shook my head. 'I don't think he's in a humorous mood.'

Quinn opened her mouth to say something but was interrupted by the phone. She glanced at me as she answered. 'Yes, she's still here. Yes, I will pass that message on.' She hung up and gave me an apologetic shrug. 'Kelvin says can you nip back upstairs and make him a coffee before you go?'

My day didn't look like it was going to get much better. After spending the morning shopping for Kelvin and doing my best to fumigate the office, Kelvin sent me back out again to buy a sleeping bag and pillow.

'Why don't you book yourself into a hotel?' It seemed the obvious solution to me. I didn't ask about crashing at a friend's house in case he didn't actually have any friends. Even I wasn't that cruel.

'Are you mad? This could go on for bloody months. I'm still paying the mortgage for a house I'm not allowed in. I can't afford a hotel bill on top.'

'So you're going to stay here? In your office?'

I added air freshener to my shopping list.

I tried to get hold of Erin to have a brief gossip, but I was either whizzing around town or she was too busy to come to the phone and I could hardly leave a message with the girl at the next desk about Kelvin and his state of undress. The only chance I got to speak to Erin was in person at the end of the day. I rushed into her office, making Richard leap away from Erin's desk in shock at my sudden entrance. I wondered if he knew about his parents' troubles but knew better than to ask.

'Are you ready to leave?'

Erin checked her watch and seemed surprised that it was after five and the rest of the office had drifted home. 'Yep. Just give me a minute.'

I waited while Erin shut down her computer and gathered her belongings, almost bursting with gossip. Erin bustled me out of the office and grimaced.

'Ugh. He's been slobbering over me all day.' She shuddered while I took in her outfit, which may have fuelled Richard's obsession with her. Her red dress was short, barely covering her crotch, her boobs pushed up to balance above the neckline and the fabric moulded itself to her frame like a second skin. If it hadn't been Erin in the dress, I would have said it was highly inappropriate for work.

'You can hardly blame him in that get up, can you?'

Erin slid her hands over her hips. 'What, this old thing? I thought Stuart might like it.' From the wicked grin on her face, I assumed Stuart had liked it very much.

'Speaking of clothes, you'll never guess how I found Kelvin this morning.'

Erin stopped in the corridor and grasped my arm. 'He was in a dress?'

'If only.' I swallowed back a tiny bit of bile before I continued. If it wasn't such a juicy piece of gossip, I'd have removed the image from my memory. 'He was almost naked, wearing just his underpants.'

Erin's face paled. 'He wasn't trying to shag you, was he?'

'No, no, no.' I covered my ears but it was too late. 'Susan's kicked him out so he's camping out in his office. He didn't have any spare clothes and he wanted me to take his suit to the dry cleaners.'

'Susan's kicked him out?'

I nodded, relishing being the bearer of such news. 'I thought she was being dramatic with the divorce thing, but it turns out she's serious.'

Erin started walking along the corridor again, tugging me with her. 'Let's go to the pub. I want all the details.'

'I can't. I have spinning class.' I never thought I'd pass up the chance for a gossip in the pub for exercise in a million years. 'I can meet you later though.'

Erin shook her head. 'I can't. I'm seeing Stuart.'

'Again?' This was even more shocking than finding Kelvin that morning.

'It turns out he's quite good company. And surprisingly good in bed.'

'You already knew he was good in the sack.' That was the only reason she'd gone back for seconds.

'And it was a surprise the first time. Anyway, come on. I've had enough of this place.'

I rushed home, even managing a sort of jog at one point, stopping by the boutique for only a few seconds to ogle The Dress. I ate quickly and changed into my gym gear so that I was ready when Jared arrived to pick me up for our class. I was still feeling optimistic about the class by this point and so I was quite content to follow Jared into the room lined with bikes, arranged in a semi-circle and facing a singular bike in the middle. A few people had arrived before us but I didn't feel out of place with Jared by my side.

'Good evening, everyone.' The instructor strode into the room and I was delighted to see it would be Courtney taking the class. He looked divine in a pair of tight black shorts displaying his muscled thighs and calves and a tight white T-shirt which showed every contour of his body beneath. It would be worth the class just to see Courtney again. Or so I thought.

'I see we have a couple of newbies today. Hi, Ruth and... I'm sorry. I didn't catch your name.' My knees felt soft beneath my frame and I felt an old-fashioned swoon coming on. *He'd remembered my name!*

Courtney took the class through some stretches, which I found quite strenuous, and couldn't wait until they were over. At least the exercise would be more gentle on the bikes.

Ha!

'Right, on your bikes.' Courtney clapped his hands together before he straddled the bike in the centre.

'And remember — Strength, Stamina and Speed. Let's start gently.'

I could do gentle and began pedalling in unison with the class, our legs happily swishing round and round. I felt my lips pull up into a smile. This class was a dream for me: easy, light exercise while in the presence of the magnificent Courtney.

Music was suddenly piped into the room, music with a fast beat that made my gut churn with uneasiness. The music did not fit our soft footwork and I was afraid of what was to come. My instincts were correct.

'Remember: Strength, Stamina, Speed.' Courtney focused his eyes on the group as he gripped his handlebars. 'Let's kick it up a notch!' With a flurry of movement, the class began pumping their legs faster and faster, cycling like their lives depended on it, their knuckles white from their grip on their handlebars. I glanced sideways and saw that Jared was cycling like a maniac.

Fuck.

I pumped my legs as fast as I could, panting and weeping within seconds. My chubby legs were not made for mad dashes.

I was relieved when Courtney spoke again. He was going to tell us to slow down again — or even better, stop completely.

'We go faster in ten.' *What*? 'Ready?' And Courtney, who had moments ago appeared gorgeous and kind, turned into a mean bastard as he began to count down. 'Go!' The legs around me pumped even harder, the beat of the music and Courtney's watchful eye spurring them on. I willed my own legs to keep up but they were having none of it. They were going as fast as they were ever going to go, which wasn't very fast at all.

'Ten more seconds now.'

I didn't think I had *two* more seconds left in me, but I managed to keep going, albeit at a quarter of the speed of the others. Relief washed over me as Courtney reached zero.

'Now up you get.' Courtney, feet still on the pedals, stood, pedalling away as his body bobbed up and down. The class duly followed suit while I attempted to copy. My knees trembled, my calves cried out and I didn't dare imagine what my face looked like as I grunted with each rotation.

'Now press-ups. Go!' Courtney, while still pedalling, bent down towards his handlebars before popping up again. Up and down he went, the others somehow keeping up with the mad bastard. I couldn't do a press-up on the floor, never mind on a bloody bike.

On and on he went, bobbing up and down with ease while I clung onto my bike, willing death to come and take me away from this torture. Sweat poured out of my body, prickling at my skin and I was sure there would be a puddle underneath my bike. Funny, there was no such puddle under Courtney's bike.

'Five, four, three, two, one, relax.'

I could have wept at that glorious word. Relax. Yes please. Except in Courtney's world, relax didn't mean stop, it simply meant slow down a tad. The other cyclists, while in a so-called relaxed state, were still pedalling faster than I had been during the more strenuous cycle. We did at least get to sit down, which I was grateful for.

On and on the class went. Up, down, cycling like a bitch, slowing down, press-ups, more resistance, less resistance. I couldn't last much longer, my body ready to keel over, and I hadn't even been going at the same pace as the sadists around me.

'Resistance down, legs speed up. Go!' I would never look at Courtney with lust again. I would project only hate. 'Now quicker. Come on everybody, keep up!'

I was openly weeping, sweat and tears mingling on my cheeks. I wanted to go home, to curl up on the sofa with Billy and a family sized bag of peanut M&Ms.

'Slow down now.'

I was convinced I'd hallucinated those words but my watery eyes spotted the pace around me drop. It dropped further and further and then Courtney was clapping and telling everyone how well they'd done. He picked up a blue towel with the Roxy logo on it and wiped the sweat from his face. Part of me was glad he'd sweated too, but mostly I just wanted to crawl off the bike and rip the bastard's nuts off. Jared helped me off the bike, my energy completely depleted, and helped me towards the female changing rooms. My throat was raw from gasping so it was a good while before I could speak again. By the time I could, we were sitting in The Bonnie Dundee, glasses of orange juice in front of us.

'I would rather be fat than do that ever again.'

'You're not a fan of spinning class then?'

I shook my head. It hurt. *Everything* hurt and I knew it would be even worse in the morning. 'Even being massaged by a naked Courtney couldn't make up for that.' I almost smiled at the thought but my muscles refused to respond.

'Doesn't your boyfriend mind you lusting after other men?'

I gave Jared a blank look, wanting to convey confusion but being physically unable to do so. 'I don't have a boyfriend. Why do you think I'm putting myself through this torture?'

Jared, who had barely broken out in a sweat during the class, found it easy to convey a look of confusion and I found myself feeling jealous that *his* face worked properly. 'But the bloke I saw you with outside your house the other day...'

'Messy brown curls?' Jared nodded and I'd have laughed had I had the energy resources. 'That's Billy, my housemate. I've known him all my life. Kissing him would be like kissing my brother.' I attempted a shudder but none was forthcoming so I voiced my disgust instead. 'Yuck.'

'Oh. I see.' Jared took a sip of his orange juice. 'So we're not doing spinning class next week?'

Was he mental? 'No.'

'How about another class?'

'Do you want to drink that orange juice or wear it?'

Jared smiled and moved his glass out of my reach. It was a lovely smile that sent a warm gush to my stomach. 'There are loads of classes to choose from. They won't all be like spinning.'

It must have been the smile that did it because I found myself scrutinising the noticeboard the following evening, choosing the women-only aerobics class. Not only would my wobbly bits be hidden from male view, the class took place on Thursdays, giving me a few days to recover from the hellish spinning class.

TWENTY-SEVEN

Billy

Clare stood in front of Billy in the hallway, her fingers tugging at the knot of his tie. He'd thought it was pretty neat but apparently not.

'There we go. Perfect.' Clare smiled at Billy and smoothed down his charcoal jacket. Clare had picked out the suit for him, along with the navy tie to match her calf-length dress with beaded sash. She'd teased his hair into neat, respectable curls that bounced from his skull and made him feel like a bit of a dickhead. 'Shall we get going? We don't have to be at the church until two but I said we'd meet Mum and Dad outside so we can have a quick chat first. They're dying to meet you.' Clare grinned at him as though this was a normal occurrence while Billy felt dread swirl in his stomach. He fought the urge to muss up his hair, tear off the tie and run upstairs to hide under his covers. This was happening way too quickly.

Clare grabbed her clutch bag and checked her reflection in the mirror in the hallway, making sure no stray hairs had worked their way loose from her up do. Grasping Billy's hand, more to tug him out of the house than for affection, she led him out to her car. Billy looked so worried at the prospect of meeting her parents, she considered buckling him into his seat herself and locking the car door to prevent him from escaping.

'Relax. They're nice people and pretty decent as far as parents go.' She gave Billy's knee a squeeze before they set off for the little church in Hartfield Hill, a village not too far away and where her cousin was getting married.

'I'm relaxed, I'm relaxed,' Billy said, though clearly he wasn't. His jittery legs and fumbling fingers were a dead giveaway.

'You'll love Abbie and Jon. Abbie's so lovely. We were like best friends growing up and Jon's a really nice bloke. Laid back but funny. He runs his own IT company, so you'll have something in common.'

'It's his wedding day. I doubt he'll want to stand around talking about computers. And Abbie won't be impressed if he does.'

Clare gave a wave of her hand. 'Oh, Abbie's not like that.'

Yeah, right, Billy thought. All women were like that. One minute they're fun and up for anything, the next they're picking out your clothes and slapping gel and shit in your hair. And they went particularly nuts on their wedding day. Abbie would have poor old Jon on a tight leash from now on.

Their conversation wilted and Clare turned on the radio in the end, humming along until they reached the church. The church sat upon a hill, overlooking the village, with a stone path leading the way up to the small building and graveyard beyond. Both the church and grounds were beautiful and Clare could imagine no better setting for a wedding. She grabbed hold of Billy's arm as they wandered towards her father's car. Her parents jumped out of the car to greet them, smiling and shaking hands, wafting perfume and aftershave all over Billy and almost choking him.

'How lovely to finally meet you, Billy. I'm Liz and this is Derek.' Clare's mother kissed Billy on the cheek, leaving behind a peach smear, before turning to Clare. 'We thought we'd go to the little café on the village green before the service.' She checked the tiny silver watch on her wrist. 'We have plenty of time and we can have a good old natter and get to know Billy before the crowds arrive.'

Billy didn't seem to have much say, as Clare clamped her hand on his arm and the foursome wandered through the village to a little tearoom. He wondered whether he'd have a choice of what he could drink.

'Shall we get a pot? And how about one of those lovely scones? The reception isn't for a good couple of hours and I'm a bit peckish.' Liz didn't wait for an answer before she summoned a waitress and placed their order. Billy didn't usually drink tea but he drank it to be polite, trying not to grimace with each sip. He was interrogated over the pot of tea and scones, questions firing from both Liz and Derek, and though they smiled and nodded at his answers, Billy was scared of saying the wrong thing. He was exhausted by the time they left the tearoom and made their way back to the church.

'You were great,' Clare whispered to Billy as they wandered up the stone path. 'They love you.'

'Really?'

Clare nodded and gave his hand a squeeze. 'They couldn't stand my ex. They thought he was vain and arrogant and only interested in himself. Which he was.' She gave his hand another squeeze. 'But you're not like that. You're lovely, and Mum and Dad think so too.'

The service was a bit dull but it didn't last too long and soon they all spilled out into the churchyard while the wedding party posed for photos. Billy felt a bit out of place when it came to the group shot of all the wedding guests, having not been introduced to the bride and groom yet. The reception took place back in Woodgate, in the huge function room of a posh hotel, red and gold balloons fastened to every available surface and the tables laid meticulously with handmade place settings and red and gold confetti scattered generously across the white tablecloth.

'It looks like Christmas,' Billy whispered as they were seated. Clare shot him a look, her eyebrows knitted and mouth puckered as she removed her shrug and draped it across the back of her chair. 'What? I'm not saying that's a bad thing. Who doesn't like Christmas?' Clare's features softened as she thanked the waiter who was moving along their table to fill their glasses with champagne. 'Must have cost them a fortune though.'

'The cost isn't important. This is the wedding Abbie wanted.'

What kind of wedding did Jon want? Billy thought but he kept his gob shut.

'I think it's lovely. Abbie and Aunty Jill have worked really hard to make it perfect.'

And perfect it was. The meal was sumptuous, the champagne and wine flowing, the speeches touching yet humorous. After the meal, the tables were whipped away and a band set up in the corner of the room. More guests arrived, filling the large room.

Clare clasped Billy's hand and pulled him to his feet. 'Come and dance with me.'

Billy sat back down again. 'I can't dance.' And he hadn't sunk enough booze to attempt to.

'I'm not asking you to morph into Patrick Swayze.' Clare gave his hand another tug. 'Just hold me and sway. Even you can do that.'

Billy dragged his eyes to the dance floor in front of the band. There were several couples entwined and shifting their feet in rhythm to the music and a group of preteens waving their arms in the air and giggling at the slushy golden oldie music. How hard could it be to sway? And it would make Clare happy.

'Ok, but I won't be held responsible if I somehow break your ankle.'

'How could you break my ankle dancing to this?' The song hardly required any vigorous movement.

'Trust me, it could happen.'

Billy felt like a condemned man as he was led to the dance floor. He looped his arms around Clare's waist while she draped her arms around his shoulders, resting her head in the crook of his neck. She smelt nice, as she always did, and this dancing lark wasn't so bad.

The song came to an end and the intro of 'Iris' by the Goo Goo Dolls began. The lead singer of the band grabbed the mic to speak over the intro. 'Please welcome the new Mr and Mrs Blackman to the dance floor.' Abbie and Jon skipped onto the dance floor as the crowds oohed and aahed at the couple.

'Doesn't she look radiant?' Clare was watching her cousin, a little sigh escaping her lips. Abbie and Jon were gazing at each other with such adoration that it made her chest ache. 'Have you ever thought about getting married?'

'What?' Billy was glad they were now watching from the chairs at the sidelines because if they'd still been dancing, he'd have fallen over and brought Clare tumbling down with him. 'How can you even be *thinking* about getting married? We've only been seeing each other for a few weeks.' Billy felt his throat close up and looked around in desperation for a drink or an emergency exit.

'It's been *three months*, Billy, and I wasn't proposing. I meant have you ever thought about getting married in general. Not to me, right now. But it's nice to know that the idea of marrying me is so horrifying.'

Billy watched as Clare pushed her way through the crowds, grabbed her shrug and elbowed her way outside for some fresh air. What was he supposed to do now?

TWENTY-EIGHT

Ruth

I hadn't quite forgiven Courtney for the horrific spinning class, but the sight of him in his shorts and tight T-shirt (and not a bike in sight) made me thaw a little as I followed him into one of the rooms off reception. Six weeks had passed since my initial fitness assessment, so it was time for a follow up and I was looking forward to seeing any improvements. I *felt* fitter and no longer batted an eyelid at my walk to and from work when Jared wasn't giving me a lift so I was more than a little disappointed to learn I had lost a measly two pounds.

'How often do you use the gym?' Courtney's tone was conversational rather than accusing but I still felt like a naughty school girl on the wrong end of a ticking off.

'Once or twice a week.' More like once. My enthusiasm for the gym had waned quite quickly and my daily visits had plummeted. I attended the women-only aerobics class with perky Tahlia, spending the whole hour wanting to slap the sprightly look from her face, and while I didn't exactly enjoy the exercise, I stuck with the class despite the annoying instructor because I could just about keep up and somehow managed to retain the ability to walk afterwards. I occasionally dipped my toe into the women's gym but I found it dull and repetitive.

'I'd recommend exercising three times a week to further your weight loss and increase your fitness levels.' Courtney's lips widened into a grin at the face I pulled. 'It doesn't have to be on a rowing machine or a treadmill. There are loads of classes on offer.' I was well aware of the classes on offer. It was how I'd ended up prancing about with the lycra-clad Ms Perky every Thursday. 'In fact, I've got a Zumba class starting in half an hour. Don't pull that face, Ruth.' He grinned again. 'It's fun, I promise.'

'Hmm.' I picked up my bag. 'I'll think about it.'

Jared was waiting for me in reception and responded with enthusiasm when I mentioned the Zumba class.

'You want to go?'

'Yeah. Why not?'

I could think of a million reasons why not, mostly my laziness and lack of co-ordination, but I kept quiet. I was there to lose weight and Zumba had to be more exciting than rowing towards a wall.

'Fine. We'll go.'

The class was made up of a mixture of people wearing baggy T-shirts like myself and the more serious wore lycra and vest combos. The baggies seemed to linger at the back of the room, which was where I headed, feeling safer hidden away. Jared was somewhere in the middle clothing wise, wearing loose shorts and a sleeveless T-shirt, but he stayed against the back wall with me.

The music had a strong beat that had me tapping my foot before Courtney had started the class. We began with some simple footwork and I was lulled into thinking this was a class I could actually do. Of course Courtney soon shattered that illusion by adding arm movements and more intricate footwork. I tried to keep up but I was beyond useless. It seemed the kinder option was to give up but then Courtney started clapping. Even I could clap! But then the clapping was joined by twirling and hip action and I was lost once again. Everyone in front of me was perfect, keeping up with the moves and smiling as they went. It was only when I looked to the left and right of me that I realised those at the back of the class – the baggies – were all as terrible as I was. The baggies were crap, at least five seconds behind everybody else and moving either their arms or legs but never both at the same time. I doubted any of them even knew where their hips were located never mind how to shake them. But, bizarrely, they were still smiling and laughing like the lycras.

The exception to the rule was Jared who, despite being against the back wall with us baggies, was amazing. His body moved with ease and was fluid and sexy. The sight of his muscly legs did something strange to my stomach and I had to take a couple of deep breaths before I could continue. By rights, Jared should have been at the front of the class with the lycras, perhaps even side by side with Courtney. He caught my eye and gave me a wink. Blushing at being caught ogling, I turned my attention back to Courtney who had begun to shimmy. I attempted to copy the action and he'd moved on to the next set of steps before my arse stopped wobbling.

Zumba was undoubtedly more complicated than aerobics with tricky footwork that left me in a muddle but, in the end, I found myself letting go like the rest of the baggies, flinging myself all over the place. I was nowhere near performing the correct moves but Courtney had been right when he'd said it was fun.

With two regular classes to attend per week, I took Courtney's advice and signed up for a third. The thought of yoga appealed to me, curling up on a mat and relaxing for an hour, and I was pleased when Jared said he would join me as I would have a perfect view of his perfect bum. Such a shame he was gay!

The instructor arrived, looking as hippyish as they come, with long, straggly blonde curls, held off her face by a tie-dyed scarf. She wore an electric blue leotard with matching leggings underneath, a fringed sarong tied at her waist and her feet were bare.

'Good evening, class. I see we have a couple of new faces. My name is Camilla and I am here to teach you yoga.' Camilla smiled at me and Jared, her eyes crinkling in the corners as she did so. 'Yoga is often thought to be associated with Hinduism, but yoga is actually older. The word "yoga" means to merge, join or unite.' She placed her palms together and interlinked her long, slender fingers. 'Yoga allows us to escape from the chaos of our lives, using breathing techniques, movement and posture, relaxation and meditation.' She smiled at us once again. 'Shall we begin with a warm up?'

The class wasn't the excuse for a nap that I was expecting. My body was curved, stretched and curled into various positions but Camilla paid special attention to me, showing me time and again the positions with patience and plenty of encouragement. I left the class feeling refreshed and energised and knew I would be back the following week.

'Shall we go for a drink?' I linked my arm through Jared's as we left the gym. It had become a habit to stop off at the pub after a workout for a drink or two before Jared dropped me off at home.

'Sorry, I can't today. It's my sister's birthday and I said I'd go round. Would you mind if I dropped you straight off at home?'

'Of course not but you should have said.' I gave Jared a playful tap on the arm. 'You could have given yoga a miss tonight.'

Jared shook his head. 'I enjoyed it. Camilla's lovely, isn't she?'

'She is. I thought she was going to be annoying with that little speech at the beginning, but she isn't. I actually really enjoyed it.'

We reached the car park and climbed into Jared's car, continuing our dissection of the class. Jared admitted that he didn't usually like to sit around doing nothing, that he didn't like being inside his own head for too long but that he'd found the class strangely calming. I was glad Jared was getting something out of the class too. I sometimes felt incredibly selfish, dragging him to classes so I could lose weight, but I was too fond of his company to cut him free.

'I'll see you tomorrow then.' I unclipped my seatbelt as Jared pulled up outside the house.

'We should meet up for lunch. To make up for missing the pub tonight.'

'That would be lovely.' Heat rose from my chest, rising to my throat and cheeks, and the corners of my mouth lifted until I was grinning at Jared. I tried to smooth my lips down but it was impossible. The thought of spending time with Jared made me incredibly happy and while I could pretend it was because we were becoming good friends, deep down I knew that wasn't the whole truth.

'We won't eat the rubbish from The Bonnie Dundee though.'

I shook my head, while wondering what we'd eat instead – digestive biscuits from the kitchen cupboard?

'I'll bring us something.'

'Great.' Without thinking, I leant towards Jared and pecked him on the cheek. He smelled good, freshly showered after our yoga session, and it was a wrench to pull myself away again. 'See you tomorrow.' I dived out of the car before I did something stupid, like throw myself at Jared completely, and ran into the house. It was quiet inside and I assumed the house was empty as I dumped my gym kit in the wash and made a cup of coffee. It wasn't until I was pushing the sitting room door open that I heard the low hum of the television, but I was confused by the darkness. Then the door opened fully and I noticed the flickering tea lights scattered on the coffee table and my eyes roamed to the sofa, where Billy and Clare were huddled. My eyes turned to the television where a romantic comedy was playing and back to the coffee table where, among the candles, were the remnants of a meal Billy had ordered from Cosmo's and passed off as his own.

I'd gate-crashed a romantic evening.

'Sorry. I didn't know you were in here. I'll take this upstairs.' I lifted my cup of coffee and started to back out of the room but Billy stopped me.

'Don't be silly. Come and watch the film with us.

There's plenty of food left in the fridge if you're hungry. It just needs reheating.'

I turned to Clare, who I was sure didn't want me hanging around.

'It's fine, really.'

The television caught my attention and I realised it was *You've Got Mail*, one of my all-time favourite films. How could I resist? 'If you're sure.'

Billy sat up on the sofa and patted the space beside him. 'We're sure.'

Jared had put together a little picnic of sandwiches, salad, mini quiches and fruit, along with a bottle of sparkling flavoured water, two plastic cups and a blanket. He whisked me off to the grass verge beside the car park and set out the blanket and food.

'This is lovely.' I sank onto the blanket and accepted a plastic cup before tilting my face to the warm sun. 'Much better than The Bonnie Dundee.'

'*Anything* is better than The Bonnie Dundee. It's a hole. I don't know how it stays in business.'

'It's because of us.' I gestured at the looming grey building of H. Wood Vehicles before us. 'I think it relies on our parties to keep it afloat. And now Kelvin's bar bill is keeping it going.' Kelvin was still crashing on the office floor, too stubborn and cheap to rent a room while he battled Susan for the house. It was now in my job description to ship his clothes to and from the dry cleaners, keep his supply of deodorant and shaving gel stocked up and to nip to the supermarket late each afternoon to bring him food for the evening. Kelvin spent most of his evenings in The Bonnie Dundee, spitting venom about his wife to the landlord, before stumbling back to the office and climbing into his sleeping bag. Both the office and Kelvin had an unfortunate whiff about them and even Angelina had refused to visit for their private 'meetings'.

'But seriously, this is lovely.' I picked up my cup and clinked it against Jared's, careful not to spill the contents. For the thousandth time I rued the fact that Jared was gay and that I wasn't a supermodel. Life was beyond unfair.

'I'm glad you like it.' Jared smiled at me and it was fortunate that I was sitting down as I was sure my lust would have weakened my knees and sent me tumbling to the ground. Damn Jared and his love of willies.

TWENTY-NINE

Jared

Jared had never had any inclination to join a Zumba class but when Ruth suggested it, he couldn't turn down the opportunity to spend time with her. After attempting the spinning class, Ruth had crawled back into her shell and the only class she'd consider was the women-only aerobics, which Jared couldn't attend for obvious reasons. So when Ruth seemed almost keen to try out Zumba – more to perv on Courtney than anything, Jared suspected – he'd gone along with it and now they were taking part in their third class. Beside him, Ruth was being her adorable clumsy self and he was finding it difficult to follow Courtney's instructions as he was too busy watching her. Her cheeks were puffed out, her hair slicked to her head with sweat and her movements were all over the place, but Jared didn't think she'd ever looked cuter.

Jared tried to banish the thought, but it was

becoming increasingly difficult to deny his attraction to Ruth, particularly after their picnic lunch, which had been practically a date and all Jared's idea. The kiss she'd given Jared in the car, though only a chaste peck on the cheek, had turned his insides to jelly and he'd feared he was going to act on his desire to kiss her properly. Luckily she'd hopped out of the car with her usual cheery wave and saved him the humiliation. It was quite clear Ruth didn't fancy him, and quite clear she did fancy Courtney with his bulging muscles.

Jared's jaw clenched and he had to concentrate on his breathing to calm himself down enough to loosen it. It didn't matter if Ruth fancied Courtney. In fact, it was probably better that way because any encouragement from Ruth would only complicate things and Jared was puzzled enough as it was.

'That was fun. I think I'm getting the hang of it.' Ruth caught his eye as they made their way out of the class and burst out laughing.

'You'll get there. We've only been to a few classes.' Jared didn't want Ruth to give up on the class, more for his benefit than hers. He looked forward to the Zumba and yoga classes each week more than anything.

'I doubt I'll ever get there but never mind. It's fun and I'm exercising, which is good enough for me.' They reached the doors to the changing rooms and went their separate ways. 'Meet you out here, yeah?'

Jared's favourite part of their classes was the drink in the pub afterwards as they had the opportunity to chat. He showered and changed quickly before heading out to reception to wait for Ruth. She emerged looking radiant after her workout and Jared averted his gaze from the cleavage her wraparound dress showcased.

'Pub?' he asked and was pleased when Ruth nodded

and led the way. The Bonnie Dundee was a dive but it meant that he and Ruth were never disturbed and they had the run of the juke box, even if Ruth did keep trying to convert Jared towards her preference for cheesy pop.

'There's nothing wrong with S Club 7. They were happy and cheerful and that's what I want from my music. I don't want to be miserable and heartbroken.' Ruth and Jared returned to their table by the window after stuffing the juke box with coins and loading it with enough songs to last the evening.

'I bet you even liked Hanson, didn't you?'

Ruth gave a shrug of her shoulders. 'They were alright, yeah. Although I did think the middle one was a girl for a long time. That must have confused a lot of young men at the time. Not you, obviously.' Jared's eyebrows bunched together but Ruth didn't elaborate before she changed the subject. 'We're lucky Kelvin's not in tonight. Can you imagine having to socialise with him outside work?'

'I can't imagine socialising with anybody but you from work.'

'Not even Angelina?' Ruth grinned at him, teasing as she knew that Angelina was still after Jared, relentless with her seduction.

'Especially not with Angelina.'

Ruth shook her head and her freshly washed curls danced around her face. 'Hasn't she worked out that she's barking up the wrong tree yet? You should just tell her.'

'I have.'

'You have?' The teasing smile that had been playing on Ruth's lips during the conversation wilted away.

'I've made it quite clear, but she either doesn't listen or doesn't care.'

'It's because you're so handsome.' Ruth reached out to rub his cropped hair, but the smile didn't quite return to her face. Jared wasn't sure whether she was taking the piss or not because she obviously didn't find him attractive, as she'd told him often enough. 'Are you really not seeing anybody? Not even casually?'

Jared shook his head.

'That makes two of us.' Ruth pulled a face. 'That's why I'm so desperate to lose weight for the reunion. It wouldn't be so bad showing up like this if I had a boyfriend, but I don't.'

'Why do you need to impress these people anyway? They sound like a bunch of tossers to me.'

Ruth took a sip of her orange juice, eyeing Jared over the rim as she considered telling Jared about Zack. It had been the most humiliating experience of her life and the only person she'd told the whole story to was Erin. She hadn't even told her parents why she'd had to flee so suddenly, and she'd told Stephen and Billy that Zack had been her boyfriend but he'd dumped her. Although she'd only known Jared a short time, she trusted him and so she told him everything. Her cheeks burned remembering the fake date and her eyes pooled with tears. It had happened ten years ago and yet it could have happened seconds ago.

'He sounds like a wanker.' Jared reached across the table and took Ruth's hand, giving it a squeeze. 'And you don't need to lose weight for him. You're beautiful as you are.'

Ruth attempted a smile. 'That's easy for you to say. You don't have to see me naked.'

Jared hated to see Ruth so upset, so damaged by a teenage boy with no tact or compassion. He longed to throw out a cheeky, flirty response, to let Ruth know that he would very much like to see her naked, but the familiar barrier rose, the solid wall that he couldn't seem to rid himself of whenever he thought of being with another woman. His words remained at the back of his throat, glued into place along with his yearnings.

'The worst bit is I really thought I was finally being accepted. I thought I was in love with him.' Ruth gave a bitter laugh. 'I've never been in love since. Sometimes I think I've built up a fence around me to stop myself from falling in love so I don't get hurt again. Does that make sense?'

'It makes perfect sense.'

Ruth gave a small smile, feeling better that she wasn't some sort of freak with a steel heart. 'Have you ever been in love?'

'Frances.' Jared nodded as he murmured the name. It had popped out of his mouth without his permission and brought with it a searing pain through his chest. Though he thought of Frances every day, he rarely spoke about her as it was still too painful, especially with people who didn't know her.

'It didn't work out, I guess?'

'Something like that.' Jared cleared his throat and concentrated on draining his glass, wishing he'd never brought Frances into the conversation.

'How long were you together?'

'I don't really want to talk about it.' Jared's words came out harsher than intended and he saw the flash of hurt on Ruth's face but, although he wanted to soothe her, he really couldn't bring himself to discuss his relationship with Frances. 'Sorry.'

'It's okay.'

'It's just difficult, you know?'

Ruth nodded and this time it was Jared's hand being

given a comforting squeeze. 'Shall I get us another drink?'

Jared nodded, fighting the urge to jump in his car and drive home so he could be alone, possibly with an awful lot of beer to drown out his thoughts and feelings.

It took a couple of days for Jared's body to unwind, for his jaw to unclench and the need to soothe the ache inside with alcohol to abate. He knew he was being foolish, that feeling down wasn't going to help anybody, especially himself, and the last thing he wanted to do was ruin his friendship with Ruth. She didn't know about Frances and what had happened. She didn't know about their baby, the son Jared had never had the chance to hold before he was whisked away from his life. He didn't even know what colour eyes Barney had. His only reassurance was that he was with Frances and Jared knew, above all else, that Frances would be a wonderful mother.

So Jared picked himself up and as he came through the fog once again, he felt the need to see Ruth. Not to explain – he didn't feel ready for that – but to spend time with her, to hear her laugh and see her smile. To try to make up for being such an arsehole over the past few days. The urge was so sudden, he found himself driving to her house without calling first. He was at the door, finger pressing the doorbell before it occurred to him that Ruth may not even be in and, even if she was, would she want to see him on a Saturday afternoon? Weekends were her free time and he was invading her precious day away from work, but it was too late. The bell had rung and he could hear footsteps in the hall.

'Jared, hi.' Ruth looked surprised to see him but she

was smiling so that was a positive sign.

'Hi.' Jared faltered. What was he supposed to do now? Tell her that he'd been desperate to see her? Perhaps not. 'It's a lovely day, so I thought we could go for a run in the park.'

Ruth barked out a laugh, the noise sudden and filling the air around them. 'I hate to break it to you, Jared, but I don't run.'

'We can walk then.' They could sit on a bench if it meant they could spend the afternoon together.

'A walk? Yes, I suppose we could do that. Come in for a minute while I change.' Ruth moved aside, closing the door behind Jared as he stepped into the hallway. 'Do you want to wait in the sitting room? Don't worry, the others aren't home. Billy's out with his girlfriend and Theo didn't come home last night.'

Jared perched on the sofa, taking in his surroundings while he waited for Ruth. The sitting room looked like a stand at a technology convention with every conceivable games console set up by the television, including retro consoles such as a SNES and a Megadrive. Various controllers were scattered about the room and a laptop was closed on the coffee table.

'Sorry about that. I couldn't go for a walk in those shoes.' Ruth glided into the sitting room wearing black jogging bottoms, a white long-sleeved T-shirt and a purple fur-lined gilet and trainers. 'Shall we get going?'

They drove across town to a large park, which was packed with families spending their Saturday wandering through the animal centre, picnicking on the vast expanse of parkland, tossing a Frisbee or racing through the woods. Ruth and Jared made it once around the large boating lake before they collapsed on a bench with an ice cream.

'My mum and dad used to bring us here when we were kids,' Ruth said, glancing around at the dozens upon dozens of families milling around. 'I used to love going to see the peacocks. Do you think they're still here?'

'We can go and have a look if you want.'

Ruth's head almost bounced off her neck as she nodded, leaping from the bench. They strolled through the park towards the animal centre, which housed goats, pigs, chickens, ducks, rabbits and, to Ruth's delight, peacocks.

'They're beautiful, don't you think?' she asked as a peacock opened his tail feathers to reveal the blue and green plumes that always reminded Ruth of jewels.

'Yes. Beautiful.' But Jared wasn't watching the peacock. His eyes were on Ruth, on her bright eyes and wide smile, her hands against the mesh to be as close to the birds as possible.

'My brother used to tease me and say we were going to take one of the peacocks home for tea.' Ruth laughed at the memory. 'I used to go mental, begging my dad not to kill the poor peacock and offering to make us cheese on toast instead. I fell for it every time.'

'Are you close to your brother?'

Ruth forced herself away from the peacock enclosure and looped her arm through Jared's as they made their way to the animal centre's courtyard, which housed the visitors centre, a café and gift shop. In the centre of the courtyard was a wishing well and Ruth automatically reached into her purse for a coin.

'We are but I don't get to see him very often any more. He lives in New York with his wife and kids.'

'You must miss him.'

Ruth nodded. 'A lot. But I have Billy, and he's like a

brother.' She stopped at the brick wall of the well, closed her eyes and made a wish before dropping the coin, listening to hear it plop at the bottom. Jared copied the action, wishing for Frances to return with their son, even though he knew it was never going to happen.

'Shall we go for a coffee?' he asked, needing to be away from the wishing well and his crazy dream. The café was crammed but they bought their coffees to take out and returned to the courtyard, perching on a low wall. Children ran around the courtyard, chasing one another and climbing on the small green tractor that had been stationed outside the visitors centre for as long as Ruth could remember. She watched them, fascinated by their different personalities. You could tell which children were going to grow into mean girls in their teenage years, their hair already perfect and with the hint of eye shadow and lip gloss, their clothes on trend. They carried an air of importance about them and sent the less bolshie girls to do their bidding. There was a chubby boy on the outskirts, clearly wanting to join in the fun but too shy to ask and Ruth felt for him, willing him on.

'Do you ever think about having kids?' Ruth blew on her coffee before taking a tentative sip. She didn't notice Jared stiffen beside her.

'It's complicated for me.'

'But not impossible. Not these days.'

Jared sloshed his hot coffee down his leg as he leapt from the wall. 'Shall we start heading back to the car? It's getting late.'

Ruth checked her watch. It wasn't yet three o'clock but perhaps Jared had plans. 'Good idea. I said I'd meet up with Erin for a quick drink before her date with –'

She stopped herself but pretended it was to take a sip of coffee. 'Before her date. Are you okay? You're looking a bit pale.'

'I'm fine.' Jared offered a smile, but he was far from fine. It was so frustrating. One minute he could feel a sense of contentment and the next he was back to square one, desperation gnawing at his gut.

'Are you sure?' Ruth slipped her arm through Jared's but he inched away. He couldn't act like everything was normal because he doubted it ever would be.

THIRTY

Ruth

My hand automatically went up to my mouth at the top of the staircase, my lungs taking in their last bout of fresh air before I scurried into the office and threw open the windows. The fog dissipated but refused to leave completely. Kelvin had been camping in his office for weeks and there was a permanent staleness to the air now, no matter how wide the windows were wedged or how much air freshener I blasted the rooms with. I now needed regular breaks from my desk, to take a few deep breaths of fresh air before I passed out. It was like working in a teenage boy's sock drawer and I didn't know how much more I could take.

'Ruth? Is that you?'

I braced myself as I made my way towards Kelvin's office, both for the smell as I opened the door and the sight that would greet me. I'd seen more of Kelvin since Susan had given him the boot than I'd wish on my worst enemy and often dreamt about his pale, saggy chest, waking in a cold sweat.

'Yes, Kelvin?' Thankfully he was fully clothed, already sitting behind his desk, his window wide. I expected to be sent out on an errand – perhaps he needed new underpants or a new pack of razors.

Kelvin's gaze dropped to his fingers poised on his keyboard. He spoke briskly and without looking up at me. 'I need you to send flowers to Susan. The biggest bouquet you can.'

'For Susan? Your wife?'

Two patches of purple appeared on Kelvin's cheeks. 'That's what I said, isn't it? Do it now. Send them to the house with a nice note. Make sure it says sorry and that I... well, you know.' He wafted his hand and rolled his eyes.

'Love her?'

'Mmm. Go on then, get on with it. My back can't take that floor anymore.' To demonstrate, he placed a hand on the small of his back and groaned.

I smiled to myself as I retreated from his office. Susan had won the war and so had my nostrils.

I ordered the most expensive flowers and dictated a gushing note before phoning Jared to tell him the good news. I'd found having Jared to gossip with a godsend as Erin was usually too busy planning secret dates with Stuart from Accounts. Things seemed to be going well with the pair and they'd even gone away to Paris for the weekend, yet I was still sworn to secrecy. It was strange to witness my best friend falling in love, no matter how much she protested that they were merely going on the odd date and having amazingly hot sex, and I couldn't help feeling a tinge of jealousy. Not only was Erin blissfully happy, I felt like she was slipping away from me. But still, I had Jared and we were becoming quite close. He'd already told Erin and even Angelina that he was gay so I thought I was imagining our growing bond until he confided in me about Francis, his ex-boyfriend. He hadn't said much as it was obviously still raw and I didn't want to push him, but I was pleased he'd finally let me in when I was beginning to suspect he never would.

It was a glorious summer day, so Jared and I met at the bench in the corner of the car park. It had once been mine and Erin's meeting point, but Jared and I used it more often these days, meeting there most lunchtimes with our sandwiches.

'Good news about Kelvin.'

I nodded as I plonked myself down next to Jared on the bench. 'My lungs are very relieved. We may be able to breathe properly by the end of the week.'

'*If* she takes him back.' Jared took a huge bite of his sandwich, his cheeks bulging as he smiled at my aghast face.

'She has to.' The carrot had been dangled before me. Susan couldn't tease me like this.

Jared patted my knee, his fingers brushing the bare skin where my skirt had ridden up slightly, and I felt a stirring in my gut. A whimper catapulted itself from my chest but I managed to catch it in my throat.

'I'm sure she will. And if not, Kelvin will have to find somewhere more permanent to live. He can't sleep on his office floor forever.'

'Can't he? He's a stubborn bastard and stingy too.' I lifted my face to the sun, closing my eyes against the glare. Perhaps I should have wished for a reconciliation between Kelvin and Susan at the wishing well a few weeks ago instead of wishing to miraculously drop to a size 10 before the reunion.

'Haven't you got your assessment at the gym tonight?' I was grateful when Jared changed the subject. I could worry about Kelvin and his stench when I returned to the office after lunch. 'I bet you're looking forward to seeing the wonderful Courtney.'

I gave a shrug of my shoulders, the shine having started to dim on the gorgeous Courtney. He was still gorgeous of course but I'd become accustomed to his beauty and no longer drooled when he came into view.

'I'm looking forward to seeing how much weight I've lost.' I'd been much more active over the last six weeks, attending the Zumba and yoga classes each week, walking to work and then home again on the non-gym days. Jared and I also met up at the weekend for a stroll in the park or a wander around town (hey, shopping *is* exercise). I loved yoga and Camilla had managed to contort my body into positions I didn't think were possible – if I ever found myself a boyfriend, I would be sure to put them to good use. And, quite surprisingly, I enjoyed the Zumba class too. I was still useless and as co-ordinated as a drunken three-legged donkey with a blindfold, but it was fun and I had a laugh with Jared. I also enjoyed the drink we had in the pub afterwards, even if Jared did mock my (far superior) choice of music. I no longer bothered with the women-only aerobics as Tahlia was beyond annoying and I didn't have Jared there to join in with taking the piss out of her perkiness. Besides, I felt fantastic with the exercise I was doing and was sure the pounds must be falling off.

'Three? *Three pounds*?' I stared at Courtney and then back at the scales before jumping off as though they had scalded the soles of my feet. 'Three pounds in six weeks is... is...' I struggled to find the words to describe the direness of my weight loss. 'It's shit.'

Courtney placed a hand on my arm and gave a small shrug. 'It is coming off. Slowly. Let's review your diet and exercise and see if there's any way we can tweak it to see some more improvement.'

Some more improvement? I needed vast improvement and fast. The reunion was a month away and although my clothes were feeling a little loose, I hadn't even dropped one measly dress size. Drastic action was needed.

Courtney suggested swimming as an all-round exercise and so I started to go to the women-only session on a Sunday afternoon to avoid being ridiculed in my swimming costume. I wasn't the best swimmer but I gave it my best shot, powering my way from one end of the pool to the other until my vision blurred and I started to see stars. By that point I barely had the energy to crawl out of the water and couldn't speak for a good half an hour, but I knew I'd pushed myself as much as possible.

'Doesn't the lack of nearly naked men bother you?' Erin had taken a break from servicing Stuart from Accounts to meet me for a drink in the pub and couldn't understand why I would attend a women-only session at the pool and sacrifice a good ogle. But then she was thin.

'Nobody would fancy me in my swimming costume, so what would be the point?'

Erin gave a tut. 'Stop putting yourself down. You're so pretty and a lovely person too. You're much nicer than I'll ever be.' Her eyes widened and she grasped my hand, suddenly inspired. 'Why don't you come with me to my salsa class? I know you've said no before, but you weren't on this stupid mission back then. Salsa is great exercise and it's a great place to meet sexy men.'

It was true that I had turned down Erin's class in the past, mainly due to my severe lack of co-ordination, but desperation was beginning to claw at me, reminding me on an hourly basis how close the reunion was. I needed all the exercise I could fit into my life so maybe salsa wasn't such a bad idea anymore.

'I could invite Jared too.' He hadn't had a boyfriend since Francis, and that relationship had ended years ago from what I could gather, given that Jared was not prepared to talk about it. With all those wriggling hips and mincing around the dance floor, I was sure salsa would be the perfect place for him to meet a man too.

'You fancy him, don't you?' Erin smirked when I tried to deny it, her eyebrows lifting to her hairline. 'It's okay to fancy him, Ruth. He's gorgeous. But you should be concentrating on men who want to jump you, not borrow your shoes.'

'Jared doesn't wear women's clothes.'

'Whatever. Are you coming with me or not?'

I did go to the class, feeling like an elephant in contrast to the slim women as they shimmied around the dance floor, tossing their hair and running their hands up and down their tiny frames, but I wasn't the only large person attending the class. I was paired with a rotund man named Jeremy who had been dragged to the class by his sister, eager for him to meet a nice girl and settle down. Unfortunately, Jeremy was even clumsier than I was, and I left the class with a black eye, courtesy of his elbow, and a suspected broken toe.

'I'm never going back there.' I slumped on my sofa, a bag of frozen peas pressed to my right eye.

'Why don't you try a different kind of class? I go to

one on a Wednesday evening and it's women only, just like you prefer, and it doesn't involve partners with pointy elbows.'

I studied Erin through my good eye. 'Women only you say?'

So I found myself meeting up with Erin the following Wednesday evening, my right eye still tender but the bruising fading and hidden behind a layer of foundation. We ended up on an industrial estate, making our way towards a small shutter-fronted unit.

'Don't worry, it's much more glam inside,' Erin assured me. I followed Erin into the unit, turning straight back around and heading home again as soon as I spotted the poles.

THIRTY-ONE

Billy

Billy woke feeling suffocated, one of Clare's legs thrown over his thighs, her arm across his chest pinning him to the bed. The sun was already blaring through the curtains despite the early hour, heating the room, which only added to his sense of being smothered. Turning, he tried to ease Clare's body to the other side of the bed but she only clung on tighter. He tried again, pushing a little harder and Clare successfully rolled away. The movement stirred Clare so Billy clamped his eyes shut, pretending he hadn't purposely pushed her away.

'Billy?' She grasped his shoulder and gave him a gentle shake. 'Billy, it's time to get up. You'll miss your train.'

Billy made a show of murmuring before rubbing his eyes and stretching. Clare waited, propped up on her pillows, until Billy had woken fully.

'Sorry to wake you but you don't want to get to the

station too late. You'll hardly have time to see your dad if you get a later train.'

'You're right. Thanks for waking me.' Billy shifted into a sitting position, avoiding Clare's gaze as he knew what was coming next. It was a conversation they'd had plenty of times already.

'Are you sure you don't want me to come with you? It's about time I met your dad.' Billy and Clare had been together for five months now, but Billy still felt it was too soon. 'You've met my parents a few times now.' That was true, even if Billy would have done anything – *anything* – to avoid seeing them. Visiting parents was all a bit scary and serious for Billy's liking. What if they thought he was a prick? He was hardly wonderful boyfriend material, was he? He was floppy haired, a bit scruffy and, let's be honest, a bit of a geek while Clare was none of those things. She deserved somebody better than Billy, somebody better looking and with better prospects. Like that Jared guy Ruth hung around with. He was a proper man, someone who could take care of Clare financially, physically and emotionally.

Billy's fingers clenched into fists on his lap at the thought of Jared and his good looks, sniffing about the place. Billy was surprised Clare hadn't dumped him upon sight of pretty Jared and made a play for him herself.

'You have no problem with Ruth going with you,' Clare pointed out, dropping her lashes, her mouth turning down at the corners.

'That's different. Ruth isn't my girlfriend. She's known my dad almost as long as I have. Our dads used to go to the pub together and we were always in each other's houses as kids.'

'Exactly. *I am* your girlfriend. You should want me to

meet your dad, to be a part of your life.' Clare looked at Billy, her green eyes wide and moist. 'Are you ashamed of me or something?'

'No. Don't be daft. Look at you.' Billy grasped Clare's hand and swept his fingers along her soft, pink cheek. Jesus, look at her. She was beautiful and angelic. Any man would be proud to show off Clare. It was just... Billy didn't know what it was holding him back. 'You're perfect.' He kissed her on the lips and felt Clare's arms wind around his shoulders, pulling him in closer.

'You know, if I came with you, we could go in the car. We wouldn't have to wait around for the train. We wouldn't have to get up just yet.' Clare bit her bottom lip as she lay back down on the pillows, pulling Billy down with her and how could he refuse?

Billy was a nervous wreck for the duration of the journey to Liverpool, his hands and feet jittery and his mind unable to concentrate on anything for more than a few seconds. It was silly to be so nervous and he really had nothing to fear. Clare was perfect and his dad would be so pleased that Billy had a girlfriend, in much the same way Billy had been pleased when Brian met Pearl. The stuffing had been knocked out of Brian when his wife passed away, but Pearl brought him back to life. Billy got on well with his stepmother and was glad his father finally had someone to share his life with again. His dad deserved to be happy and Billy knew it didn't mean he'd forgotten about Patricia or stopped caring.

'They are expecting me, aren't they?' Clare asked as they pulled up outside Brian and Pearl's little terraced house. She cut off the engine and clasped her hands on her lap without removing her seat belt and Billy realised she was nervous too. She was just better at hiding it than him, the first signs only seeping out now.

'I phoned them when you were in the shower.' Billy unclasped his own seat belt and then Clare's. 'Come on, I bet Pearl's got the kettle on already.' He gave Clare's hand a squeeze before they climbed out of the car and made their way to the house. Pearl answered the door, beaming down at them.

'Clare! How lovely to finally meet you. Billy never shuts up about you so I feel like I already know you.' She enveloped Clare in a brief hug before ushering her into the house, shooting Billy a wink. Billy hadn't mentioned any hint of a girl until that morning. 'The kettle's on, so sit down and I'll make us all a nice brew. Your dad's out in his greenhouse as usual but I'll give him a shout. He's looking forward to meeting Clare.' Pearl hesitated on the threshold, watching Clare as though she may have been a figment of her imagination. Then, realising what she was doing, she flashed a smile before darting into the kitchen.

'Is this where you grew up?' Clare glanced around the small but cosy sitting room, photos of a younger Billy framed on the walls.

'No, I grew up in Oldham. Dad moved here with Pearl when they got married. I think there were too many memories back home for Dad. He's more settled here now.'

Clare leant across to kiss Billy's cheek, to offer some little comfort. She couldn't imagine losing a parent, especially so young.

'Hey, I'll have no canoodling on my sofa.' Brian strode into the sitting room, wiping his hands on a tea towel, a grin filling his whole face. 'You must be Clare.' He leant down to peck her on the cheek before settling himself in an armchair. 'It's very strange for Billy to bring a girl to meet his old dad. He usually only brings our Ruth with him.'

'Don't tease the boy, Brian.' Pearl bustled into the room, a tea tray in her hands, which she set down on the coffee table before sitting down in an empty armchair.

'I'm not teasing. Just saying.'

'Well don't.' Pearl shook her head at her husband before turning to Clare, asking her a million questions and listening intently to the answers. Billy learned more about Clare over his cup of coffee and a plate of Jammy Dodgers than he had during their five months together.

'I've got a lovely piece of beef in the oven for lunch,' Pearl said after draining her cup of tea. She bit her lip. 'You're not vegetarian, are you?'

'No, I'm not vegetarian.'

'Good. It's all a load of nonsense if you ask me. I'll just go and check on the potatoes.' Pearl heaved herself out of the armchair and disappeared into the kitchen.

'Speaking of nonsense, how's Ruth getting on with those silly diets of hers?' Brian asked Billy. 'Still eating cabbage, is she?'

'She's not doing the diets any more. Not the daft ones anyway. She's trying to eat more healthily and cut down, and she's been going to the gym a lot. She's doing really well, isn't she, Clare?' Clare nodded and was about to say something, but Billy hadn't finished. 'She's looking really well too. She's got a bit of a glow now and you can tell she's happier than she has been in a long time.'

'Good, I'm glad. She's a lovely girl, our Ruth. Is she courting?'

Billy shook his head. 'Not that I know of.'

'What about Jared? They're always together and she

never shuts up about him.'

Billy gave Clare a funny look. 'Jared's gay. Ruth said so.' And it had been a relief to hear it.

Clare gave a hoot. 'You've got to be kidding. Haven't you seen the way he looks at her?' No, Billy hadn't noticed anything peculiar about the way Jared looked at Ruth. 'He's smitten. And I'd say she is too.'

'Don't be daft.' Billy began to roll his eyes but paused midway. What if Jared wasn't gay? He did spend an awful lot of time with Ruth. Perhaps he saw her as more than just a friend. Did Ruth realise? Billy wasn't sure but he wasn't about to go sticking his beak in, just in case Clare had got the wrong end of the stick.

'You young ones don't half complicate things,' Brian said with a shake of his head. In his day, if you liked a girl you let her know. You didn't go around pretending to bat for the other side or shove your feelings away and out of sight.

Pearl poked her head around the door. 'Lunch will be ready in a couple of minutes. Do you want to come through?'

The four squeezed around the small round table in the kitchen, the plates in front of them piled with beef and the potatoes and vegetables from Brian's greenhouse, all smothered in thick gravy. Billy's dad had survived on microwave meals, Pot Noodles and the odd portion of fish and chips before he met Pearl. He'd attempted to cook when Billy was younger but, with Brian having to work long hours to provide for them, Billy spent most of his time at the Lynch household where he was fed food that hadn't been reduced to lumps of charcoal.

'This is grand, love,' Brian said, tucking in with gusto.

'Yeah, it's lovely.' Billy matched his father's

enthusiasm. He may have had a weedy frame, but he could put away food like the rest of them. When he was little, his mother used to joke that his food was stored down in his toes to make room for more.

'There's plenty of beef left. You'll have to take some home with you. Ruth loves my beef sandwiches. She's not still on those silly diets, is she?'

'Nope but she's been spending her time at the gym,' Brian answered.

'The gym, eh? Has she got her eye on a fella then?' Pearl giggled. 'It's about time the girl found herself someone decent. Wish her luck from me, won't you, Billy?'

'I don't think she's got her eye on anybody specific.'

Clare immediately thought of Jared but she kept quiet this time. Billy didn't want to believe Ruth fancied Jared and Clare was afraid to push him, afraid it would open up a Pandora's box of trouble.

```
To: s.lynch
From: billy.worth
Subject: Meet The Parents

I finally did it. I introduced Clare
to Dad and Pearl. It went well. I
think.
```

```
To: billy.worth
From: s.lynch
Subject: Re: Meet The Parents

Good on you. It'll be me meeting her
next. Only a few more weeks until I'll
be home for the reunion. I'll be able
to show Clare where all the
```

embarrassing stories I have up my
sleeve took place. I think I'll start
with you being caught behind the stage
curtains with your hand up Lisa
Piper's blouse…

To: s.lynch
From: billy.worth
Subject: Re: Re: Meet The Parents

You're only jealous because you
fancied Lisa Piper as well.

Anyway, Clare isn't coming to the
reunion. I only have one ticket and I
think it's too late to buy another.

THIRTY-TWO

Ruth

The room began to empty, towels flipped over shoulders, mats rolled up and tucked under arms, chatter and laughter fading as I was left on my own, slumped on my mat, too weak to open my eyes, let alone drag myself to my feet. They wouldn't have kept me up anyway, my body too exhausted by the exercise programme I'd devised for myself over the past few weeks. In desperation and with time stampeding away, I'd made a last-ditch attempt to lose weight, packing my days with classes and time in the women's gym. I'd tried everything from Legs, Bums and Tums, Total Tone, and step classes to aqua aerobics with the irritating Tahlia and I even returned for a tortuous spinning class. So desperate was I to shed a few more pounds, I'd even taken to using the pool during general hours, swimming for an hour each morning before work. Luckily it was usually just me and Jared and a couple of hard core fitness freaks, who were more interested in their breathing techniques than my fat arse squeezed into a swimming costume. And speaking of mortification, I'd also taken part in a street dance class with Courtney. My cheeks burned remembering my flailing arms and legs moving to a different rhythm to everybody else, even now, as I slumped on the floor, unable to coerce my muscles into attempting to work.

The lights were switched off as I lay on my mat but I didn't care. I'd sleep on the floor and resume my crazy exercise regime in the morning. I'd swim with Jared first thing, fit in half an hour on the treadmill if there was time and dash back over at lunchtime. After work I'd use the women's gym, pushing myself until I could no longer blink, before Jared dropped me off at home. And then I'd sneak back for a class on my own in the evening. Jared didn't know I took an extra class in the evenings as he was concerned I was pushing myself too much already. And he was probably right. Everywhere ached from the moment I opened my eyes in the morning until I collapsed on the bed at night, grateful for rest at last. But then my dreams were plagued by dumbbells and spinning bikes and horrific dance classes and my mind ached along with my body. The only thing keeping me going was the thought of Zack's mocking face when I turned up at the reunion still fat. I couldn't. I had to keep going, to lose the weight, *any* weight. I no longer had The Dress as motivation and the grief I'd felt as I'd passed the boutique's window and found a different dress on the mannequin was still with me.

I'd flown into the boutique that day, the first time I had dared to cross the threshold. It was a tiny shop with only a couple of rails of clothing, another mannequin beside a blue curtained changing room and a cash register squeezed into the corner. The owner noticed me straight away – how could she miss the woman who was taking up her entire shop? She was pencil thin with shiny auburn hair and dark eyes that narrowed when she saw me.

'Can I help you?' Her voice was incredulous. How could *she* help *me*? I thought she was about to start wafting her hands, shooing me out of her shop, reserving her precious space for the thin and beautiful.

'You had a dress in the window. A pink one with beading but it's not there any more.'

The owner flicked her head, more of a tic than a nod. 'It was sold this afternoon.'

It was as I feared and I felt my stomach – along with all my hopes and dreams – plummet to the tiled floor. 'Do you have another?'

The owner pursed her lips, deciding whether it was worth explaining or if it was easier and kinder all round if she simply ejected me from her shop. 'I create one-off garments.' She looked me up and down, thinking it wouldn't have fit me anyway. And she was right – it wouldn't have, but while it was in the window, the dream was still burning inside, urging me on. 'Besides, I don't think my designs fit in with your style, do they?' She attempted a smile but couldn't stop it turning into a sneer as she strode towards the door, opening it as wide as possible to allow me to thump my way back out into the street.

So The Dress was gone and for a few minutes so was my motivation. What was the point? Who was I kidding? I was never going to be thin enough to change Zack's opinion of me. I imagined the disgust pass across his face as I stepped into the room, followed by sneering and the jibes of old. He wouldn't be taken aback and ashamed of his actions. He'd probably still think it was funny.

And that's when the anger began to build up, a tight ball in the pit of my stomach spreading its branches throughout my body, taking hold of my muscles and forcing them into action. I wouldn't let him win. I wouldn't. He'd reduced me to nothing but a blubbering wreck the last time I saw him but he wouldn't do that to me again. I was better than that. I was better than Zack.

I turned away from the boutique, feeling the owner's eyes on me as I began to walk away. The anger inside stretched and I felt my pace picking up, my breath becoming haggard as my legs powered their way home. My chest and the back of my throat burned, but still on I went, faster and faster until somewhere along the way I began to jog. On and on I jogged, my body working on autopilot as my mind wondered what the fuck my legs thought they were up to. I reached Oak Road and instead of slowing down, my feet were spurred on and I found myself running, actually running, every part of my body screaming for mercy yet refusing to give up. I barrelled into the front door, my legs working quicker than my fumbling fingers as they attempted to slot my key into the door. Stumbling into the hallway, I collapsed on the bottom step, head hung low as I took in sharp breath after sharp breath, fighting the urge to throw up all over the hallway carpet.

I'd done it. I'd pushed myself more than I ever thought possible and, though I felt like shit at that moment, I'd survived. The nausea and exhaustion subsided, making way for euphoria. I'd survived! I could do this. I could push myself more and more. I could lose the weight. Perhaps not as much as I'd originally planned but I could lose *something*. I could feel good about myself as I walked into that reunion, head held high, mocking faces passing me by unnoticed.

And that's when the crazy schedule began.

'Oh, I'm so sorry. I didn't see you there.' The Pilates instructor flicked the lights on and wandered back into the room. 'Are you okay?' She towered above me as I lay slumped on my mat, willing my body to move. I'd assumed Pilates would be similar to yoga, which was by far my favourite class at the gym, but I was wrong. Pilates was an exercise plan devised by Lucifer himself and I didn't think my stomach muscles would ever stop hurting.

'It's Ruth, isn't it?' The instructor dropped to her knees and I managed a nod. 'Do you need a hand?'

The humiliation of being yanked to my feet by the instructor, who probably thought I was too fat and lazy to stand up, was enough to release the reserves of energy I'd secretly stored up and I inched myself up onto my hands and knees, eventually rising to my feet.

'I'm okay. Thank you.'

The instructor cocked her head to one side. 'You look exhausted.'

Did I? That's funny because I felt exhausted too. My body was utterly spent. But more than that, I was devastated. I'd worked so hard over the past few weeks since the disappearance of The Dress and it hadn't been good enough. The reunion was just over a week away and I'd only managed to drop one dress size. I should have been celebrating my triumph, but it was nowhere near enough. I'd failed miserably, despite my efforts. I thought back over all those diets, the salads and the cabbage soup, and the humiliation of wearing a swimming costume in public for the first time since I was a teenager. Had it all been worth it?

With my eyes to the ground, I left the gym and wandered to the bus stop. I usually walked home from my secret sessions at the gym to snatch a few more minutes of exercise, but that day I felt too dejected. I didn't notice the streets passing me by as I sat on the stuffy bus but rose automatically at my stop and shuffled my way home.

'What's up with your face? You look even more miserable than usual.' Theo and Billy were playing on the Playstation in the sitting room, and Theo looked taken aback when I refused to respond and instead flopped onto the sofa, still wearing my gym clothes. 'Jesus, it must be bad. I'll fuck off upstairs so you two can chat.' Theo raced out of the sitting room, his feet thundering on the stairs while Billy turned off the console and sat beside me.

'I haven't showered,' I warned him as he wrapped his arms around me.

'Do you think I care about that? Come here.'

It felt good to be wrapped in Billy's arms. It felt safe and being fat didn't matter for the moment. I'd known Billy forever and we'd been through a lot together. I'd only been eight when his mum died, but even then I'd felt his pain and wished I could take it away. I'd known Patricia was really ill because we weren't allowed to go over to Billy's house to play any more and when we were playing out at the front we had to keep the noise down as Patricia was resting. But I didn't know she was going to die. Death was for old people and hamsters, not mums of ten-year-old boys. But she did die, and our house was filled with a strange atmosphere that day. Mum's eyes were red and swollen, though she tried to hide it and was overly jolly, making us bacon sandwiches for breakfast. I remember the clump of bread lodging in my throat as she told us about Patricia, telling us we had to be extremely kind to Billy because he would be very upset. I was confused and afraid. Would *my* mum die too? I followed her around the house until it was time to go to school and I clung to her at the gates, crying because I didn't want her to leave me like Billy's mum had left him.

Billy wasn't at school and he didn't come to our house at home time. I'd grown accustomed to him being there for tea over the past few months, thinking it was fun to have him around all the time and not realising it was because Patricia was too ill to take care of him any more. So while Billy's dad was at work, Billy came round to our house but he wasn't there that day.

'He's gone to say goodbye to his mummy,' Mum explained and my little brow furrowed.

'So she's not dead yet then?'

Mum had dropped to her knees and pulled me into a hug. I thought it was Mum comforting me until I felt her shoulders shaking and I wrapped my little arms around her and held her as tightly as I could, like she did when I was upset. Mum didn't explain about the saying goodbye thing but I knew Patricia must have been dead because why else would she be crying?

It was late when Billy turned up. I was already in bed but I crept out onto the landing when I heard the knock at the door. Billy and his dad were in the hallway talking to Mum.

'He wanted to come over and see Stephen. I told him it's late but...'

'No, no it's fine. Go through to the sitting room and I'll go and get him.' Mum had smiled down at Billy, stroking his curly hair with the palm of her hand. When she turned to climb the stairs, there were tears already streaming down her cheeks.

Mum didn't say anything as I passed her on the stairs, tiptoeing into the sitting room in my pyjamas, my favourite teddy tucked under my arm. Billy was sitting in Dad's chair, stiff and staring at the wallpaper on the opposite wall, while Dad and Brian went into the kitchen for a slug of whiskey.

'Hi, Billy.' I crept towards the chair, hesitating before climbing up onto his lap. Billy looked different, his eyes hollow and swollen, the skin around his lips pink. 'Are you alright?'

Billy nodded and smiled but his lips wobbled and a tear fell onto his cheek.

'Me and Stephen will look after you. I promise.' I kissed Billy on the cheek and wrapped my arms around him, resting my head on his chest.

Not that I'd been much good at looking after Billy. It had always been the other way round, even before I turned up on his doorstep, heartbroken over Zack. He'd looked out for me at school, helped me with my homework and acted as a go-between whenever Stephen and I fell out. I was a grown woman now and he was still looking after me.

'What's wrong, Ruth?'

I wiped my eyes but found I was too exhausted to even cry. 'Everything. Look at me.'

'Well, you're a bit sweaty but other than that you look fine.' Billy smiled at me and I tried to join in, but I couldn't.

'The reunion is next Saturday and I'm still fat. I wanted to be thin and gorgeous by the time we went.' I laughed at my foolishness but my still tight chest repelled the action and turned it into a coughing fit.

'Ruth.' Billy's tone was hard and when I looked at him, his jaw was set, his brown eyes focused on mine. 'When are you going to realise you *are* gorgeous? You don't need to lose weight for some prick you haven't seen in years. You're perfect the way you are.'

I smiled at Billy, still taking care of me and trying to make me feel better about myself despite my obvious flaws. I didn't know what I'd do without him.

'Thank you, Billy.'

'I mean it, Ruth.' He kissed me on the cheek, as I had done when we were kids and he'd been hurting, and for one crazy moment I imagined turning my head and kissing him on the lips. I'd never thought about kissing Billy in any way other than as an act of friendship but found myself wondering what it would feel like to kiss Billy, to feel his arms around me in a non-comforting capacity. The thought shocked me and I shook it from my head, angling my body away from Billy's as I reached for the remote.

'Shall we watch last week's *Beginner's Guide*?' I'd been so busy at the gym I'd neglected our weekly ritual.

'Yeah. Let's watch it.'

I put the show on but I didn't really pay any attention to it, my mind still on the reunion. I had a matter of days to go and while I couldn't lose the weight I'd planned in such a short space of time, I could give it my all.

It was time for Plan C.

THIRTY-THREE

Jared

Jared's eyes flickered open but he shut them again quickly, squeezing his lids down as tightly as he could, willing sleep to consume him again. If he was quick, he might be able to get back to his dream and feel more alive than he had in years. It was a familiar dream yet he hadn't had it for over a year. In it, Frances came back to him, apologising and crying and vowing never to leave him again and pleading for his forgiveness. But forgiveness was not in question. Jared pulled Frances into his arms, his lungs filling fully with air, something they hadn't done since she'd gone. The air was fresh and sweet and cleared his head and heart.

'Don't cry, baby. Don't cry.' His fingers swept over Frances's face, cleansing her cheeks of the salty tears. 'You're back. That's all that matters.'

'I am so sorry I left you, Jared. So very sorry.'

Jared smiled as he brought his lips to Frances's

forehead. He'd missed the feel of her soft skin and the smell of her hair. 'Stop saying sorry. It's done now. We'll forget the past five years ever happened. I love you, Frances.' He took her face in his hands and she smiled then, relieved both that she was back with Jared and that he didn't hate her. Frances had never looked so beautiful.

'I love you too, Jared. I'll never leave you again. I promise.' And Jared believed her. He knew Frances and she would never lie to him about something so important. 'I've brought somebody to meet you. A very special little boy who wants more than anything to meet his daddy.'

Jared had never met his son. He'd seen his boy squirm about on the monitor during the scans and he'd felt him kick and stretch from within the womb, but he'd never seen his son in the flesh. Frances was eight months pregnant the last time he'd seen her, Barney still tucked up inside her, just weeks away from giving birth, and so he had no idea what Barney looked or sounded like.

'Barney, come here, darling.' Frances reached out a hand and the boy shuffled forward, two fingers posted between his lips in a nervous gesture. Barney wasn't the tiny, helpless baby Jared expected to see the first time he met his son but it didn't matter. The boy was only five but tall for his age with white blond hair and bright blue eyes, a dimple in his left cheek as he gave a faltering smile. He was beautiful. Utterly beautiful and Jared heard himself gasp behind the hand covering his mouth.

'Barney? It's me, daddy.'

The boy smiled then, the dimple deepening, his eyes shining brighter as he ran towards Jared, his arms pummelling at his sides in his eagerness for speed.

'Daddy!'

And then, cruelly, Jared woke without his son ever reaching him and no matter how much he willed sleep to envelop him and whisk him away to his perfect dream, he couldn't drift off again and he was forced to face the agony of another day without his son.

One day, Jared thought as he wrenched the covers from his body. *One day he'll run to me and he'll reach me, and I'll never let him go.* He dragged his feet out of bed and pulled himself up before wandering to the bathroom. He used to have this dream every night in the beginning, meeting his son for the first time night after night. Barney was a baby in Frances's arms, growing up as the dreams became less frequent. Barney had been a toddler the last time Jared had seen him and now look at him! He'd have started school by now and have his own little friends, his own personality and preferences. Jared began to wonder about his favourite foods and cartoons but shook the idea from his head. It was no use thinking about that kind of thing. He'd learned to keep those things at bay, but the return of the dream had knocked him off kilter. Try as he might to keep thoughts of Barney at the very back of his mind, Jared couldn't resist plucking the framed photo of Frances from the mantelpiece, the twenty-week scan photo tucked into the corner. It was the only image he had of his son and he ran a finger over the grainy grey face. They were supposed to be married by now, a happy little family. Perhaps they would have had another baby, a girl with Frances's curly brown hair and eyes like melted chocolate. They would have had to move from their little house, would have moved to somewhere bigger with a large garden for Barney and his little sister to run around in. Their days would be filled with fun and laughter, every day like Christmas. Jared's mother would dote on her grandchildren because he knew, despite her putting on a brave face, that she was as gutted as he was at missing out on her cherished grandson's life, unable to watch him grow from a playful little boy to a charming young man. She was a grandmother but she didn't get to play the role.

Jared placed the frame carefully back into place with a heavy heart. Perhaps his family were right. Perhaps it was time he moved on, as scary as that thought may be. He couldn't keep living in the past, wishing for something that was never going to happen. As difficult as it sounded, Jared had to let go and try to live his life.

Jared checked the time and shot one last look at the photo before he rushed out of the flat. He was supposed to be meeting Ruth and now he was running late. The thought of seeing her lifted him from the slump the dream had created, and it made him wonder if it was possible to find someone new. His mum and sisters had been trying to get him to date in vain because he could never even contemplate the idea, but that was before he met Ruth. A few months ago he would never have considered putting himself through potential heartache again, but maybe Ruth was worth the risk.

'I didn't think you were coming.' Ruth was already in the pool when he arrived for their early morning swim but she swam to the side when she spotted Jared approaching. It was just after seven-thirty but that didn't stop Ruth. Her determination had been boundless recently and Jared suspected she would camp out at the gym if she were permitted to.

'Sorry. I slept in.' Jared slipped into the cool water

and together they set off towards the opposite end of the pool. Jared had slowed down his pace so Ruth could keep up with him when they first started using the pool together, but now she met him stroke for stroke and even beat him to the wall before turning and setting off for the opposite wall. He found her efforts truly amazing and inspiring, even if he thought they were for the wrong reasons.

They dried off after their swim and met for a juice in the gym's bar before they had to head across to work. Jared had taken his time in the shower, thinking about Frances and Ruth and his future. His life wasn't as bleak with Ruth in it, so wasn't it foolish to ignore his growing feelings? Ruth had told him on quite a few occasions that he wasn't her type, but there were times he doubted her words. He'd catch her watching him out of the corner of his eye and she often caught her breath ever so slightly when he touched her. He'd thought he was imagining it to begin with, projecting his own feelings onto her, but he was sure she felt the same way.

Ruth was already sitting in the small bar, two banana and raspberry smoothies in front of her, and he felt an ache in his chest as she glanced up and a smile spread across her face. He decided then that she was worth the risk. It scared him and his pulse raced as he neared her table and his head felt light and fuzzy, but he was going to do it.

'Are you okay? You look a bit... funny.'

'I'm fine.' He attempted a smile as he reached for his drink, but the smoothie was too thick for his dry mouth and it took a Herculean effort to swallow it. 'I was just wondering if you fancied going out tonight after work. We could go and watch a film. Get something to eat after.'

There. He'd done it. He'd asked her out on an actual date.

Ruth wrinkled her nose and Jared felt the euphoria flush out of his body before dumping itself at his feet. 'I'd love to, really I would, but I can't. You remember Clare, Billy's girlfriend? It's her birthday and she's having a party and Billy's asked me to go.' She pulled a face. 'I don't really want to. I don't think Clare likes me very much, but I couldn't say no to Billy.' She took a sip of her drink through her straw and her eyes lit up. 'Why don't you come? I'm dragging Erin along for moral support as well. It'll be a laugh.'

Jared doubted he would be laughing any time soon. He'd put himself 'out there' for the first time in years and had been knocked back. It would take him a little while to lick his wounds.

'It's not really my thing. Sorry.'

Ruth gave a little shrug. 'Don't be sorry. I'm only going for Billy's sake.' She checked the time and drained her drink. 'Shall we get going?'

Jared nodded, leaving his drink barely touched. He was looking forward to the sanctuary of his office and his plan to lock himself in to ward off Angelina. 'Are you okay?' He reached out for Ruth as she staggered back, clutching her temple.

'Yes, I think so. Just got a bit of a headache.'

'You've been pushing yourself too hard.' Jared took Ruth's arm to steady her as they left the bar and headed through reception. It felt good to be almost holding her.

THIRTY-FOUR

Ruth

When I started my very first diet, I tried to distract myself from the hunger pains by imagining what it would feel like to be thin. The clothes I would wear. The appreciative glances I would receive when I stepped into a bar. I'd carry myself with a confidence that I would no longer have to fake and there would be a glow from within that shone through for all to see. I'd still be me but a better version. I should have felt ecstatic as I slipped the dress over my head and found it hanging off my frame, a size too big. But when I looked in the mirror, I didn't see the weight loss. I saw the excess weight still there, the multiple chins wobbling away. I wasn't glowing, not even a little bit. I wasn't *thin*. Plan C had come along too late and now there were mere days left before I had to face Zack and co.

My dress was a one-shouldered fuchsia tunic dress that now hung from my body like I was wearing a sack, so I added a contrasting aqua belt to cinch it in at the waist. The effect wasn't bad and certainly an improvement, so I moved on to my make-up, caking it on to paper over the cracks. Glittery eye shadow, thick, dramatic lashes, rosy cheeks and a flash of red lipstick, fiery and confident. A mask to portray the person I wanted to be. I tousled my short blonde curls and added a giant daisy clip to one side. There. I was as good as I was ever going to be.

The shower was still going as I left my bedroom so I went downstairs to wait for Billy and Theo, pouring myself a large glass of wine in the kitchen. I could have done with something a bit stronger to get me through the evening, to blank out the iciness Clare had been secreting towards me more and more. I had obviously offended her in some way but I couldn't see how and Billy assured me I was imagining it all.

'What's that smell?' Billy paused in the doorway of the kitchen, his wrinkled nose giving a tentative sniff. 'Are you back on that stupid Cabbage Soup Diet?'

'I'm not on any diet.' It was too late for that and I wasn't sure even starvation would work now. 'The reunion's on Saturday.'

'There's no need to look so glum about it.' Billy, against his better judgement, stepped into the room, trying his best to breathe only through his mouth. 'You'll have me and Stephen to keep you company, and Aubrey will have so many baby photos to show you, Zack won't get a look in.' Billy put a hand on my bare shoulder and gave it a squeeze. 'And who gives a fuck what this Zack thinks anyway?'

I did. I gave a very big fuck what he thought.

'You're right.' I drained my glass, ignoring the dull throbbing in my head. 'Shall we get going?'

'Theo's still faffing with his hair. He could be a while.' Billy grabbed another glass and filled it with wine, refilling mine too. 'I think he's borrowed your straighteners.'

'What?' I leapt up from my seat at the table, wincing as pain crackled across my skull. Stressing about the reunion and Clare's party had brought on a headache and the sudden movement intensified it. I knew thundering up the stairs would only cause me more pain and was it really worth it? As long as he returned the straighteners – and promised never to enter my bedroom without permission again – it didn't really matter.

We finished our wine, hurrying Theo along between sips and eventually we were able to leave the house. The party was being held at our local and Clare had done a great job of transforming the slightly shabby pub into a pink, glittery palace with balloons and banners. A DJ had been set up in one corner and the bar had been hijacked by Clare's cocktail menu, which the barman was trying his best to follow.

'There you are. I didn't think you were coming.' Clare swept towards us in a glamorous floor-length gold-sequined dress and threw her arms around Billy.

'We had to wait for Theo. You know what he's like with his beauty regime.'

'Never mind. You're here now.' Clare lifted herself onto her tiptoes to kiss Billy on the cheek, leaving a bronze smear behind. 'Come and say hello to Mum and Dad.' She tugged at Billy's hand but I stopped her before she could disappear and handed over the gift bag and card I'd brought along.

'Happy birthday. This is from me and Theo.' Only because Theo had 'forgotten' to buy either a gift or a card.

'Thank you, Ruth.' Clare flashed a smile that I'd have missed if I hadn't been paying close attention. 'Come on, Billy. Mum and Dad are waiting.'

The pub was full to the brim but the only people I knew were Billy, Theo and Clare, and they were all busy either chatting to parents or pretty girls. I ordered a mojito, ignoring the pounding in my head, and sipped it at the bar, watching everyone having a fabulous time. Relief washed over me when Erin arrived looking magnificent in the shortest dress I have seen on a non-street walker. She kissed me hello before ordering a cocktail, chatting up the barman as he fumbled with the ingredients. Patrons of The Grey Horse never required cocktails, so he was a beginner and didn't know his margaritas from his daiquiris.

'Bless him.' Erin took a sip of her Singapore sling as we left the bar, the poor barman now on his hands and knees as he swept up the shards of broken glass behind the bar, a casualty of his lacklustre Tom Cruise impression. 'Let's find a seat. My feet are killing me in these heels.'

'That's because they're about nine inches.'

Erin gave a shrug. Aching feet were a sacrifice she was willing to make to look so fabulous.

We'd been at the party for over an hour and I had yet to see Billy since Clare whisked him away. Theo was busy floating from girl to girl, collecting phone numbers and the odd sneaky kiss before moving on.

'Doesn't Clare know any fit men?' Erin scanned the room but gave a dissatisfied tut upon finding nobody of interest.

'What happened to Stuart from Accounts?'

'We're not married, and you know me. I don't do serious.' She tipped the last drop of her cocktail into her mouth and licked her lips. 'And we've had a bit of a tiff. Another?'

'Yes please.' My head was still hurting but the alcohol was dulling the pain.

Erin rose from her seat and earned quite a number of appreciative glances as she tottered to the bar. Her dress was riding further up her thighs with each step but she either didn't notice or didn't care.

'You're Ruth, aren't you?' My head turned from Erin's exposed thighs as a body seated itself next to me. I vaguely recognised the girl but didn't think we'd ever had a conversation or been introduced. 'I'm Becki, Clare's best friend.'

'Hi.' I smiled but the gesture wasn't returned. Feeling uncomfortable, I turned back towards Erin and was alarmed to see her being chatted up by Theo. He was leaning against the bar as the barmaid made up his drink and I watched on in horror as he reached out to Erin, tucking a strand of hair behind her ear.

'Oh God.' I turned to Becki. 'Would you excuse me? I need to go and rescue my friend from a letch.'

Becki sneered at me and I shuffled backwards in my seat as she bared her teeth at me. 'You can't help interfering with other people's relationships, can you? Why don't you get a boyfriend of your own, you sad, fat cow?'

I felt like I'd been punched in the stomach, winded by her words. Confusion, hurt and anger soured in my veins as I stared at her, still sneering at me just inches away. I wanted to slap her and demand to know what I had done to deserve such nastiness. I didn't even know the woman! But I also wanted to slink away and hide, to protect myself from her poison. I felt small and humiliated and was back to being the fat kid nobody liked. The anger stepped up a gear then, surging up through my body, the force of it causing my body to shake. I hadn't deserved to be mocked and ridiculed when I was a child, and I didn't deserve it now.

'What is your problem? Do you think you're better than me because you're a size 10? Do you think I'm a lesser person because I'm fat? Because I'm not. I'm a human being, just like you. I'm not a freak and I have feelings. You have no right to sit there and call me names just because you feel like it.'

'Is there a problem?' I was still shaking as I looked up and saw Billy, here to rescue me yet again.

'Oh, look. Here's your knight in shining armour.' Becki's top lip lifted into a snarl as she rose from her seat, glaring first at me and then Billy.

'What the hell is her problem?' Billy sat next to me as Becki sauntered away, throwing us one last dirty look before she disappeared into the crowd.

'I have no idea.' I shoved my hands under the table so Billy couldn't see them trembling. 'But she's gone now so let's forget about it.' But though I tried to shove Becki to the back of my mind, her words echoed through my mind. *Fat cow. Fat cow. Fat cow.*

'Do you want a drink?'

'No thanks. Erin's getting me one.' I glanced back at the bar where Erin was now holding our drinks but was stood still, laughing at something Theo was saying. He had his phone in his hand and was tapping away. Oh, God. Not Erin too. Of all the women in the world, Erin was the last I'd expect to fall for Theo's phony charm.

'Billy!' Clare strode towards us, her dress swishing with each step. 'There you are. Come and dance with me.'

Billy groaned beside me. 'You know I don't dance.'

'But it's my *birthday*.' Clare stopped in front of Billy, her hands on her hips and a pout on her lips. 'Please? Just one dance.'

Billy looked pained as he rose to his feet and allowed Clare to lead him towards the DJ and the makeshift dance floor. Left alone, my eyes scanned the room for Becki but I was relieved when I spotted Erin making her way back to our table.

'He'd be quite cute if he wasn't so arrogant.' She placed the drinks on the table and sat down, seeking out Theo in the crowd to wiggle her fingers in a wave.

'You think Theo's cute?'

Erin lifted her shoulders a fraction. 'I've seen worse. I've *slept* with worse.'

'But you wouldn't sleep with Theo, right?'

Erin ignored my question, taking a long sip of her drink instead before changing the subject. My hands eventually stopped shaking as we chatted and laughed. The *fat cow* echo subsided and I began to relax again but the moment was ruined as Erin's phoned beeped into life. A smile spread across her face as she read the text before slipping her phone back into her handbag. She was already on her feet and draining her latest cocktail.

'Would you mind if I left a bit early? Like now?'

'Was that a booty call?' My voice was laced with jealousy. I'd never been summoned for sex in my life. The closest I'd got was one time when Gideon turned up at the house at two o'clock in the morning, pissed and horny but it turned out he was too inebriated to do anything about it.

'Maybe.' Erin grinned down at me. 'You don't mind,

do you?'

I shook my head. What else could I do? 'Of course not. Have a great time.'

'Thanks, Ruth. You're a star.' She stooped to plant a noisy kiss on my cheek. 'We'll meet for lunch tomorrow, yeah?'

I felt small and awkward as Erin sashayed out of the pub, hammering a reply into her phone, and my headache returned with a vengeance. I searched the pub for either Billy or Theo, but Billy was nowhere in sight and Theo was sauntering after Erin, winking at the barmaid before strolling out of the pub. I stayed for another drink, but my headache increased with each sip so in the end I sent Billy a text to let him know I was going home, citing work in the morning as my excuse.

I didn't expect Billy to come home that evening, with Clare's house being slightly closer to the pub than ours, but shortly after midnight the front door opened followed by drunken tiptoeing on the stairs. I knew it wasn't Theo as his bed springs had been having a workout since I'd returned home myself. I was pretending it wasn't Erin in there, howling and grunting away, as I'd never be able to look her in the eye again. If I was honest, I'd lost a bit of respect for her. She knew what Theo was like – she was exactly the same herself and I thought they cancelled each other out. At least neither of them would spend the next few days wandering around like a love sick puppy while they waited for a phone call, so I suppose there was some good in the situation.

I just wished I didn't have to listen to it.

I hadn't been able to sleep – and not just because of the rutting couple across the hall. My headache had doubled its efforts and worrying about the reunion didn't help. Becki's words had returned, belittling me from within my own head. *Fat cow. Fat cow. Fat cow.* It's what everyone would be thinking as I waddled into the school hall and I only hoped they wouldn't openly ridicule me like they did when we were kids.

How had it come to this? Six months ago I was happy. I had a boyfriend (even if it was Gideon) and I wasn't obsessed with my weight and food and exercise. People's opinions of me didn't matter so much back then, but now I was paranoid, convinced everyone was thinking how disgusting I was, an abomination of the human race. A blimp. *A fat cow.*

The pain in my head was unbearable, a constant thudding that made me clench my fists and grit my teeth against it. Pulling myself out of bed and covering my ears to block out Erin's crescendo howling, I'd made my way downstairs to the kitchen and poured myself a glass of water, gulping down paracetamol and praying they'd act fast. I couldn't face returning to the racket upstairs, so I sat in the kitchen, fighting against the ache in my chest, but it was no use and I began to weep, truly feeling sorry for myself. How could I go to the reunion like this? Fat and single – just as I'd been ten years ago. I was so caught up in my private pity party that I didn't hear the footsteps on the stairs again and it was too late to wipe away the tears as Billy stepped into the kitchen.

'Hey. What's the matter?' Billy rushed forward and knelt in front of me, his brow furrowed and his eyes doleful as he looked up at me.

'I've tried everything, Billy.' I crossed the kitchen to grab a sheet of kitchen roll before sitting back down and blowing my nose. 'Diet, exercise and now these useless diet pills.' I took the bottle out of my dressing gown pocket and dumped it on the table.

'You've been taking diet pills?' Billy picked up the bottle, examining its label.

'Yes, but they haven't worked.' I wasn't expecting miracles. I'd bought the pills on the internet weeks ago but had decided to go ahead with Plan C way too late, but I was expecting something other than the stomach cramps, insomnia, headaches and gas.

'It doesn't even have a list of ingredients.' Billy thrust the bottle at me, his eyes no longer doleful but burning with rage. 'You could have been taking anything. Promise me you won't take any more.'

'I won't.' There wasn't any point. It was too late.

'Is this the only bottle?' Billy asked as he unscrewed the top and tipped them down the sink. 'You haven't got any stashed away anywhere?'

'Stashed away?' I managed a small laugh, which was a triumph under the circumstances. 'I'm not a drug addict or an alcoholic.'

'Do you realise how dangerous diet pills can be?' Billy twisted around to face me so fast he was in danger of snapping his neck. And he was lecturing me about dangerous activities?

'Yes. I know. But I won't be taking them again.'

'Good.' Billy pulled a chair close to mine and sat in front of me, taking my hands in his. 'We've known each other a long time. I care about you. You know that, don't you?'

'I care about you too.' We smiled at each other then and I actually started to feel a little better.

'I'll always look after you, Ruth. Always.' Billy reached up to wipe away a stray tear that lingered on my cheek and I felt myself leaning into his touch. I didn't know what I would do without Billy, how I would have survived the past ten years without the support and laughter. He was like my best friend but more, much more, in a way I couldn't put into words.

'Thank you, Billy. That means a lot.'

Billy's hand was still resting on my cheek and the anger had vanished from his eyes and was replaced with something I didn't recognise. Neither of us spoke as we sat in the kitchen, fingers entwined, one of Billy's hands on my cheek and it should have felt uncomfortable to be so close, but it didn't. It felt natural, as though we were supposed to be touching and our bodies had been waiting for years for this contact.

'Ruth.' Billy's voice was strange in the quiet that I had become accustomed to, familiar yet intrusive. He opened his mouth to continue, but a crash in the hallway jolted us both to our feet. Billy was first out of the kitchen, skidding to a halt when he saw Theo trying to extricate himself from a pile of coats.

'Sorry.' The howling woman, blonde and most definitely not Erin, bit her bottom lip as she glanced from Theo, to Billy and me and back to Theo again. 'We didn't mean to disturb you.'

I wished she'd been this courteous for the past couple of hours, but I remained silent, my brain too confused to form words. The moment in the kitchen was forgotten as I tried to merge 'Erin' upstairs and this blonde woman who was now wrestling the coats off Theo and helping him to his feet. I was so sure Erin had hooked up with Theo, but clearly not.

'Isn't that Caitlin from The Grey?' Billy whispered to me.

I looked at the woman and realised it was. I was more used to seeing her pulling pints than pulling my housemate, but it was indeed Caitlin. I was a little disappointed in her to be honest. I'd thought she was a sensible girl, thwarting Theo's charm offensive at every turn, but she had finally succumbed. I wondered if she was aware that Theo's interest in her would be non-existent from now on. Still, at least it hadn't been Erin's groans of pleasure I'd had to witness through the wall.

Ah, Erin. If the booty call hadn't been from Theo, then it had to have been from Stuart from Accounts. They'd obviously made up after their little tiff. Perhaps their relationship was more serious than Erin would admit.

THIRTY-FIVE

Jared

Jared's body was sluggish as he changed into a pair of old, grey jogging bottoms and a plain white T-shirt, almost as though it suspected what his brain already knew. Yoga wasn't a good idea. Not today, when the dream was still fresh in his mind despite the hours that had passed since he woke. Yoga gave him the space and freedom to think, which was dangerous, given the circumstances.

Camilla was as warm and calming as ever as the group filed into the yoga class and unrolled their mats. Jared's body mirrored hers as she took them through the warm-up and he followed her instructions throughout the class, concentrating on the moves and poses instead of allowing his mind to wander, but his downfall was the end of the class as they settled themselves for their usual meditation session. He tried to think of other things – anything other than Frances and Barney. He'd known the class was a mistake but he couldn't let Ruth down and so it was his heart that led him to the gym and not his mind or body.

Ruth. He pictured her in his mind and felt relieved to find he could focus on something else. She was mere inches away and he wondered what thoughts lurked in her mind. Hopefully, better ones than his memories. Memories of Frances – of losing her and being denied the chance to be a father to their son. Barney wasn't planned, but their relationship was solid and they'd already moved from their beloved bedsit and into the little two-bedroomed house, almost as though they knew what was on the horizon. They were thrilled to discover they were about to be parents and threw themselves into planning for the new arrival. They found out the sex of the baby so they could decorate the spare bedroom and they named him as soon as they left the hospital after the scan, naming him after Frances's grandfather.

Jared had been working late one night. It was his birthday and while he'd rather have been out celebrating with Frances, he was trying to prove himself at work. There was a promotion coming up and he was determined to get it, to improve himself and be better able to provide for Frances and Barney. It was dark by the time he left the office but there were no lights on in the house, which was odd. Frances should have been at home. She'd said they'd order a take away and snuggle up on the sofa, their own subdued celebration as she was only a few weeks away from her due date and too exhausted to contemplate a proper night out.

The house was empty. He checked downstairs first before moving upstairs to the bedroom, expecting to see Frances curled up in bed. But the bed was empty and Jared began to worry. He even checked Barney's room but that was empty too. He rushed down the stairs and this time he spotted the handwritten note on the mantelpiece, folded in half with his name on the front. That was when the worry really set in, swirling in his gut and closing his windpipe as he plucked the paper from its resting place and unfolded it, seeing Frances's familiar scrawl.

Surprise! Meet me in the pub. And bring your dancing shoes!

Frances had secretly organised a party at their local pub, complete with a DJ and had invited all their friends and family. Everyone Jared loved was under the same roof and it was all down to Frances.

'I love you,' he whispered as they danced to 'their' song.

'I love you too. And do you know what? This doesn't just have to be a birthday celebration. It could be an engagement party too.' Frances wasn't down on one knee, but she was proposing and how could Jared refuse? He loved Frances more than anything and they were about to have a baby. His life couldn't be more perfect.

Their mums cried when they announced their engagement that evening and were eager to start preparations immediately. Jared and Frances decided to wait until after Barney was born as she was already eight months pregnant and didn't fancy giving birth soap-style at the altar, with everybody gawping at her nether regions. But they were happy to start making plans, booking their local church and asking Jared's sisters to be bridesmaids. Barney would wear an adorable baby suit and tie and would be carried down the aisle in his mother's arms.

Jared was at work when he received the phone call. He grabbed his jacket as soon as he realised it was the hospital, but his arm froze halfway in the sleeve. Frances wasn't in labour and never would be. A car had sped through a pedestrian crossing, ignoring the red light and Frances as she crossed the road. She'd died at the scene, along with their precious son. Jared's life had buckled around him, splintering his mind and body and altering him beyond recognition.

Jared's eyes snapped open and his body jerked into a sitting position. He'd tried so hard not to think about Frances and the accident, but she was always there, nestled in his heart and mind. She'd come to him in his dream again the night before, only this time she hadn't brought Barney with her. She'd taken Jared's face in her cool palms, kissed him on the lips and smiled her beautiful smile at him.

'I'm not coming back. You know that, don't you?'

Jared hadn't answered. Of course he knew she wasn't coming back but he couldn't bring himself to acknowledge the fact.

'But that doesn't mean I don't love you. And I know you love me. Moving on won't change that. I've gone, Jared, and you must get on with your life. Enough time has passed. You'll never forget me and you'll never stop loving me, but it's time, Jared.'

Jared knew it wasn't really Frances telling him these things. It wasn't an apparition visiting him from the other side. It was his mind letting him know it was okay to be happy, to find love and risk heartbreak again. But that didn't make it any easier to deal with.

'Are you okay, Jared?' Camilla had crept across the

room and placed a warm hand on his shoulder. 'Would you like a glass of water?'

Jared glanced around the room, hoping he hadn't disturbed anyone. Or made a show of himself. But everyone else was still relaxed, breathing deeply, envisioning white sandy beaches and warm breezes.

'No thank you. I'm fine.' He settled himself back down on his mat and spent the remainder of the session pretending to be relaxed. Camilla ended the session, and everybody rolled up their mats and filed out of the room while Jared remained seated, still contemplating his future. His family had spent months trying to coax him to move on but he hadn't been ready then.

Ruth rolled up her mat and tucked it under her arm. 'Ready?' she asked him.

Jared nodded but remained seated for a moment longer. 'I think so, yes.'

THIRTY-SIX

Ruth

'Fantastic session today, guys. I'll see you all next week.' Camilla smiled at the group dotted around the room and we all crouched on the ground to roll up our mats and filed out of the room. There was no chance of me losing weight in time for the reunion now and I'd probably end my membership to the gym pretty sharpish and never set foot on a treadmill again, but I quite liked yoga. It was calming yet energising and I liked having that bit of time to myself. I'd have to look into a class outside the gym after the reunion. Perhaps there was one at the church hall or something.

'Drink?' I asked as Jared and I met in reception after changing. It was a silly question after so long. Going to the pub after the gym had become our ritual, our cooldown stretches and a time to unwind, but Jared didn't respond with his usual 'Good idea! Where shall we go?' and, come to think of it, he did look a bit shifty.

Nervous, perhaps.

'Are you okay?'

'I'm fine. Never better. Drink?'

I eyed Jared but simply nodded my head. Maybe he was fine and I was sensing my own nerves and projecting them onto Jared. I had an important question to ask him and wasn't sure how he would take it.

The pub was as dead as ever but we soon livened the place up with a bit of cheesy pop and this time Jared didn't try to dissuade me from playing a medley of Steps and S Club on a loop. Something was definitely bothering him but I was too caught up in my own dilemma to pay too close attention to what it could be. We sat at our usual table with our orange juice and packets of crisps. The crisps were a new addition to our ritual as I'd come to terms with the fact that I was going to the reunion fat and had even bought a dress. It wasn't quite The Dress but I'd have fallen in love with it under normal circumstances so it would have to do.

We ate our crisps in silence. I was inside my own head, contemplating how to broach my proposal and Jared seemed happy enough with the quiet. I couldn't come up with a sensible or even witty way to ask Jared and so I decided to just wing it.

'You know it's my school reunion on Saturday?'

Jared nodded and managed his first smile of the evening. 'I've heard it mentioned on an occasion or two.'

I started to laugh but clamped my mouth shut when I realised it sounded slightly manic. 'I have an extra ticket and I was wondering if you'd like to come with me.'

Jared studied me for a moment, his head cocked to one side and I started to feel warm under his gaze. 'As your date?'

'Sort of. But more like as my boyfriend.' I offered a grimace-like smile as I heard the words out loud. They hadn't sounded quite so desperate in my head. 'Pretend boyfriend,' I added quickly so he didn't think I'd gone completely cuckoo.

'*Pretend* boyfriend?'

The day after Clare's party, I'd met up with Erin at the bench for lunch, desperate to know about her text from Stuart from Accounts. She could no longer deny the growing seriousness of their dalliance. Except Erin did.

'I'm not seeing Stuart from Accounts.'

I'd rolled my eyes at her. 'Come off it, Erin. This is me you're talking to, your best friend. I know you and I can tell you're into him. I've never seen you gooey-eyed about anyone and your eyes are well and truly gooey.'

'Am I really gooey-eyed?' Instead of being angry at the description, Erin was amused.

'The gooiest. You have feelings for him, don't you?'

I expected Erin to erupt, to deny any such nonsense. I expected her to be indignant and remind me that she didn't *do* feelings or any of that bollocks. I expected a fiery response but all I received was a little sigh. Erin plucked a Malteser from the family sized bag we were sharing and rolled it between her finger and thumb.

'Oh my God, you do. Jesus, Erin. Are you in love with him?' The notion was so ridiculous I almost laughed but managed to rein it in.

'I don't know. Maybe.' My mouth gaped open and Erin shoved her Malteser inside the cavity.

'Thanks.' I crunched the Malteser while I tried to get my head around the fact that Erin, Ms Love Is For Losers, had not only fallen in love but was freely admitting it. 'God, Erin. I never thought this would happen.'

Erin giggled, a proper girlish titter that surprised us both. Her eyes widened as she smothered the giggle with her hand. 'I didn't either. It kind of crept up on me.'

'And does Stuart love you?' He'd never come across as the settling down type to me but then neither had Erin until thirty seconds ago.

'No.'

The grin I hadn't noticed on my face until now began to droop. 'Oh, Erin.' I reached out to take her hand in mine, knowing how horrible it was to be in such a situation. And for Erin, who had always stated she wasn't weak enough to fall in love, it must have been a hundred times worse.

'But I'm not in love with Stuart either.'

My hand froze on her fingers, my brow creasing in a most unattractive manner. 'But you just said you were.' She had, hadn't she? I wasn't going la-la here.

'I said I was in love. But not with Stuart.' Now I was beyond confused. What the hell was she talking about? 'I haven't been dating Stuart from Accounts. I just pretended I was seeing him because I was too embarrassed to tell you who I was really seeing, which I feel awful about now because Richie's a really great guy once you get to know him.'

'Richie?' Who the fuck was *Richie*? I gasped then, my hand covering my mouth as I shook my head. No way. 'Richard?' Erin nodded her head. 'Richard Shuttleworth?'

'Yes.' Erin didn't look mortified, in fact quite the opposite. She was beaming.

'You mean Richard, the Ginger...' I couldn't continue

with the insult, not now he was Erin's *boyfriend*.

'The Ginger Bastard. Yes, I'm afraid so.'

'But you said he was fantastic in bed.' My hand flew to my mouth again as an image of a naked and very ginger Richard popped into my head. He reminded me of the lion from *The Wizard of Oz*. I'd never be able to sit through the film again.

'He is.' Erin beamed again while I shook my head, trying to piece it all together and make sense of the situation. It took eight Maltesers before I was able to speak again.

'So you've been pretending you were seeing Stuart? You never even went on one date with him?'

'Not one.'

I suddenly leapt up from the bench, sending the remaining Maltesers scattering across the grey concrete of the car park but I didn't even care. That was it! A pretend boyfriend! Plan D was conceived on the farthest corner of H. Woods' car park and all I needed to do now was work out a few tiny details.

'You want me to *pretend* to be your boyfriend?'

Jared looked at me as though I were crazy, which I probably was but I was also desperate. My first thought for the faux boyfriend had been Billy as he was already going to the reunion and he was sort of cute in a shaggy dog sort of way. But I assumed Billy would be taking Clare so that option was out. Erin then suggested Theo, pointing out he was very good looking (and didn't the arrogant sod know it) and he'd do anything for a bit of free grub and beer. But even I wasn't desperate enough to put myself through the humiliation of asking Theo.

Which left Jared. He was gorgeous – even more so than Zack – and it didn't matter that he was gay. He'd only be pretending to be my boyfriend and he wasn't camp. Zack and co wouldn't be able to tell.

'It'll only be for one night. And don't worry, we won't have to kiss or anything. I'm not after your body. I'm not that delusional. Or desperate.' Well, I'd have to be desperate to throw myself at a gay man, wouldn't I?

I sat back and awaited Jared's answer. It was a strange request but I wasn't asking too much of him. All he had to do was show up on my arm looking gorgeous, which, let's face it, wasn't a difficult task for Jared. He'd make any woman's knees go weak. Particularly mine, but I brushed that thought away.

'So what do you think?' I prompted when Jared failed to respond.

Jared's hands clasped the edge of the table as he eased himself out of his seat. His face was blank but his clenched jaw flagged a warning. 'No, I won't pretend to be your boyfriend. I've got better things to do than play silly games.' Grabbing his jacket from the back of his chair, he swung around and began to stride out of the pub, pausing to glance my way as he reached for the door handle. 'You might not be desperate and neither am I.'

My own jaw clenched then, either because I was angry or to prevent myself from crying. Probably both. I'd thought Jared and I were close and that he cared about me, but he was just like the others. I was just a fat cow to him too. Someone to be seen with in public only if you were beyond desperate.

'If you don't want to do it, then fine, but there's no need to be so nasty about it. I thought we were friends but clearly you think differently.'

'Yes, Ruth, I do think differently.' Jared's tone was sombre and he gave a sad shake of his head before he tugged at the door handle and left me sitting there, tears thankfully not yet falling.

I somehow managed to keep the tears at bay long enough to track Erin down. She'd been at Richard's but met me at my house as soon as she heard how upset I was. She listened as I told her about my disastrous proposal, wiping my eyes with a tissue as yet more tears wormed their way down my cheeks. I didn't understand how our friendship had disintegrated so quickly.

'It's a bit more than friendship for you though, isn't it?' Erin dabbed at my eyes with the damp tissue. 'That's why you're so upset.'

'What do you mean? It can't be more than friendship. Jared likes men, not big fat women.'

'Hey!' Erin grasped my chin and turned my face towards her own. 'Don't you ever let me hear you talking about yourself like that.'

'But it's true.' And the devastating thing was Jared thought so too. Jared, who had become one of my closest friends. I'd told him about Zack and he'd been sympathetic, but he must have been agreeing with Zack the whole time. Oh God, how embarrassing.

'You are a wonderful person, Ruth. You are beautiful and smart and funny. And gay or not, there is no excuse for acting like a wanker.'

I bobbed my head up and down. I didn't entirely agree with Erin but her fingers were digging into my chin.

'Good girl.' Erin released my face and I rubbed at the tender skin. 'Now, why don't I come with you to the reunion? Richard's supposed to be taking me to his mum and dad's at the weekend, but I can't think of anything I'd rather do less. Apparently, Susan threatens

Kelvin with divorce at least twice a day. I'll cancel and we can have a laugh and get pissed.'

A glimmer of hope shone through my misery. That could work. In fact, it could be pretty bloody perfect. 'Erin, you're a genius. Imagine Zack's face when he realises I've pulled a woman as gorgeous as you. Nothing grabs a man's attention like a couple of lesbians. He'll probably suggest a threesome and I'll get to tell him to get stuffed in front of everyone.' I grinned at the thought of humiliating Zack but Erin soon put a dampener on my jubilation.

'Erm, that's not what I meant, sweetie. I meant we could go as *friends*. To have a laugh.'

'Oh.'

Erin gave my hand a pat. 'Do you think you're desperate enough to ask Theo yet? Because it sounds like you are.'

THIRTY-SEVEN

Ruth

I was officially a failure as I arrived at my parents' house the day before the reunion. The school was only a few minutes away from my childhood home, so I would be staying with mum and dad to make it easier. With my suitcase at my feet, I rang the doorbell and waited.

'You'll never guess what he's planning on doing with the shed.' Mum didn't bother with a greeting as she ushered me inside, taking my suitcase from me. '*A sauna*! He wants to turn the shed into a bloody sauna. What do we want with a sauna?'

'I'd quite like a sauna actually.'

'Well, let him build one for you then.' Mum took my jacket from me and hung it up on the coat stand in the hall. 'You've lost weight, Ruthie.'

'I have.' Pride about my weight loss crept into my voice for the first time. 'I've dropped a dress size.'

'Well done.' Mum beamed at me as she pulled me

into a hug. 'You look fantastic. Let's go and show your dad. He's up in the attic turning it back into a bedroom for you. You don't mind sleeping up there, do you? It's easier to have the little ones close to Stephen and Aubrey.'

'It's fine. I don't mind.'

'Let's get your things up there then. I'll make us a nice brew while you unpack.'

Dad had transformed the attic into a cinema with a giant TV and two short rows of flip-down seats he'd sourced on the internet, but Mum had made him unscrew the seats and store them in the soon-to-be sauna and a single divan had been made up. I unpacked as best as I could and hung my new dress up on the back of the door. Mum brought me a cup of coffee up when I failed to return downstairs, wondering what had kept me. I had very little to unpack but I needed a few minutes to myself.

'Your brother should be here any minute,' Mum said, knowing seeing Stephen would cheer me up. I followed Mum back down to the sitting room, pushing all thoughts of the reunion out of my head and trying to forget the humiliation of not only explaining the situation to Theo but actually asking him to pretend to be my boyfriend. He was working that day but would be meeting me at Mum and Dad's the following evening in time for the reunion. Suddenly the idea of a pretend boyfriend seemed ludicrous and childish but the alternative was turning up alone, which wasn't an option as far as I was concerned.

I sat with Mum, watching crappy daytime telly but before long the house erupted as Stephen and his family arrived. Mum's eyes filled with tears as she took in how much her grandchildren had grown since the last time she'd seen them, but she hid her upset quickly as she gave them each a great big hug.

'Your grandad's out in the garden. Shall we go and find him?' Mum led the three little ones out to the back garden, leaving Stephen, Aubrey and me alone. I surveyed my brother, searching for hints of change but he was still Stephen, my big brother. I ran to him, throwing my arms around him. I missed Stephen every day but it always seemed to catch me off guard when I saw him again, all my emotions rushing to the surface.

'Did you bring them?' I asked a moment later.

'Of course.' I released Stephen so he could unzip one of his suitcases. After rummaging around he pulled out a bag containing five small boxes of Sweet Tarts, my favourite American sweets. I opened a box immediately and popped one into my mouth before offering them to Stephen and Aubrey.

'So has Billy been looking after you?' The three of us sat down in the sitting room, ignoring the pile of suitcases by the door. The sound of laughter could be heard out in the back garden as Mum and Dad became acquainted with their grandchildren again.

'Yes, but he's been a bit distracted lately with his new girlfriend.'

'Ah, Clare. Billy hasn't told me that much about her. What's she like?'

'She's nice.' I didn't mention the air of frostiness she reserved for me. 'And for some reason she really likes Billy.'

'He didn't mention any head injury she'd suffered but I assume there has been one.' Stephen and I grinned at each other and popped another Sweet Tart into our mouths while Aubrey nudged Stephen with her elbow.

'Billy is lovely. A woman could do a lot worse.'

'A woman could do a lot better,' Stephen quipped and we both laughed, though we both thought Billy was pretty fantastic. Stephen wouldn't have entrusted Billy with my care if he didn't think so.

'You must be exhausted after your flight,' I said, and Stephen responded with a yawn.

'We didn't get any sleep. Ryder slept all the way from take-off until we landed but Austin and Riley were too excited to settle.' He yawned again. 'The joys of family life, eh?'

It was great to see Stephen again and the kids were hilarious. Ryder was almost two and everything piqued his curiosity, from next door's cat to the washing machine. Austin tried to teach Dad how to play American football with a taped-up T-shirt, and Riley was convinced Buckingham Palace was within walking distance. We all went out for a meal that evening and, for the first time in months, I didn't even think about the food I was putting in my mouth. I enjoyed the food for what it was and relished having my family so close. With the children tucked up in bed, Mum, Aubrey and I shared a couple of bottles of wine while Dad and Stephen worked on a bottle of whiskey. I floated up to bed that evening, not even noticing I was in an unfamiliar bed as my head hit the pillow. I was drifting off to sleep when my mobile rang and jolted me awake again. Worry spiked in my gut when I saw Billy's name on the display.

'Are you still looking for a pretend boyfriend? Because I'm on your doorstep.'

THIRTY-EIGHT

Billy

Billy wasn't quite sure how he'd ended up on Ruth's parents' doorstep at almost one o'clock in the morning, clutching the doorframe to stop his body from keeling over, partly from exhaustion but mostly due to the large amounts of alcohol he'd consumed. He'd already had a few drinks in the pub before the row with Clare erupted and that had probably added fuel to the argument. He hadn't let Clare rant, hadn't told her what she wanted to hear to soothe her and so the row had escalated until he found himself on a late train to Oldham.

The door opened and there was Ruth in her cow-print pyjamas, her feet bare apart from the shocking pink polish on her toenails. 'Billy? What are you doing here?' She spoke in a hushed tone, her eyes darting towards the stairs, making sure she hadn't woken anybody on the way down.

'I wanted to see you, Ruthie.' Billy clutched the

doorframe harder as he began to sway.

'Are you drunk?'

'A bit.' There was no point in denying it. She could probably smell it on his breath and he could barely stand. Billy suspected he'd given the taxi driver a rather hefty tip in his dazed state.

'Come in but please be quiet. Everyone's asleep.'

Billy stumbled after Ruth, following her into the small kitchen where she made sobering cups of coffee before leading Billy into the sitting room. He flopped onto the sofa and patted the space beside him.

'What's going on, Billy? Why are you here so late?' And so drunk, Ruth wondered but remained quiet about that.

'I'm your knight in shining armour, aren't I?' Billy threw his arms wide, but Ruth still didn't understand so he struggled into a more upright position to elaborate. 'I'm here to offer my services. You wanted a pretend boyfriend and so here I am.'

Ruth studied her friend for a moment, wondering just how much he'd had to drink. 'I'm going with Theo, remember?'

Billy spluttered and gave a wave of his hand. 'Theo's an arsehole. He'll cop off with one of the stupid cows who used to bully you. You don't want that when you can have me. I promise not to cop off with *anyone*.'

Under normal circumstances Ruth would have preferred the company of Billy by far, but there was one tiny snag in his plan. 'And what about Clare? Aren't you already taking her?'

Billy shook his head. 'I never was and definitely not now. We've split up.'

'Oh, Billy. Why didn't you say? Come here.' Ruth pulled Billy into a hug and he was quite comfortable, his head resting against her ample bosom. He closed his eyes and contemplated falling asleep right there.

'What happened?'

Billy thought back over the night's events. He'd stumbled out of a taxi minutes earlier after emptying his wallet into the beaming taxi driver's outstretched hand. He'd taken a train from Woodgate to Oldham, almost getting the shit beaten out of him when he yelled at a youth to turn the tinny music on his phone down. He'd called him an inconsiderate fucking prick, not caring that the kid probably had a knife tucked down his sock. He didn't feel any fear in confronting the lad and he wasn't even relieved when a seriously huge guy a few seats down stood up and told the youth to sit back down, to shut the fuck up and turn the music off. The youth, towering above Billy with a sneer on his ugly, rat-like face, eyed Billy and then the seriously huge guy before deciding it was in his best interest to put his arse back in his seat and keep quiet for the remainder of his journey.

Before that train journey, Billy had been in the pub. Clare had been there and she was yelling at him. Ah yes, now he remembered.

'She says I don't love her.' Had Billy been sober, he probably would have stopped there, but he wasn't sober and so he ploughed on without considering the consequences. 'She says I'm in love with someone else.' There was still time to keep quiet, to limit the damage but Billy's alcohol-addled brain didn't even pause for thought. 'You, Ruth. She says I'm in love with you.'

Billy's head began to jangle as Ruth's bosom vibrated with laughter. 'Don't be ridiculous. Whatever gave her that idea?'

Had he been sober, Billy would have laughed along

and claimed he had no idea. But Billy was far from sober. 'Because it's true.'

Billy wasn't sure when his feelings had developed into something more than friendship, but it must have been some time ago because it was something he and Louise used to argue about, and in the end Louise couldn't handle the three of them living under the same roof and she'd moved out. Billy had thought she was crackers at the time and had told her so on many occasions, but it turned out she was right. He should apologise, really. He'd track her down on Facebook or something and – Billy's head dropped as Ruth's bosom was snatched away.

'What?'

Billy thought back over his conversation with Ruth. Ah yes, he'd just told her he was in love with her, hence the open mouth and startled eyes.

'It's not Clare I'm in love with, Ruth. It's you.' And then, because he was drunk and not thinking straight, he propelled himself at Ruth and kissed her. Her lips, though clamped shut against his, were as soft as he'd imagined and although he'd wrecked their strong friendship in a matter of seconds, Billy couldn't help thinking it was worth it.

And then something miraculous happened. Ruth responded. Not by slapping him across the chops as he'd expected, but by opening her lips and allowing Billy's tongue to dip inside to meet her own. Billy shifted position so he could kiss her properly, taking her precious face in his hands. It was the best moment of Billy's life thus far.

THIRTY-NINE

Ruth

It was disorientating to wake in the former home cinema, squashed into a single bed, which seemed to have shrunk overnight. Stretching out my leg, it met with a solid mass which, with closer inspection by my toe, seemed to be soft, warm and hairy. And all at once the events of the early hours hit me full force. Billy on the doorstep, telling me about him and Clare, confessing his feelings for me. And we'd kissed! *More* than kissed if my memory served me correctly.

Oh cripes. I'd had sex with Billy.

Billy. He'd been drunk but what had been my excuse? I remembered him kissing me and feeling shocked at first but the shock soon dulled and I was left with a strange mix of feelings. Part of me was appalled, feeling like I was snogging Stephen on our parents' sofa. But part of me felt safe and cherished. This was Billy. Billy would never hurt me, would never make me feel repellent and he loved me. I loved him too, perhaps not in the same way that he loved me, but I could love him like that, given time, I was sure.

'Morning.' Despite knowing Billy was there, his voice startled me, but I tried to hide it as I turned over in the tiny bed. It was then that I realised I was still naked. And so was Billy. 'This is a bit weird, isn't it?' Weird? *Weird*? Fucked up is what it was. I was *naked. Billy* was naked. 'But it's also fantastic. Last night was amazing, wasn't it?'

Last night was a mistake. A huge *mistake*. I realised that as soon as I became aware that Billy's little friend was right there in the bed with us and I wanted to run as far away from it as possible. But I couldn't tell Billy that when he was grinning at me, his face full of euphoria while I tried to mask the horror on my own. What was I going to do? I couldn't get out of bed, not when I was in the nip.

'It was the most amazing night of my life.' Billy dipped his head to kiss my bare shoulder and I tried my hardest to repress a shudder. 'I can't believe we've ended up together.'

Ended up together? All hope that Billy would realise we'd made a mistake washed away and left a sense of dread in its place. How was I going to get out of this without hurting Billy? Because I couldn't bear to hurt him. I might not care for him in *that way* but he was still one of my best friends and I *did* care about him. A lot.

Billy kissed my shoulder again, his lips moving up to my throat, and then my cheek and they were about to meet with my alarmed lips when there was a knock at the door. Relief prickled my very naked flesh as I was given the excuse to jump away from Billy, sitting up and tugging the covers with me.

'Ruth, love, we're off out,' Mum told me from the other side of the door. Thank God she didn't come inside. 'We'll be gone most of the day because we're off to the Trafford Centre.'

'Under duress,' Stephen added from a distance.

'You can come with us if you'd like. You'll have to hurry up though. We're setting off in ten minutes or so.'

'Thanks, Mum, but I think I'll stay here. I don't want to wear myself out before the reunion.'

'Alright, love. We'll see you later then.'

I waited until Mum's footsteps ceased on the stairs before turning to Billy. His face was ashen and I was hopeful again. Perhaps hearing Mum's voice had been like throwing a bucket of iced water at him and he'd come round from whatever trance he'd been under.

'Shit, Stephen's here.' He placed a hand over his mouth as I nodded. 'I forgot. He can't find me, not like this. He'll kill me.'

'You're right. You stay here and I'll get up. I'll let you know when it's safe to come down.' Seizing my chance, I leapt from the bed and grabbed my robe, shielding my body as rapidly as possible before hurrying down the stairs. I needed a bit of space to think, to find a way to dig myself out of this great big shitting hole. It seemed like an age before my family filed out of the house and divided themselves between Dad's car and Stephen's hire car.

'Do you need anything while we're out?' Mum called as she fished in her handbag for her set of keys.

A rewind button for my life? 'No thanks.'

'Alright, love.' Mum patted my arm as she kissed my cheek. I watched as she joined the others, waving as the cars pulled away from the kerb.

Now what?

'Ruth!' I was about to close the front door when I heard my name being called. I thought I was still dreaming as I saw Jared jogging up the path towards me. Oh, please let me be dreaming. Please let my night with Billy be down to my sordid imagination and too much wine.

'Jared? What are you doing here?' If I wasn't dreaming, how did he know where to find me?

Jared had reached the door and was standing in front of me looking as gorgeous as ever. I kicked myself for thinking such thoughts. 'I ran into Erin yesterday. I asked her where you were and she eventually told me.'

'You'd better come in then.' I kept my voice cool and detached, despite my pneumatic-drill heart. 'Do you want a cup of coffee? I'm making one anyway.'

Leaving Jared in the sitting room, I escaped to the kitchen to gather my thoughts. I'd slept with my closest friend, who was up in the attic waiting for me, naked, while the man I really wanted to sleep with but couldn't because he was gay and thought I was a heifer, was in the sitting room. And I was naked apart from a pink fluffy robe. Great. Fantastic. Best day ever.

The kettle boiled and I had yet to come up with a solution so I made the coffees and carried them through to the sitting room. The least I could do was find out why Jared was here.

'I'm sorry about our argument,' Jared said before I'd even placed the cups down. 'I was angry and upset that you would ask me to pretend to be your boyfriend. I've been going through some... stuff. But that isn't your problem and I shouldn't have taken that out on you.'

'What kind of stuff?' I'd been pissed off and angry myself, but seeing the anguish on Jared's face made me soften. It must have been something serious because I'd never seen anyone looked so pained.

Jared closed his eyes for a moment, seeming to be gathering strength before he opened them, looking directly at me. He looked tired, as though he hadn't slept for weeks. 'Do you remember me telling you about Francis?' Oh God, they'd got back together and were going to live happily ever after. Which was fabulous for Jared, obviously, but I couldn't help feeling a stab of jealousy. Francis was a very, very lucky man. 'I told you we were together and how much I loved Francis, but I didn't tell you that she died.' *She*? 'And that she died while carrying our baby. My son, Barney.' *She*? 'It was five years ago, but it's still so painful and I find it hard to deal with. My family think I should have moved on by now and they're always trying to set me up with women, but I haven't been ready.'

She? 'But you're gay.'

'I am?' Jared's anguish turned to confusion. His eyebrows hung low over his eyes as he looked at me, his head cocked to one side. 'You think I'm gay? Why would you think that? Oh, I get it.' He snatched his eyes away from me, observing the ceiling instead. 'It's the ballet. You think I'm a big poof because I loved to dance.'

'No, that's not it.' Not entirely. 'Erin told me you were gay. *You* told her you were gay.'

Jared hooted but he didn't sound amused. He sounded angry again. This was not going well. 'I can assure you I did not.'

'But Erin said...' I thought back to our conversation months ago. Erin and Jared had gone out and he'd told her he was gay. 'She tried it on with you and you knocked her back.'

'And that makes me gay?'

Yes, it sort of did. 'Erin's gorgeous and beautiful and sexy. All men fancy her.'

Jared gave a shrug of his shoulders but the anger had dispelled now and his voice was back to its usual gentleness. 'Erin is all of those things but she isn't my type. She's also loud and vulgar and arrogant. And also, I like somebody else.'

I wanted to shove my hands over my ears. I did not want to hear about another woman. It was bad enough when men had been my competition.

'You, Ruth. I like you.' Eh? 'I think you're beautiful and you make me smile and I absolutely adore your laughter.'

Me? How could he be attracted to me? He'd seen me at my absolute worst, sweating and panting at the gym, my face puce, hair slicked back, struggling to keep up with everybody else. Oh, sweet Jesus. He'd seen me in my *swimming costume*.

'I think you're amazing, Ruth. You're strong and loyal and you make me feel alive again. I never thought that would be possible after Frances.'

Jared seemed to be overlooking my bad points. I was also judgemental, lazy and greedy and I swore too much. But if he wanted to overlook such qualities, who was I to object? I still didn't understand why somebody like Jared would like me and my head was still reeling after discovering Frances was in fact a woman. And God, I hadn't even expressed my sorrow at Jared's loss. He'd lost the love of his life *and* his child and I had yet to offer an ounce of sympathy or comfort. I should add selfish and unfeeling to my list of bad points.

'The only problem is you don't seem to like me the same way.' The pained look was back on Jared's face. The fool!

'Are you kidding me? I fancy the bloody pants off you. You're gorgeous and have the patience of a saint. Anyone who can put up with my attempts at the gym is very special in my eyes.' I dared to raise my eyes, which had been observing my clasped hands on my lap throughout my confession. I was relieved to see Jared smiling at me. It was going to be okay after all.

'Babe? What's keeping you? I heard everyone leave ages ago. Are you coming back up to bed? I was hoping for Round Two.' Billy wandered into the sitting room, thankfully with his nether regions covered by a pair of boxer shorts. He leapt back behind the door when he spotted Jared on the sofa, only his head poking into the room. 'I'll wait upstairs, shall I?'

I closed my eyes as Billy disappeared but felt Jared jump to his feet.

'I wish I could say it isn't what it looks like,' I said, attempting to inject a bit of humour into my voice.

'And I wish I could say I didn't feel like the biggest idiot on the planet.'

'Jared. Wait.' I reached out as I rose from my seat but Jared was already striding out of the room, refusing to look back as he left the house. I tried running after him but only made it as far as the garden gate as I was in nothing but a dressing gown and I wasn't Bridget Jones.

Shit, shit, *shit*. How could I have stuffed this up so badly? I'm usually pretty good at driving men away, but it usually didn't happen until we'd at least kissed or been on a date. I'd managed to offend Jared and given him the impression I was a bit of a bike in a matter of minutes. Well done, Ruth.

I ran back into the house, belted it up into the attic where Billy was perched on the bed, still clad only in his boxers (but at least he hadn't removed them, I suppose).

'Sorry about that. I guess the cat's out of the bag now, but everyone would have found out sooner or later.'

Would they? God, I hoped not.

'Have you seen my phone?' Choosing to forget the whole sleeping with Billy thing for the moment, I flew about the room, opening drawers and lifting pillows. I needed to speak to Jared and try to explain. Though how I would explain what had happened with Billy when I didn't understand it myself, I had no idea. But I had to try. Jared liked me. *Me*!

Billy joined the search and I tried to avert my eyes from his almost naked body. The phone was finally located between the bed and the wall, wedged in tight.

'I need to make a call downstairs. Why don't you get dressed?' I hoped I didn't sound too abrupt but I didn't have time to agonise over my words. I needed to speak to Jared, to let him know how I felt before it was too late. Jared had been through so much already and I didn't want to add to any distress he may be feeling.

'*No*.' Jared's phone went to voicemail but I tried again anyway, a couple more times just to be sure. He'd turned his phone off. He didn't want to talk to me. What the hell did I do now? I couldn't sit back and watch possibly the best relationship of my life pass by. Because it would have been a fantastic relationship. Jared and I were already close and I loved spending time with him. Imagine our friendship but more, much more.

'Ruth?' Fully dressed now, Billy found me in the sitting room, my head in my hands as I tried to figure out a way to right this mess. 'What's going on? Last night was amazing, but now...' He shook his head, his features morphing into that of a puppy's and I felt awful. Billy was one of my best friends and I didn't want to hurt him, but what else could I do? Jared or no Jared, I didn't want to be with Billy.

'I'm sorry Billy, I really am, but last night was a mistake.' There, I'd said it out loud. I'd kicked the puppy in the gut and there was no going back. 'I know you think you have feelings for me –'

'I don't *think* I have feelings for you, Ruth. I *know*. They're real and you can't brush them under the carpet because you don't feel the same. You don't, do you?' I shook my head, unable to look at Billy. How could I have done this to him? Selfish was already on my bad points list but it needed to be put in capital letters and bold. 'You like him, don't you?'

I didn't need Billy to clarify who 'him' was so I nodded my head. 'I'm in love with him.'

'And you couldn't have told me that last night?' Billy's question seemingly didn't require an answer as he stormed out of the house, slamming the door as he went. I was hoping we could salvage our friendship after this whole debacle, but it seemed unlikely from the thunderous look on Billy's face as he left.

FORTY

Jared

Jared felt like the biggest dickhead as he drove home, kicking himself for putting himself back out there only to be crushed. It was the first time in years that he'd contemplated a new relationship, which was a massive step forward and his mother would be thrilled, but why couldn't he have picked someone who was available? He'd just humiliated himself and in front of Ruth, his closest friend. How would this affect their friendship? Surely he'd trampled it beyond repair with his big gob. He knew Ruth had tried to phone him but he'd switched his phone off immediately, not able to face talking to her at the moment. He needed a bit of time to lick his wounds and figure out how to move forward from the mess he'd created.

He drove back to Woodgate, still without any answers, and pulled up outside his house to see Erin sitting on the doorstep. She was fiddling with her phone but dropped it into her handbag when she spotted Jared and leapt to her feet.

'We need to talk.'

'Do we?' Jared wasn't in the mood for talking, especially not with Erin. How dare she go around telling people he was gay? Who did she think she was?

'Ruth phoned to tell me she's stuffed everything up.' *She'd* stuffed everything up? She hadn't been the one declaring their feelings to someone already involved with another man. 'I told her not to worry, that I'd sort everything out.'

'That was kind of you. And how do you propose to do that? Do you have a time machine tucked away in your handbag?' Jared unlocked the door and stepped into the foyer, hoping Erin wouldn't follow him up to his flat but she did.

'No, I don't have a time machine. But I do have a bit of common sense.' Really? That was news to Jared but he kept quiet. 'And I also have the facts. Ruth *did* sleep with Billy.' The thought jabbed at Jared's insides and he flopped onto the sofa with a grimace. 'But she doesn't have feelings for him. She has feelings for you.'

Jared spluttered. 'If she has feelings for me, why was she with her housemate last night?'

'Don't you know Ruth at all?' Jared thought he knew her quite well but from the way Erin was glaring at him, he wasn't so sure anymore. 'She has told you about Zack, hasn't she?'

'Yes, but I fail to see what he has to do with last night.'

'He has everything to do with last night. He's the reason Ruth has settled for shitty boyfriend after shitty boyfriend. He made her feel so crap about herself that she thinks it's okay to be treated like shit and she should be grateful that they would want to be with her.'

'But what has that got to do with Billy?' He'd always come across as a decent bloke to Jared.

Erin sighed, as though the answer was obvious. 'Ruth pretends she's confident, that she doesn't care what people think, but she cares very much. Her self-esteem is beyond low and she'll take any scrap of affection on offer. You only have to look at her ex, Gideon, to see that. The man was revolting and I swear he didn't bathe for the duration of their relationship. He treated Ruth like crap and she put up with it because he was slightly interested in her.' Jared was still bewildered. 'Ruth doesn't like Billy in that way, but she went along with it anyway because she thinks she should be grateful that any man would fancy her, whether she fancies him or not.'

Jared didn't know what to make of the situation. On the one hand he hated to think of Ruth feeling so bad about herself but on the other he couldn't stop the image of her and Billy from popping into his head. The sight of Billy in his tiny boxer shorts may one day make him laugh, but for the moment it filled his chest with hot rage.

'Can I get you a coffee or anything?' Jared needed a bit more time to ponder what Erin had said to him but wanted her close to hand in case he had any further questions – and they still had the matter of his outing to discuss.

'Thanks. Coffee would be great.'

Jared still couldn't get his head around the situation. It was difficult enough admitting he was ready to move on after Frances and the guilt that ensued without adding the complications of other lovers. Why couldn't his life be simple? Why couldn't he meet a woman he liked, who liked him back, so they could live happily ever after?

But perhaps it *could* be that simple if only Jared would allow it to be. If Ruth was able to take Billy out of the equation, why couldn't he? Why had he run at the first bump in the road?

Because he was terrified. Terrified of getting hurt again. Perhaps he wasn't as ready to move on as he thought he was.

Jared grabbed the coffees, his mind still in turmoil as he returned to the sitting room. Erin was fiddling with her phone once again.

'Are you meant to be somewhere else?' he asked, nodding at the phone.

Erin gave a wave of her hand. 'Richie's been chasing me for years. Making him wait will only keep him on his toes.' She dropped the phone in her handbag and took the proffered cup of coffee. 'Besides, I'm not leaving here until you agree to go back and talk to Ruth.'

'I'm not sure I can agree to that quite so soon.' Jared flopped onto the sofa and turned to Erin, who was already itching to retrieve her phone. 'So I'm gay, huh?'

Jared thought Erin would look abashed but she simply gave a shrug of her shoulders. 'What was I supposed to think? I made a move on you and you backed away, saying I *wasn't your type*, which everyone knows is code for "I'm gay".'

'So you assumed I was gay because I knocked you back?' The woman was incredible. 'You do realise you're the most arrogant person *on earth*, don't you?'

'I do.' Erin took a sip of coffee. 'And you do realise that if you let Ruth go, you'll be the most moronic person on earth, don't you?'

FORTY-ONE

Ruth

I was soaking in the bath when Mum and the others
arrived back from their shopping trip, the sound of their
chatter and laughter wafting up the stairs. I lowered
myself further into the bubbly water to muffle out their
happy sounds. I was in no mood for jolliness. I'd heard
from neither Jared nor Billy since they'd stormed out of
the house that morning and I wasn't relishing the
thought of the reunion that evening. What if I bumped
into Billy? I couldn't stand the thought of seeing the
hurt on his face again, and what if Stephen found out
what had happened? I didn't know who he'd blame
most: Billy for sleeping with his sister or me for hurting
his best friend.

I remained in the bath for as long as possible, my
body wrinkled and cold, only emerging because Stephen
and Aubrey had to get ready for the reunion too.
Locking myself in the attic room, I pulled my new dress

down from its hanger and held it in front of me. It was a strapless cobalt blue dress with a jewelled bodice and I'd felt fabulous when I'd tried it on in the shop, but I doubted I'd feel quite so special in it now.

Dumping the dress on the bed, I dried my hair and twisted it up on top of my head, leaving stray curls to frame my face. After applying my make-up, I slipped on the dress and my matching shoes and I had to admit the overall effect was pretty good. If only I felt it inside too. Finally, I emerged from the attic, plastering a smile on my face for my family's benefit.

'I'll drop you off,' Dad offered. 'It'll be like old times.'

I slid into the back seat with Aubrey, making sure I didn't crumple my dress. Dad was about to set off when a figure flew at the car, waving like a maniac. My breath caught in my throat as I craned forward to see who it was, my first thought being Jared. I slumped back down with disappointment when I saw that it was Theo. In all the drama I'd forgotten I'd begged him to come along to play the part of my fake boyfriend.

'Sorry I'm late. Train was delayed. Shove over, Ruth.' Theo squeezed into the car, introducing himself to Aubrey with an outstretched hand and a wink.

Dad chuckled from the driver's seat. 'Are we expecting anybody else?'

I thought of Jared. 'No. Nobody else.'

We set off for the school and pulled up a couple of minutes later. My stomach churned at the thought of seeing all my old classmates and I suddenly realised Erin was right – I didn't *have* to be here. Why put myself through the torture?

'I bet it feels weird being back here, huh?' Aubrey looped her arm through mine and I had little choice but to scuttle along with her.

'Very weird.' And petrifying and nausea-inducing.

'So what was Stephen like at school? I'm guessing he wasn't a ladies' man. More like a computer geek.'

I forced a smile while my insides looped around themselves. 'That's pretty much it.'

'I take it Billy's meeting us here.' Aubrey turned to Stephen now and my insides tightened their knots.

'I think so. I haven't heard from him today. Have you, Ruth?'

I shook my head but couldn't speak. It was almost a relief to step into the school hall, the sound of a thousand conversations engulfing me. I scanned the room, crammed with people of all ages, from pensioners to late teens, all saying goodbye to their former school and reacquainting themselves with old friends. I didn't spot anyone I recognised and fresh hope surged through me. Perhaps the other people in my year wouldn't come.

'We're going to get a drink,' Stephen told me. 'Do you want one?'

I nodded, still assessing the room. I couldn't see a single familiar face but I didn't dare hope it would remain that way for the entire evening. If only. Brad and Ryan, former and possibly present friends of Zack's, were jostling through the crowds towards me and I dipped back, hiding behind a group of orange-tanned women before they caught sight of me. Who had I been kidding, thinking I could turn up at the reunion with my head held high? A decade had passed, but I was still the same Ruth, still destined to stick out and never be accepted for who I was.

And then I saw him, sticking out from the crowd like a sore thumb, his hair unruly and almost to Sideshow Bob standards. Billy spotted me too but he refused to meet my eye. At least his humiliation and possible heartbreak hadn't driven him off a cliff or something equally as dramatic. Still, I had to talk to him. I'd hurt and embarrassed him and while I could never undo my actions, I could apologise until he believed how sorry I was.

'Billy!' I pushed my way through the crowded hall, my eyes on Billy at all times. He saw me moving towards him and began pushing his own way through the crowds only in the opposite direction to me. 'Billy, please!' I had to talk to him. I had to explain somehow. I had to fix our friendship, if that were even possible, but I couldn't do that if Billy insisted on running away. 'Billy!' There was a pocket of space in the crowd and I surged forward, colliding with a body coming from my right.

'Sorry. I was in a bit of a rush.' I attempted to laugh the collision off but any mirth died in my throat when I looked at the person's face. It was Sasha Bloom, the most popular girl in my year and she was as gorgeous as ever, still slim with waist-length blonde hair and flawless make-up.

'Oh my God, it's Ruth, isn't it?' I prepared myself for the names and for the laughter they would cause. Sasha had always been gifted at creating a guffawing crowd at my expense. 'I'm glad I ran into you. I was hoping to see you here.' Oh God, she'd been planning the ridiculing. I didn't stand a chance. 'I just wanted to say sorry for the way I treated you. I don't expect you to forgive me. I was awful to you, we all were, but the thing is, I have a daughter now. She's eight and like the most amazing person ever, but she was bullied at school last year. It destroyed her confidence and we're working to build it back up again, but it made me think of you. I truly am sorry, Ruth.'

I waited for the punch line but it never came. She was being earnest. 'Thank you, Sasha.'

Sasha gave a humble smile before she backed away and then she was gone. I appreciated her apology but it didn't leave me with the feeling of triumph I always envisioned it would. I didn't feel much at all, to be honest. It was refreshing to realise I no longer cared what Sasha Bloom thought of me. She wasn't important, but Billy was. I scoured the crowds for him but he was no longer in sight. I turned around and barrelled into Zack.

Shit. I wasn't expecting to do this now and not after I'd almost rammed him to the ground. 'Hello, Zack.'

'Hello.' Zack narrowed his eyes as though trying to place me but I saw the glint in his eye and the way they danced around the room, making sure nobody saw us conversing. Some things never changed – I was still fat and Zack was still an arsehole.

'It's Ruth.'

'Ah, yes, Ruth. Of course.' He bobbed his head up and down, eyebrows knotted. He was pretending he still didn't recognise me. 'We had... science together?'

'Something like that.' I really couldn't be bothered having this conversation. I had more important things to see to and I realised then that even if I had managed to slim down to a size 10, Zack would still have been a wanker about the whole thing. He wouldn't have regretted humiliating and hurting me, no matter what. 'Anyway, it was nice to see you again.' I flashed him my brightest smile to show I didn't care about our past, even if it still rankled, and rejoined the crowds in pursuit of Billy. I didn't have to look far as he appeared by my side.

'Is that him? Do you want me to knock him out?' He nodded towards Zack, who was flirting with a slim, blonde girl barely out of her teens.

I laughed, relieved that Billy still cared enough to get his arse kicked for me. 'Are we going to be alright? Can we still be friends?'

'I'm sure my embarrassment will fade enough for us to remain friends. Possibly even before we draw our pensions.'

I reached for Billy's hand and gave it a squeeze. 'I do care about you. A lot.'

'Just not in the same way as I care about you.'

I shook my head and lowered my gaze to Billy's shoes. 'I'm sorry.'

'Don't be. You can't help how you feel.'

'But I can help how I act. I shouldn't have...' I couldn't continue as an image of Billy and I together came to mind, and my face burned brighter than the sun.

'Perhaps not but it's done now. Shall we forget about the whole thing?' If only I could. Life would be simpler. But I nodded anyway. 'How about a dance?'

I glanced around the room. Most people were standing in clusters and chatting, but a few were dancing. Mostly the old timers and a couple of people who had been pissed before they'd even arrived in true school disco style.

'I thought you didn't dance.'

Billy's skinny shoulders rose into a shrug. 'I'll make an exception for my best mate.'

I didn't know how we would ever mend our fractured friendship, but I knew I wanted to more than anything. Billy and I had been through a lot together over the years and he'd become my surrogate brother when Stephen moved to New York. I really didn't know how I would cope without him in my life.

'What about Clare? Are you going to get back together with her?'

Billy twirled me around, catching me by the waist. An image of his hands on my naked flesh popped into my mind but I elbowed it away.

'No, she deserves better than me. Someone who cares about her and not some other woman.'

'You'll find someone else, Billy.'

'I hope so.' Billy dipped me but stopped moving as he pulled me back into an upright position again. 'And what about you and Jared?'

'Oh that.' I shook my head. 'Not going to happen. He stormed out of Mum and Dad's and hasn't spoken to me since. It doesn't help that he thinks I'm a tramp.'

'I wouldn't be so sure about that.'

I batted Billy's arm. 'I could be a tramp if I really put my mind to it.' And I hung out with blind people.

'I didn't mean that.' Billy twirled me around again but grabbed me by the shoulders to stop me halfway round before pointing towards the door where Jared stood. He was studying the room, searching for me but I was frozen to the spot. Jared was here and I didn't dare think what that meant. I saw Billy wave his hand from the corner of my eye and then he was gone as Jared strode towards me. His eyes were on mine the whole time, their gaze burning but I was unable to turn away. Jared was *here*.

'You're here.'

'I am.'

'But how did you get in without a ticket?' Like that was the important bit! I'd have kicked myself but my shoes were a bit pointy and I didn't want any injuries.

'When you're this hot, you don't need tickets.' Jared winked at me and we both laughed. It felt great to be able to joke around with him and I allowed myself to hope that our friendship could remain intact. 'But seriously, I had to do a bit of flirting. I think the woman at the desk thinks we're engaged.'

'Congratulations. This calls for a glass of champagne.'

'Hardly. The woman on the desk is about a hundred years old.' Jared gave a shrug of his shoulders. 'And I sort of like someone else.'

'Oh?' Hope, hope, *hope*. My heart hammered and my palms began to ooze sweat, which was unfortunate given the circumstances and most unsexy.

'And I'm hoping she feels the same way about me.'

My heart pretty much exploded from my chest and splattered against Jared's lovely suit. Which, by the way, he looked *hot* in. 'She does. Very much so.' Throwing my arms around Jared, I kissed him, feeling far from safe as I had the previous night. My insides sizzled as flesh met flesh and I wished we were somewhere slightly more private than a school hall crammed to the brim with other people.

'You did mean me, didn't you?' I asked, pulling away.

'That was very presumptuous of you but yes. I definitely meant you.'

I doubted I had ever felt happier than I did that evening in Jared's arms. I found I didn't actually care that we were surrounded by people. There would be plenty of alone time for Jared and me, I was sure about that.

'Erm, Ruth?' Theo was tugging at my arm and wouldn't stop, no matter how much I swatted at him. In the end I tore myself away from Jared's lips to glare at my annoying housemate. 'Does this mean I'm dismissed from fake boyfriend duties?'

What fake boyfriend duties? I hadn't seen Theo since we'd arrived, the useless git. 'Yes, you're dismissed. Thank you for all your help.'

I rolled my eyes but Theo didn't notice. 'You're welcome. So I'm free to be Theo Logan, hot, single guy?' I rolled my eyes again. 'Good, because there's a girl who's been giving me the eye all evening.'

'Go, Theo.'

He grinned at me and then he was gone, the girl in question's heart already half broken.

'Shall we get out of here?' Jared asked and I nodded, taking his hand in mine. I wasn't thin when I left the reunion and I hadn't proven anything to Zack, but I couldn't have cared less. I was happy and that was all that mattered in the end.

ACKNOWLEDGMENTS

The hugest thanks to my family, particularly my husband Chris for all your support and encouragement and for listening to me bang on about covers (you were almost always right with your advice – and that's the best you're going to get).

Thank you to my mum, who has always encouraged my writing and kept me stocked up in books throughout my childhood. I've almost forgiven you for reading my rubbish stories, even though I hid them so well.

Thank you to my daughters, Rianne and Isobel. Just because.

Millions of thanks to all the authors (aspiring and published) and readers who I've met through Twitter and my blog.

Thank you to Google (my very best writing friend) and YouTube. Without you, I may have had to actually attend a spinning class myself.

Thank you to 'the other Ruth' Durbridge for editing the book.

Finally, thank you to Ruth Lynch, who inspired me to finally get off the sofa and join the gym.

A SPECIAL NOTE REGARDING THE ACKNOWLEDGMENTS

It's been several years since I wrote A Beginner's Guide To Salad and almost as long since I attended the gym. I thanked Ruth for inspiring me to join the gym so now I must apologise for reverting to my lazy ways. But I'm sure Ruth will understand.

I hope that you enjoyed reading A Beginner's Guide To Salad. If you did, why not leave a review? I'd love to hear what you think and it helps other readers find books they'd enjoy too!

If you'd like to keep up to date with my new releases and book news, you can subscribe to my newsletter on my blog (jenniferjoycewrites.co.uk). I send out newsletters 4-5 times a year, with short stories, extra content, a subscriber-exclusive giveaway and more! Plus, you'll receive my ebook quick read, *Six Dates,* which is only available to subscribers, for FREE.

Printed in Great Britain
by Amazon